GREENBEAUX

David Bergheim

FTB Press, LLC
Chandler, AZ USA

ISBN-13 978-0692575734

For more information about the author and book, please
visit
www.greenbeauxforpresident.com or
www.facebook.com/greenbeauxforpresident.

For my parents,
who shaped my love of politics and the arts.

PROLOGUE

The candidate moved with determination from house to house, leaving footprints in the snow much larger than one would expect from an ordinary six-foot six-inch tall man. One more house, he told himself to stay motivated. One more house.

Each door that slammed in his face was a reminder of why he was running. His people did not enjoy the freedoms that others took for granted, and his quest was a solitary march to open minds and win a larger measure of dignity. In his deepest moments of self-doubt, he wondered if he were more Don Quixote than Mahatma Gandhi, but he kept moving forward against the biting December wind, determined to expose and eradicate a prejudice that few others could see.

Even his mother who believed in him unconditionally did not think that he would be elected.

And she was his campaign manager.

He had no volunteers on the ground to speak of, and his headquarters was in the unused portion of a storage building behind an industrial supply company. There he had a folding table with leaflets wedged up against drums of chemical solvents and a wrapped pallet of toilet paper. The whole operation resembled not so much a political campaign as a missionary expedition going from house to house to convert nonbelievers.

Sometimes the person answering his knock would step outside to talk, but his presence was disquieting to most, and he was rarely invited inside. Society had become accustomed to seeing his kind as clumsy oafs, or worse, as psychotic killers in horror movies, and he could often sense the fear when he showed up at a house unannounced.

He was familiar with the signs of rejection. A curtain would sometimes move behind the force of a finger, eyes darting in the background while the threat of his imposing presence was assessed. At the next house on this day the door opened almost immediately when he rang the bell.

"Hello. My name is Russell Greenbeaux, and I am running for president."

The pause on the other end was telling. Perhaps this household was tired of the campaign. Every four years, Iowa was invaded by an army of politicians, operatives, and reporters from around the country. Some people liked the attention and special favors the state garnered from its caucuses, while others just wanted it all to go away.

More likely, though, it was the sight of an extremely tall man in a clown outfit with a shock of bright green hair that had turned off this homeowner.

As the door slammed in his face yet again, Greenbeaux exhaled deeply and turned to navigate his way down the icy porch stairs, which was never an easy task in oversized orthopedic clown shoes.

The odd discomfort of the campaign greeting could be a two-way street, and there were times when he was the one who felt the need to exit. The day before, he had arrived at a house filled with toddlers who were gathered for a

8

birthday party, and he could hear the cries of disappointed children as he hurriedly left the scene.

There was no such drama today, and Greenbeaux took little time to process the rejection of another slammed door.

One more house, he told himself as he moved on. One more house.

CHAPTER 1

The kickoff of Russell Greenbeaux's presidential campaign would have received no press coverage whatsoever if a French television news cameraman had not been shooting B-roll footage on the steps of the Lincoln Memorial when the event started. The camera was focused on Greenbeaux as he made his first stump speech to a crowd of two-dozen clowns and a slightly larger number of amused tourists.

That night, footage from the announcement made newscasts in Paris, where clowns were held in especially high esteem. The spectacle of a man with a French-sounding surname wearing greasepaint to announce his candidacy for president of the United States was too good a story for the media there to ignore for a day. But no longer.

At the feet of Abraham Lincoln, the candidate made an impassioned plea for tolerance toward his people that was almost completely ignored by the intended audience. Greenbeaux then spent the next week scrambling about Washington in search of reporters to cover his campaign. To no avail.

He didn't really expect to change the world right away, but it was a little disheartening that his message was not being heard. At low moments like these he sought solace in the wisdom of the smartest person he knew. So once again, it was time to listen to his mother.

With the week-old campaign failing to gain traction, Greenbeaux and his mother, Ruth, met for lunch at an Italian restaurant to chart out the path forward. After they were seated, she started off the conversation bluntly:

"If you pack it in, you won't look the worse for it because nobody knows you are running anyway. If you choose to carry on," she continued, "you will have to decide whether you want to be a candidate or a politician."

Greenbeaux tried to let this sink in for a few moments, but he was coming up short. "What's the difference?"

Ruth smiled slightly. "Politicians talk on the air. Candidates run on the ground. You've been trying to talk like a politician, but nobody knows you yet. You are just a man in a clown suit crying about a problem that doesn't exist in anybody else's mind. Without building a ground game first, you might never get the chance to talk on the air."

"So, you're suggesting that I should start knocking on doors to tell people about my campaign?"

"Well, yes and no."

Greenbeaux furrowed his brow at his mother's circumspect way of getting her point across. He glanced around briefly to see the waiters in the corner pointing and whispering about the clown sitting at his table. He was used to it, and he wasn't bothered by it in the way she was.

"The purpose is not to just knock on a door and tell someone what you want them to hear," Ruth continued when she saw that she had his attention again. "You also have to be prepared to listen to what's on their mind."

This made sense. A big part of Greenbeaux's own frustration with Washington was that the people in power seemed more interested in protecting the interests of their coalitions than in serving the needs of the country. When a congressman was in front of a voter, he was prepared to talk, but when he was in front of a lobbyist with deep pockets, he was ready to listen.

Over the course of the meal, Greenbeaux and his mother charted out a plan to hit the ground. They needed to establish a presence in one of the early primary states, and they settled on Iowa since she was originally from there and knew the territory. It would be easy enough to rent an apartment to serve as a home base there while they rebooted the campaign.

*   *   *

Ruth McCaslin Greenbeaux's faith in her son was unshakable, and seemed only to grow stronger when others questioned the boy's sensibilities. Her late husband Martin, for one, struggled with Russell's desire to put on makeup and dress as a clown. "What are you going to do, run away and join the circus?" he would gently chide, not always realizing the sting the barb would leave.

There was a part of her that wondered whether young Russell's clown tendencies ran in the family. Her older brother, Aaron, was secretly a clown whose alcohol-shortened life had been filled with sadness and rage about having to pretend that he was someone he was not. Ruth would have none of that for her son. If Russell wanted to be a clown in public, then she would buy him greasepaint and press his clown suit so that he could look his best.

Ruth had been born into a family of actors and evangelists on a farm in Casey, Iowa, near the Adair and Guthrie County lines. The men in her family were mostly scoundrels who traveled from one revival to another to read the good word in a fashion most dramatic. They would start from the beginning of the Old Testament, and by the time they reached the story of Moses, wallets and purses opened as though the Red Sea was being parted again. Often without the owner's consent.

She had learned of hypocrisy at an early age by studying her uncle Caleb McCaslin, who was well-known for his personal disregard of no less than seven of the Ten Commandments. Every time Caleb got into trouble, he pulled out the "we are all sinners" line as his get-out-of-jail-free card. This often helped him avoid personal responsibility, though when the indiscretion involved alcohol -- as it frequently did -- the sheriff would wait for sobriety to set in before opening the door to the cell and releasing Caleb back into the wild.

The McCaslin men came to accept sin and debauchery as but a small compensation for their worthy service to the Lord. Their ministry was built upon words, not deeds, and they granted themselves permission to live their hedonistic lives in private so long as everyone in the family could project the same wholesome image to the outside world, excepting the occasional public misstep by Caleb.

The family homestead was more of a base camp for their ministry business than a working farm. They rented out most of their land to neighboring farmers, and the corn growing in their fields was part of a theatrical set designed to convince their audience that the McCaslins were really hardworking men of the soil.

But that environment, where appearances meant everything, was no place for a clown, and it would have brought unthinkable shame on the family for Aaron to walk down the main street of town dressed as he wished. The McCaslin men talked in hushed tones about his "issues," and after enduring sermon after sermon on the subject of obedience, Aaron dutifully suppressed his clown tendencies for the sake of the family.

Ruth saw many of her brother's traits in Russell, and by the time he had reached first grade she knew he was meant to be a clown. Her parents had put forth a lot of energy trying to change her brother and hide his true nature from others. Clearly, that had not worked out well for Aaron, and Ruth decided to take a different approach. Russell's childhood was to serve as a launching pad where he would be given the freedom to learn from success and failure without false piety or a thick, protective bubble around him.

When Russell was seven, his father, Martin, bought him a cowboy outfit for Halloween, hoping that the young boy would take a liking to a more manly theme and move on from his clown phase. Martin's mother was visiting at the time, and was taking pictures when the boy reluctantly emerged from his bedroom dressed as a cowboy and burst into tears.

The scene was imprinted on Ruth's memory, not because of the hurt she felt for the little boy, but because it was to become the most courageous moment of her life.

She had listened to her husband's anxious ramblings about their son's clown tendencies for too long. Ruth went to her son, wiped the tears from his face, and said in a voice loud enough for everyone in the room to hear: "That's okay, Russell. If you want to be a clown then I will never let anyone tell you that you cannot do that."

Her husband heard enough resolve in her voice to know that he wasn't going to win this battle by putting his foot down. But just to be sure, Ruth added: "Besides, the devil is afraid of clowns, and you will always be safe if you are honest with the world about who you really are."

Her mother-in-law was oblivious to the dynamics of the drama playing out in front of her, and happily kept snapping pictures of her cute little grandson dressed as a cowboy. One of the pictures, with Ruth's mouth opening to speak as her fingers touched Russell's face, became Ruth's most cherished possession. At moments when she most needed strength, she turned to that photograph to remind herself of the power she had to stand up for what was right.

It's not that Martin didn't love his son -- quite the opposite was true -- but he had a very strong opinion about what Russell's childhood ought to be like. Boys should want to play catch and jump in mud puddles, he thought. He just wanted his son to fit in, and he couldn't understand why Russell would go out of his way to subject himself to ridicule.

Ruth didn't care so much about what other people would think. She was more interested in raising a son who would be honest in the eyes of God.

As Russell reached adolescence, an uneasy truce was negotiated in the Greenbeaux house. The young man would be allowed to dress as a clown at home on nights and weekends, but for school and events with his father's extended family, he would have to dress in a more conforming manner. He was still teased in subtle ways by his peers who knew about his clown inclinations, but his towering presence spared him the fate of physical bullying that befell so many other social misfits.

As a senior in high school, he was voted Class Clown. He felt a little bit conflicted about receiving the ceremonial title. He was not a prankster or a comedian, and there were certainly others who were more worthy. But he chose to take it as a small measure of acceptance.

He knew that there were other clowns at the school; they mostly preferred to keep to themselves in the marching band, where nobody would pay attention or know their secret. But since Greenbeaux was the only one who was open about it, the title belonged to him. Besides, he thought, he probably would have felt slighted if they had given the honor to someone else.

The journey from childhood to presidential candidate was filled with both professional accomplishments and personal disappointment. But at his lowest moments -- his nasty divorce, the death of his father, and the social isolation that came with being a clown -- his mother was always there to support him.

*   *   *

Russell Greenbeaux was unusually intense for a clown, which some people found unnerving. He was unapologetic when someone would point out that he didn't act like a clown. "And how should I act," he would sometimes retort, "like a fool or a chainsaw-wielding maniac?"

He had chosen to live the life of a clown openly, but his every move was self-consciously choreographed to avoid reinforcing negative stereotypes. He refused to make balloon animals, he didn't juggle, and he would never allow himself to be seen in a small car with a large number of clowns.

For every clown like Greenbeaux who was courageous enough to wear greasepaint in public, there were hundreds more who stayed private for fear of what their families, neighbors and co-workers would think. There were clandestine gatherings organized through the Clown Underground, where like-minded people could put on their gear, socialize, and be themselves. But there was always an ominous undertone of secrecy because of what exposure would mean.

Clowns were an invisible minority whose society was so deeply hidden that most people were ignorant of their own prejudice against them. Greenbeaux was an articulate and successful man who had built and sold two software companies, and he took derogatory comments about his people as a personal insult that demeaned his own accomplishments.

Nothing raised his blood pressure more than when his people were unfairly tarnished with the stain of political incompetence. Every time someone joked about the clowns in Congress, Greenbeaux wanted to jump out of his skin. Being compared to Congress was the worst insult he could imagine being hurled against anyone, and he had reached the point where inaction was no longer an option.

There were, in fact, plenty of clowns in Washington, including a few members of the House of Representatives and the Senate. But with one notable exception, these people generally avoided the type of grandstanding that might inadvertently lead them to being exposed as clowns. Being open about it would be a political death sentence, and they worked hard to conceal their true identities so they could keep their jobs.

Russell Greenbeaux would be the first person to admit that his campaign was nothing more than a publicity stunt to benefit the cause of clown rights. He had little interest in actually becoming president, and since he was a clown running as a third-party candidate, he didn't have to worry too much about the consequences of winning.

He had always been interested in public policy, but he was not strongly partisan. A few of his political ideas were liberal, some were conservative, and still more were moderate. But he had become disillusioned with politics in the United States. It seemed that the two main political parties were now caricatures of themselves, each more interested in feeding red meat to their base than in actually governing effectively.

When he first hit the ground, he immediately started seeking out voters to shake hands and hear what was on their minds. His talk of clown rights mostly elicited puzzled looks from the few people who were willing to talk with him, but the reaction was quite different when he engaged voters in conversations about politics.

He had detected a recurring theme: People were sick and tired of partisan gridlock in Washington. They despaired that the game was fixed to perpetuate polarization, and that the biggest problems facing the country would only get worse if the leaders from both parties didn't find the courage to change the most dysfunctional elements of the system.

*   *   *

Two months after the strategy dinner with his mother, Greenbeaux settled down to write out his thoughts. His feet were aching after 20 more miles of wear from the day's door-to-door campaigning, and he eased them into a tub of warm water as he typed the first of so many words he wanted to say.

A few paragraphs in, Greenbeaux realized that the flood of thoughts could easily turn into a manifesto, which wasn't really a practical way to get his point across in a sound bite-driven culture. That was when he decided to write an editorial.

He chose to depart from his usual pitch on the theme of clown rights and instead position himself as a role model.

Perhaps he could do more good for his cause if he was presented as a serious presidential candidate who also happened to be a clown, rather than the other way around. He cast himself as an outsider who represented a group of people who were even more powerless than the common man against the big-money influences inside the Beltway.

"Reasonable people can disagree on the issues, but reasonable people also work out their differences in a civil manner. I am running for president," he concluded the editorial, "to be a voice for the reasonable people who want their leaders to stop the partisanship and work together to address the biggest challenges we face as a nation."

The next day, the newsroom at the *Des Moines Register* erupted into laughter when an intern tasked with reading incoming e-mails walked around to show everyone what had arrived overnight. Word had been circulating for weeks that a man in a clown suit was showing up in diners and walking the neighborhoods asking for votes, and now the man had surfaced with an opinion essay for the paper to publish.

After the initial laughter subsided, one editor sat down to read Greenbeaux's piece while an available reporter quickly checked for background information on the clown. When they compared notes, they were both surprised that they had a serious and eloquent editorial written by a successful businessman.

If he wasn't a clown, he might make a formidable major-party candidate for statewide office somewhere. But he was a clown, he wasn't running as a Democrat or a Republican, and without ever having held elected office before, he was running for president. He had all the earmarks of a crackpot. And yet, there was something more there to suggest he was not.

The paper had provided a nonstop stream of coverage of the major-party candidates coming to the state since long before the previous summer's straw poll, but had paid precious little attention to third-party hopefuls. A copy of the commentary was circulated before the morning editorial meeting, and the initial amused reaction gave way to a serious discussion about the merits of running the piece.

The *Register's* editorial board was well aware of the power it had to influence the outcome of a presidential election, and the members took their role as a gatekeeper very seriously. Running Greenbeaux's editorial would bestow a measure of credibility on him, but it might also open a floodgate, with other offbeat candidates demanding equal time. The paper would be under no obligation to accommodate these requests, but there was some concern about creating unnecessary headaches where none had existed before.

Whatever concerns the editorial board had about Greenbeaux's personality quirks, they could not deny that his essay presented an insightful perspective on politics in America. It met their journalistic standards, and a consensus emerged that they would publish it on their op-ed page.

CHAPTER 2

Virgil Munsell sat anxiously in a conference room in Cleveland, Ohio, waiting to learn his fate. He had given 17 years of his life to IXM Systems as a logistics manager, optimizing the movement of billions of dollars worth of freight each year through six transportation hubs.

He sensed that he had two strikes against him at work. There was nothing he could do -- or wanted to do -- about being a black man. He always tried to work harder than everyone else to overcome lingering prejudice and prove his worth, and over the years he had been rewarded with a few modest promotions. The second strike: he was also a clown, though until very recently he had never shown that side of his personality at work.

Everything changed a few days earlier when he was reading political news stories online and came across Russell Greenbeaux's editorial. It stopped him cold. Here was a fellow man of the greasepaint who was running for president as an open and honest-to-God clown. And on top of that, he was making an argument about Washington that made a hell of a lot more sense than what most of the other fools in the race were saying.

Virgil realized that if he wanted to be judged by the content of his character, he could no longer hide that he was a clown on the inside any more than he could hide the color of his skin on the outside. The next day he dyed his salt and pepper hair a bright shade of blue, put on his greasepaint, and wore his best clown suit to work.

He was well-liked by his co-workers, and for the most part they were amused when he showed up at work in his gear. But his boss was furious, and when Virgil came to work dressed as a clown for a second day in a row, there were whispers that Human Resources was being brought in.

Virgil's boss, Riley Booth, was the most dim-witted executive at IXM Systems, and quite possibly, in all of corporate America. He was ignorant, profane, pompous, spiteful, and utterly clueless about how other people saw him. His insertion into the company and subsequent rise up the ladder was due solely to the good fortune of being the son-in-law of a prominent member of the company's board of directors.

Riley did not care much for people who were more intelligent than he, and so he went through life with a disdain for just about everybody else on the planet. Virgil was thoughtful, perceptive, and competent -- pretty much the opposite of his boss -- and his working environment had become progressively more stressful as Riley imposed irrational deadlines to execute ill-conceived projects.

For the past year, Virgil had been more careful with his money to prepare for what he came to view as the inevitable end of his professional relationship with IXM Systems. He had been actively looking for another job, and also gave some thought to just walking away. When the day came that he showed up at work dressed as himself, he knew that he was forcing the issue.

Outside the conference room, Sharon from Human Resources was coaching Riley Booth about what he could and could not say. The company had faced four lawsuits in the past two years because of his imprudent behavior and offhand comments, and if he wanted to fire Virgil, she was going to make sure that it was done legally and compassionately.

She enjoyed her job most of the time, but not on this day. She hated Riley and all of the headaches he created in her life, but she was powerless to stop him because of his protection from up high. All she could do was mitigate the risk that the company might be sued because of something the stupid man might utter.

Riley had a bad habit of saying what he thought without the benefit of a proper filter, and what he thought was often inappropriate. Sharon would not have been surprised to hear him say that he was firing Virgil because he was black. That would have set in motion a very expensive chain of events that would have consumed her life, and she didn't need that hassle, even if it meant an end game in which even Riley's benefactor on the board of directors could no longer protect him. Besides, it grated on her soul to think that Virgil might be subjected to a racist diatribe while being terminated. He deserved better than that.

In the hallway outside the conference room, she continued to coach Riley, hoping against hope that something was sinking in. Federal discrimination laws prevented companies from firing individuals on the basis of certain characteristics like race, skin color, and age. Clowns were not a protected class, and if Riley had no other good reason to get rid of Virgil, then they would have to base the termination on a violation of the company's rules governing professional attire.

Normally, Sharon remained silent in meetings when employees were being dismissed, preferring to be there as an observer who inconspicuously slides the separation packet across the table while the employee is distracted by the jolt of the news. But this time, she was prepared to take the lead to limit the risk of litigation. Riley was instructed to start the conversation but then say very little after that.

Virgil had focused on controlling his breathing to steady himself while he waited, and he appeared outwardly calm when Riley and Sharon walked into the room. He could feel his pulse quicken as everyone settled into seats and his boss started the conversation.

"We have decided to let you go."

He had braced himself for this possibility, but thought it was more likely he would be given a warning and told to not come back to work dressed as a clown. He would not have agreed to that condition, and he was prepared to tender his resignation if necessary. But that was not to be.

Virgil knew very well why he was being fired, but he decided to look his now-former boss in the eye and ask the reason anyway. Riley started to open his mouth to speak, but Sharon cut him off. Virgil was one of the first friends she had made at the company when she started there five years earlier, and her voice cracked a little as she walked through the subsections of the employee handbook that covered professional behavior and attire.

She explained the terms of his exit, including a generous 34-week pay package, two weeks for every year that he had worked at IXM Systems. That type of severance was unusual for a mid-level manager to receive, but Sharon had made the case to her own boss that this was a smart move to reduce the potential for a discrimination lawsuit.

In truth, she did it because she liked Virgil, and she didn't like what was happening to him. There were two men in the room, and the wrong one was being fired. And right before Christmas, too. Sharon felt culpable for not standing up to Riley, but like it or not, this was part of her job, and the best she could do was to make sure that Virgil walked out the door with enough of a cushion to stay on his feet.

The meeting ended cordially enough, and his friend Stan from security was waiting outside the conference room to escort him as he cleaned out his desk and walked out of the building.

No words were exchanged until they reached the front door and Stan asked him why he had thrown it all away by dressing up as a clown.

"Because, I really am a clown," Virgil said. "And I'm tired of putting on a costume and pretending to be something else."

*   *   *

Virgil drove home in a haze. He was relieved that the confrontation was over, but he was numb from the suddenness of it all and the sting of having to leave on someone else's terms. He was let go because of a technicality in the employee handbook that gave his boss all the cover he needed.

That bastard Riley Booth had finally gotten the better of him, but he knew, as did everyone else at IXM who the better man was, and he felt no shame or sense of failure.

He could forgive his friends at work if they thought he had gone a bit off the deep end, dressing as he did in his final days at the job, and he couldn't help but laugh at how ridiculous the whole scene must have seemed to someone who was ignorant of the struggles clowns faced. But in a moment of clarity, he also realized how absurd it had been for him to hide who he truly was for so long.

Like Russell Greenbeaux and so many other clowns, Virgil was divorced. He had entered into a marriage with a woman who was not a clown, and then struggled to explain himself when she found his lipstick and makeup lying around. He immersed himself in the culture of the Clown Underground, and started to emotionally distance himself from his family.

His children were both under 10 at the time of the divorce, and he waited until they were in college to explain to them that he was, in fact, a clown. He was honest in admitting his shortcomings as a father and didn't go to them seeking forgiveness, but they gave it to him anyway.

He was 54 years old and ready to live out the rest of his life openly as a clown. The severance package ensured that he would have benefits and a regular paycheck well into the next year, and he had enough set aside so that he could do something meaningful in the next chapter of his life. Even if that meant volunteering for a while or working for less money at a company that would accept him as he was.

When he got home, he packed two duffel bags for an extended trip and dropped his cat off at his daughter's house. The next morning, Virgil filled up the tank of his car and started driving west toward Des Moines.

*   *   *

Ruth had a headache to deal with, both literally and figuratively. Word of the *Des Moines Register* editorial had spread quickly through the Clown Underground message boards, and volunteers were flooding to the tiny outbuilding that served as the campaign headquarters. It was cold outside, and everyone was crammed in so tightly she couldn't get any work done, let alone organize everyone else to help.

Of all the stereotypes that people had in their minds about clowns, the image of a large number of them coming out of a small car bothered Greenbeaux the most. But Ruth thought there might be a kernel of truth behind the sight gag. As a baby, Russell was happiest when he was tightly swaddled. He seemed to enjoy being in close quarters with other people, and despite his great height, he never cared for the extra legroom afforded by first-class on a plane.

Many years earlier, Ruth had donned greasepaint and accompanied him to a Clown Underground dance party. She thought it would be a fun way to learn more about her son's interests, but found herself on the verge of a claustrophobic panic attack as the size of the crowd grew well beyond the capacity of the small space. The entire collection of clowns moved as one to the deep bass of the bluesy music pulsing through the room. Nobody else seemed to mind, and the frenetic energy rose with every new person who entered.

That was all well and fine for clown parties, but she had a campaign to run, and the crush of unusual people in the room was causing her head to throb.

Ruth had a gift for reading people and figuring out how their strengths could be utilized, but she was not particularly strong at coordinating the movement of an army of volunteers. She had told her son the previous night that she was going to start interviewing people to take over her role as the campaign manager so she could better serve him in a different capacity.

Greenbeaux had concerns about that. All of the people hanging around to help were new to the effort, and he was not sure he could trust any of them with the keys to the campaign. But his mother was adamant, and so he asked her to take on a new role as the head of personnel so she could manage the manager.

She started initiating friendly conversations with the volunteers, asking them what they did for a living in a casual way that would not tip her hand. Mostly, she was unimpressed. They were predominantly grassroots, single-issue volunteers who lacked the political savvy to run a campaign that was starting to take on broader issues than clown rights.

By midafternoon, Ruth had identified a handful of high-potential individuals to manage different aspects of the effort. Two women -- a lawyer and a retired banking executive -- were tasked with tracking donations coming in through the website and ensuring compliance with federal campaign finance laws. Another man, a recruiter with a staffing firm, was put in charge of assigning volunteers to projects.

Still, Ruth did not feel completely in control of the suddenly chaotic campaign effort. But at a few minutes past six, when Ruth stepped outside to check on the status of a batch of pizzas that had been ordered to feed the volunteers, she encountered a tired-looking clown who would change everything.

"Are you here to help with the campaign?" she asked.

"Yes, I am. I've driven all day from Cleveland, and I'm here to do what I can."

"Wow, that's a long drive. Well, come on in and we will put you to work. My name is Ruth Greenbeaux. I'm Russell's mother."

"My name is Virgil. Virgil Munsell. I'm pleased to meet you."

"What do you do for a living?" Ruth inquired.

"I am... I was a logistics manager. I left my job yesterday."

"Logistics?" Ruth said, feigning ignorance. "Tell me, what does that mean?"

"Well, basically, I was in charge of planning the movements of hundreds of trucks every day. It was kind of like being an air traffic controller, except with more advanced planning and quantitative analysis."

Ruth suppressed her urge to shout hallelujah and instead fired more questions at Virgil. "Did you supervise anyone?"

"Well, yes," He was tired and a little bit hungry, and had not expected to walk into an inquisition. "I managed a staff of 11, and most of them had direct reports as well. So there were about 50 people under me at any given time. Depending."

"Depending on...?"

"Depending on how many people my boss decided to arbitrarily fire in one of his restructuring exercises that quarter."

She had worked for a boss like that once too. "Have you ever worked on a political campaign?"

"Uh, no, not really," he said. "When I was a kid, I helped a neighbor who was running for sheriff put leaflets on cars, but he was arrested by the guy he was running against for littering. I was able to get away fast enough, and so I didn't get caught."

30

Ruth laughed. "I guess that answers my next question about whether you've ever been arrested."

"I am a man of strong convictions, but no, I never have been arrested."

"Well, that's good because we may have a job for you," said Ruth. "And I promise we won't ask you to do anything illegal."

"I would appreciate that," replied Virgil. He was weary from the long drive, but he was happy that he was being welcomed and could be of help.

The pizza was arriving, and Ruth needed to turn her attention to paying the deliveryman and getting the food inside, but she didn't want to lose sight of Virgil in the crowd before she could screen him further. "Come with me."

Virgil followed Ruth and the deliveryman into the cramped headquarters. The crowd of volunteers was starting to thin for the day, but those who remained surged toward the pizza as it came into the room. He was hungry and would have liked to grab a slice when the first box was opened, but he stayed by Ruth's side as she moved toward the back of the room.

"Okay, Virgil. Give me your first impression of our operation."

He scanned the room and immediately focused on the barrels of solvents lining the wall an arm's length away. He glanced at the labels and immediately knew there was a problem. Virgil could recite from memory the material safety data sheets for each of the different types of chemicals in the drums. He would never have allowed many of them to get on the same truck together, let alone to be stacked on top of one another in an enclosed room with people milling about.

"I think," he said, "you need to find a new headquarters for the campaign."

Ruth had been thinking that all week, but she had no time to find a new office on her own. She had asked around earlier to see if anyone had experience with real estate, but the closest she came was a very odd woman in mismatched clown shoes who had managed a trailer park.

"Do you think you could help find us new space tomorrow?"

"Yes, I can help with that." He explained that he had started his career in the procurement department of a chain of oil-change centers, and he knew a lot about negotiating. He hadn't been involved in the real estate side of the business, but he had helped his first boss double-check the contracts lawyers would send over.

Ruth liked what she was hearing. Virgil had an operational expertise that she lacked, and understood numbers and how to manage people in an organization. She also liked his calm, straightforward demeanor, but she couldn't tell how much of that was because he was tired from the drive.

There was a commotion in the headquarters as the candidate entered, and Ruth turned to see her son, towering above the crowd.

"Let's go," she said, grabbing Virgil by the arm and half-dragging him as she parted the gathering throng, now clamoring for her son's attention.

"Russell, can I see you please?" Ruth motioned for them to step outside into the cold. "Russell, I would like you to meet Virgil Munsell."

Before they could shake hands and exchange pleasantries, Ruth turned to Virgil and said: "Now you go and get a good night's sleep and meet me back here at 7:30 tomorrow morning. We have some work to do."

"Thank you," he said. "I'm looking forward to helping." He wanted to duck back inside and see if there was any pizza left, but he decided instead to make a clean break, and he turned to make the long walk back to his car.

When he was out of earshot, Greenbeaux asked his mother who that was.

"That," Ruth said, "is your new campaign manager."

*   *   *

Virgil went to a sandwich shop and grabbed some dinner to go. He was tired of road food, but a decent meal would have to wait for the next day. About two miles down the road he found a rundown extended-stay hotel. It wasn't pretty, but it would do.

The front desk clerk looked at the tired black man in a clown suit with trepidation. "How long will you be staying, sir?"

"I don't know," Virgil replied. He had never checked in to a hotel without an end date in mind. "A couple of days, I guess."

His assigned room was a considerable distance from where he was able to park, and he struggled to carry his heavy duffel bags. Once inside, he flopped down on the bed and would have fallen right to sleep if not for the hunger. He was tired, but his mind raced about what had just happened. He had just met Russell Greenbeaux, the man whose editorial and life example had given him the courage to take a stand, and he was being welcomed into the campaign.

After he finished eating, Virgil opened his computer and logged into the Clown Underground message boards to read the most recent threads on the campaign. It dawned on him that they were going to need help finding their new office space, and so he posted a short note.

"Wanted: Turnkey commercial office space in central Iowa for a short-term lease. 3,000 sq. ft+. Thx."

Then Virgil took off his makeup, brushed his teeth, set his alarm and went to sleep.

CHAPTER 3

The clown community was excited that one of their own was running for president, and everyone wanted to know what they could do to help. Clowns were far more numerous in society than most realized, but there were only so many people and resources in Iowa that could be drawn upon to help, and Virgil doubted that he would get much of a response to his query.

He woke up on his own before five a.m. and he logged in to scan the replies to his post before going out to enjoy a sit-down breakfast. A few volunteers who had been to the headquarters were posting that it was quickly becoming too small to accommodate the growing army of volunteers, so Virgil's message was taken as a hopeful sign the campaign was poised to grow.

Most of the responses were merely speculative. Did this mean they were getting ready to branch out into other states? Are they going to hire paid staff? But one reply caught Virgil's attention:

"Class A office. 6,300 Sq. Ft./room to expand. Free to a good clown. Call me."

The reply had been posted by someone named Goldfarb. There was not much information on the profile, but there was a phone number with a 202 area code that Virgil recognized as being from Washington, D.C. He wondered if this was legit, and if it was, whether the space in question would be close enough to the current operations to make sense. He wrote down the phone number so that he could call later after discussing it with Ruth.

*   *   *

The headquarters was quiet but open when he arrived at 7:20. Only Ruth was there, and she was pleased to see that Virgil had come a few minutes early. She had been working for more than an hour, trying to get ahead of the maddening crush of people that would come later in the morning, as it had every day since the editorial was published.

Most of the volunteers came out to help because of the excitement building in the Clown Underground, but there were a few who were not clowns. Greenbeaux's common-sense assessment of the state of affairs in Washington had hit a nerve, and while he was still widely unknown in the race, there were some hints that his message was reaching beyond the clown community.

There still was not much in the way of press coverage, aside from a handful of mentions at the tag end of offbeat news stories. "Just when you thought it couldn't get any worse in Washington," said one, "we now have a clown running for president." The other stories were not much more flattering.

But that was about to change. His editorial in the *Des Moines Register* had caught the attention of a production assistant at C-SPAN, and that led to an invitation to participate in the network's third-party candidate debate scheduled a few days before Christmas.

Greenbeaux was well aware that running as a third-party candidate put him at a huge disadvantage. The final presidential debates had not included a third-party candidate since 1992, when Ross Perot made the stage with Bill Clinton and George Bush the elder. In that case, the third-party candidate had benefited from a similarly rich vein of dissatisfaction with Washington that Greenbeaux was now tapping, though Perot could not have put himself in contention without a vast personal fortune.

Greenbeaux was in a comfortable financial position, but he was not a billionaire, and he had no intention of going all-out to support a futile candidacy for a job he didn't really want.

His plan was to get in, get recognition for the clown cause, and get out without selling his soul. He and his mother were running the campaign on a shoestring. Some donations were starting to come in, and that would allow him to expand his operations a bit, but it was not nearly enough for him to start advertising to get his message out to a broader audience.

The news that someone might be willing to give them office space in a Class A building sounded almost too good to be true. But the benefactor had emerged from the Clown Underground, and so it wasn't implausible that someone who believed in the cause would donate unused space for a couple of months.

Shortly after eight, Ruth and Virgil dialed the 202 number, and leaned in toward the speakerphone in anticipation. After the second ring, a gruff voice on the other end answered.

"This is Goldfarb."

Virgil took the lead. "Hello, Mr. Goldfarb."

"It's Goldfarb. No mister. Just Goldfarb."

"Yes, okay, hello Goldfarb. My name is Virgil Munsell, and I am calling on behalf of the Greenbeaux for President campaign."

The voice on the other end brightened up. "Oh yes, hello."

"You responded to a message I posted about office space in Iowa."

"Yep. Our client has an empty building in a brand-new office park, and he would rather have tenants in there with cars in the parking lot than have it look abandoned. You can have it for free, up through the election in November, if you need it that long. The space is on the second floor. A little more than 6,000 square feet is available now. The rest of the floor is ready to be finished and that could be done on short notice if you needed more room."

Ruth and Virgil looked at each other in pleasant disbelief, waiting to hear a catch that never came. They were given an address in Des Moines and the name of a leasing agent who would show them around and give them the keys if they wanted the place.

"That is very generous, Goldfarb," Ruth started. It was not in Ruth's nature to just take good fortune at face value, and she pressed him with some questions to make sure that she had everything straight. "Are you with a commercial real estate firm?"

"No. I'm in... uh.... public relations."

Ruth and Virgil glanced at each other again, this time with a little bit of concern. There had been something odd about

38

the way Goldfarb hesitated when answering their question, and he seemed a little rough around the edges to be a public relations executive. Ruth also wondered why someone would go through a public relations firm to give away office space to a political campaign.

There must be some angle that they didn't know about yet, and she prodded further, though in the friendliest way she knew how. "I see. Well, this is a very generous offer. May I ask who your client is?"

"No," came the terse response. After a few awkward moments of silence, Goldfarb continued. "My client is from a very wealthy family who prefers to keep a low profile in political matters. But he is very interested in our cause."

Our cause? So, Goldfarb was a clown too. This made Virgil feel a little more comfortable. He was probably a performer of some sort, and it made sense to him that Goldfarb might be his stage name. But Ruth still persisted.

"Oh, I certainly understand, and I can respect that. One thing… campaign finance laws are very complex, and we want to make sure that we don't get your client into any trouble."

"It's all on the up-and-up," Goldfarb said. "He has a number of political action committees that he funnels in-kind donations like this through, and he has an even larger number of lawyers and accountants who keep everything legal."

Ruth still had some concerns, but Virgil held a hand up to stop her. "We really appreciate this, Goldfarb," he said. "We will call the leasing agent to take a look at the space, and then have our compliance officer get back in touch to work out the legal details."

Ruth understood what Virgil was doing and gave him the thumbs-up sign. After the call was over, she looked over and laughed. "I think we need to find a compliance officer."

The thought had never occurred to her that they might be able to dip into the deep reservoir of money that lurked for candidates who were willing to do the bidding of special-interests. It was intriguing to think what the campaign could become with a war chest, but it also made her uncomfortable on a number of levels.

She wasn't familiar enough with the complex laws governing the permissible use of soft money, and had no interest in spending her golden years in a federal penitentiary, or worse, having Russell sent to one. She was similarly concerned about what taking any kind of a donation from a special-interest could signal to the public about her son's integrity.

He was building momentum by talking about what was wrong in Washington, and a central theme of his message was the corrupting influence of money on politicians. She didn't want her son to become part of the problem, but she was also pragmatic enough to know that they could not run a campaign for long without the help of some big donors.

Ruth started looking for background information about Goldfarb and his public relations firm, though she found nothing. She tried running a reverse phone number search. Again, nothing.

There was no trail she could find, and that worried her. But this guy had found them through the Clown Underground, and she knew that a lot of people used pseudonyms to avoid detection. She would have to give her worries a rest, and decided to ask the lawyer who was volunteering with the campaign to help sort it all out.

The office space was in a well-manicured complex of new buildings called Cedar Point, and was less than two miles away from the campaign's current headquarters. A platinum blonde leasing agent named Carol was waiting for them with a sour attitude.

She seemed particularly indignant toward Virgil. Maybe she doesn't care for clowns, he thought. It wasn't likely that she had coulrophobia; people with a fear of clowns usually acted more frightened than hostile. Or maybe she just didn't like black people. He had certainly seen that before.

Perhaps there was a little of both beneath the surface, but what really bothered her was that the owner was giving away space for free in a brand-new building, and she wasn't going to get a commission. She was in a cutthroat business, and she had busted her butt for months to land the contract to offer the property. And now this. She wasn't happy, and she knew her boss wouldn't be either. But reluctantly, she did her job.

Ruth and Virgil stepped off the elevator and into a sweeping reception area. The millwork on the curved wooden front desk was impressive, as was the view out of the wall of windows to the side of it. The short-term nature of campaigns meant that most operations had to settle for whatever vacant space a landlord was willing to pawn off to bring in some rent for a few months. But this place was a far stretch better than what even the major party front-runners had on the ground in Iowa.

Ruth imagined inviting members of the press to meet with Russell in the office's glass-paneled conference room, and what type of message that would send about the seriousness of the campaign. It was all so beautiful, but surreal and

41

almost too good to be true. As the tour of the space was winding down, Ruth pressed the leasing agent for more details.

"Who owns the building?"

"You mean you don't know?" snapped Carol.

"Well, no, not exactly. We were contacted by a friend of the campaign who works for a PR firm."

"Goldfarb."

"Yes, Goldfarb." Ruth continued. "And who exactly is Goldfarb?"

"You mean you don't know?" Carol replied again, determined to be of no help whatsoever.

Virgil stepped in this time. "No, I am terribly sorry, but we don't. He replied to a post I made on a message board,"

"And what kind of a message board was that?" Carol said with an eyebrow raised, implying that Goldfarb and Virgil might be the type of men who trolled around places on the Internet more nefarious than the Clown Underground message boards, possibly trading office space for indecent favors.

"It was, uh… just a political message board," Virgil replied

The leasing agent sighed heavily, recognizing that she was reaching the limits of how obstinate she could be before crossing the line into overt hostility. "This whole office park is owned by a very wealthy family that likes their privacy. Goldfarb is one of their political men in Washington, and if he says you can have the place, then it is yours. No questions asked."

The room fell silent for a few moments, aside from the echo of their footsteps moving through the large space. Ruth pondered the last part. Was it Carol who wasn't to ask questions, or them?

"Is there any kind of deposit you need?" Ruth asked.

"No. It's ready to go. Utilities are on. Everything is included."

The lawyer who was volunteering for the campaign was standing by to call Goldfarb if everything checked out, and Ruth saw no reason to hold her back. She told Carol they would call her later to make the final arrangements.

*   *   *

Ruth touched base with her son in the middle of the day to tell him about the new headquarters and other developments.

"How is the new campaign manager working out?" Greenbeaux asked.

"He's great, but doesn't know he's our campaign manager yet. I thought you might want to offer him the job tonight."

The campaign organization was starting to take shape, and with others worrying about the operational details, Greenbeaux's mind was liberated to ponder the bigger picture. The C-SPAN debate was coming up in a week, and he was spending a lot of time considering how to work ideas he was hearing from voters into his talking points.

He was also starting to think about how they could expand the outreach beyond door-knocking, and he was interested in finding ways for them to organize rallies. They could pull enough volunteers out of the headquarters to make a crowd look respectable, and perhaps draw a few more people through leafleting. TV cameras were starting to swarm all over Iowa for the upcoming caucuses, and a good crowd on national television could give his campaign credibility.

The Democratic and Republican Party candidates were jockeying for position to be among the few who could maintain enough momentum to keep their campaigns alive into New Hampshire and South Carolina. It was a battle of attrition, and the fight was on to be a survivor.

There had already been countless debates among the major-party primary contenders. But with the good exposure comes the bad, and some of the weaker candidates were self-destructing under the glare. Many of those would have preferred to just slink away quietly, rather than face the unwanted scrutiny caused by embarrassing gaffes and disclosures of indiscretion in their private lives.

The third-party candidates had a much tougher time getting attention. But they weren't under the same pressure to win a caucus or primary to survive, and even a late entrant could come on strong over the summer if Americans were unhappy with the anointed front-runners going into the conventions. Still, the odds were stacked against them if they didn't break out early, and if history was any guide, the best they could hope for would be a fraction of the protest vote in states where they clawed their way onto the ballot.

Greenbeaux realized that he needed some kind of an iconic gimmick to get the media's attention, and he started wearing a green bow tie as a visual cue to remind people of his name.

More than a few people suggested that he should have clowns perform wherever he went, but he was really fighting for their rights to be seen as ordinary citizens trying to live their lives with dignity, and he feared he would do more harm than good if he perpetuated any stereotypes. He wanted to prevent his campaign from becoming a circus. Literally.

He did have one idea, and he wanted to run it by his mother and the new campaign manager when he met with them that night.

*   *   *

The evening's pizza delivery arrived shortly after 6:30, and Ruth quietly grabbed a box and walked out the door of the headquarters with it after she had paid the driver. She and her son had made plans to meet Virgil in the worn-down lounge area of his hotel so that they could have more privacy. Ruth was the last one there, and the two men interrupted their friendly chat to start in on the pizza.

Greenbeaux had wanted his mother to be there when he offered the campaign manager job so that she could better answer any questions. He liked what his mother had told him about Virgil's work so far, and he instinctively trusted her judgment of people. Nothing he had witnessed in his two brief encounters contradicted Ruth's assessment, and so Virgil would be offered the opportunity to become the manager of the Greenbeaux for President campaign.

With the pizza settling in their stomachs, they started discussing business. The lawyer had spoken with Goldfarb, and everything appeared to be, as he had described, on the up-and-up. The in-kind donation of office space could be legally channeled through a political action committee without getting the donor, the PAC, or the campaign in trouble.

Ruth and Virgil had tried to research the building's ownership to see what could be learned about the benefactor and any ulterior motives, but they came up with nothing. A title search revealed that the complex was the sole asset of Cedar Point Inc., a Delaware corporation whose officers and board of directors were all lawyers from two large firms with offices in New York and Washington.

Whoever was behind this wanted to remain hidden. And for all they knew, this was just the doing of some very rich clown who wanted to help the cause anonymously. No conditions appeared to be attached, and the three quickly agreed that they should take the offer. If favors were later asked in return, Greenbeaux could always choose to decline if he felt it would compromise his integrity.

In the morning they would get the keys from Carol the curmudgeon, then walk through the office and decide how to best arrange the operation. There was sufficient money from the incoming donations to rent folding chairs and basic tables to serve as workstations, and they would also get desks for the offices of a few important volunteers.

Virgil suspected that he would be important enough to get a desk, but he was not expecting what was coming when Greenbeaux turned the conversation to the leadership team he was forming.

"I would like you to serve as my campaign manager, Virgil."

Two days earlier, he had been sitting in a conference room in Cleveland, Ohio, being fired for coming to work dressed as himself. And now, he was being asked to take the organizational reigns of a presidential campaign that was fighting for a cause dear to his heart. The long drive to Des Moines had given him time to think and clear his head, and the whirlwind of productivity since his arrival was quickly starting to revive the dead patches Riley Booth had so carelessly branded onto his spirit.

Virgil smiled.

Ruth added: "You are needed here. We can't pay you anything yet but we can cover your lodging and help with food, if you don't mind having pizza at the headquarters every night. If we keep the momentum going and raise more money, we would like to have some salaried positions on staff like a real presidential campaign. No promises, but that is the goal."

"I didn't come here for the money, and honestly, I don't care about that." Virgil said. "I came here because I believe in the cause and I want to use my talents and time to help. And so, yes, I would be honored to serve as the manager of this campaign."

"Then it's settled," Greenbeaux said, turning the conversation to how the labor would be divided. In her role as director of personnel, Ruth would be in charge of screening the volunteers for leadership roles that matched their skills. Virgil would oversee all other operational and logistical aspects of the campaign, and both he and Ruth would report to Greenbeaux. Truth be told, though, Russell always had to answer to his mother.

They talked for another hour about how to structure the campaign most efficiently around a few key goals: getting the message out, raising more money, and now that they had more space, bringing in more volunteers. The effort would be based out of Iowa for the foreseeable future, but eventually they would need to expand into other parts of the country to be close to the media frenzy that moved from state to state.

All three felt good about where this was heading. Out of nothingness, the editorial had brought a frenzy of support from the Clown Underground and others who were tired of

Beltway politics. Now, the three were forming the plan to build order from chaos.

There was one more idea that Greenbeaux wanted to float. The vision was very clear in his own mind, but he realized that it might come across as a bit batty when spoken aloud. But he felt safe enough with his mother and Virgil to throw it on the table.

"What this campaign needs is a marching band."

CHAPTER 4

Virgil woke up early again the next morning, and almost immediately went over to his computer to see what responses had come in to a query he had posted seeking volunteers for a marching band. Ruth was well-versed in the peculiarities of clowns, but she did not intuitively grasp the idea of a marching band for the campaign in the same way that Virgil had.

To Ruth, the band just seemed like a nice idea to provide musical interludes at the political rallies they wanted to organize. But both men knew well what marching bands meant in the context of the clown culture. In the awkward high school years, these bands served as a place where people could find fellowship and an escape from social isolation.

Greenbeaux understood that a band would provide him a measure of political cover to expand the message further into mainstream politics without alienating his base. There were some grumblings among the more strident elements within the Clown Underground that Greenbeaux was abandoning his clown rights platform in favor of a more populist rhetoric about the problems in Washington.

That was true to a large extent. Greenbeaux had done the political calculus and realized that he would never be more than a fringe candidate if he just ranted on about clown rights when the voting public and the press didn't think it was a problem.

The more he spoke with people on their doorsteps and elsewhere, the more he realized that voters were reaching a boiling point about the polarization in Washington. In theory, moderates liked the idea of a split government because they didn't trust that either party, if left alone to its own devices, could resist the temptation to ram through the extreme agendas of their wing nuts and special-interest benefactors. But all they were getting from the current split government was more partisanship.

What they really craved -- and what Greenbeaux himself wanted -- was for lawmakers to work together to reach pragmatic compromises from the best ideas across the political spectrum. But this wasn't happening, and Greenbeaux was finding his voice as the neutral-party candidate who could bridge the gap.

Building on the approach he had successfully taken in the *Des Moines Register* editorial, Greenbeaux wanted to portray himself as an ordinary man who happened to be a clown.

Most people thought of clowns as just entertainers who performed for children and didn't have a serious side. They didn't realize that the kindly old man who lived next door or the woman who taught them history in high school might actually be a clown who was being discriminated against.

Greenbeaux strongly believed that he could do more to elevate the discussion of clown rights if he first showed himself to be a legitimate political thinker with popular ideas. There would be a time and a place for him to press the issue that had gotten him into the race in the first place, but he had to keep the more radical elements in the Clown Underground placated for his plan to work. The marching band was a dog whistle that only other clowns could hear, and he hoped that it would buy him some time.

*   *   *

Virgil arrived at the old headquarters well before 7:00 a.m. His first full day as the campaign manager promised to be a big one, with a complete overhaul of the campaign organization and the move to the new offices on the agenda. But first, he had to start building a marching band.

Ruth recalled that one of the non-clown volunteers who showed up to help earlier in the week was a retired high school music teacher, and Ruth had come into the headquarters a few minutes ahead of Virgil to search the sign-in cards to track him down.

The man was probably 80, several years older than Ruth, but he seemed to have a sharp mind and good health. Ruth was in charge of personnel, but Virgil, who had played trumpet in his high school marching band, was better suited to interview him for the position.

The responses to Virgil's post on the Clown Underground message boards about musicians being needed for the Greenbeaux for President marching band had the desired effect on two fronts. Plenty of people were stepping forward to volunteer, including a number who were offering to take leave of their jobs and family to travel to Iowa and join. Also, the posting had calmed the voices on the board who were worried that Greenbeaux was selling out.

Ruth found the volunteer card and handed it to Virgil. Douglas Goodwin was the gentleman's name, and he lived in Urbandale, a streetcar suburb just west of Des Moines. Goodwin met Greenbeaux at a diner soon after the candidate had landed in Iowa. He was amused at first, but then was deeply impressed when he read the editorial in the *Register*.

After more than 40 years working in the school system, he was retired and free to do as he pleased, and he had decided on a whim to go down to the headquarters to see if he could be of help. Virgil had a hard time getting in a word edgewise when he called Douglas later that morning. Yes, he had directed the marching bands at two different high schools. Music was his passion, and he would love to give it one more go for the Greenbeaux campaign. The two agreed to meet at the new offices to make plans for the band.

With those wheels in motion, Virgil turned his attention to other matters. Ruth had secured the keys to the new headquarters, and he was hanging back at the old place to direct people over. He arranged for furniture rental, network and telecom setup, and other logistical details of the move, then found a few moments to lean back against a drum of chemical solvents and reflect.

Everything had started to come together at Cedar Point when Greenbeaux showed up at midmorning. Word was starting to spread through the clown community that the campaign was on the move, and the excitement was driving more donations. Nearly $11,000 had come through online overnight, more than matching the entire haul for the week.

The new address had not been updated on the website yet, and some volunteers were still coming into the old headquarters to help. Virgil loaded them up with supplies to take over, and then put a sign on the door with the Cedar

Point address, leaving only the toilet paper and barrels behind.

Greenbeaux was still at Cedar Point when Virgil arrived, and the two discussed how they would use whatever space Ruth had not already marked off. The office was configured to have a large open area where cubicles or a call center could go, and this would serve as the primary place volunteers could work at the collapsible tables to be delivered the next day.

Virgil saw another potential use for the space. Most December days were pretty cold in Iowa, and he thought the marching band might be more comfortable practicing indoors. He pointed out how the tables could be arranged flush against the walls for people to work with chairs facing outward during rehearsals, and then returned to the center of the room afterward. They wouldn't be able to call any voters when the band was playing, but they didn't even have phones yet anyway.

Ruth had stationed herself at the rounded wooden reception desk near the elevator and was directing traffic when the furniture arrived. The offices had not yet been assigned, and she was wary of poachers.

As the deliverymen started bringing in the desks, she quickly scribbled signs for office doors with titles that had not yet been assigned. "Reserved for Chief Financial Officer," read one. Another said "Reserved for Press Secretary." She gave the two nicest offices to her son and Virgil, and assigned one next to theirs for herself.

She really wanted to sit at the reception desk to welcome and screen people as they came in, but she thought that she had better hold a room where she could close the door just in case. There were 12 offices in addition to a conference room, bathrooms, the large open area, and a combined kitchen and break area that she labeled "War Room." She managed to come up with a few more imaginary titles before she gave up and posted signs that simply said, "Reserved" on the remaining office doors.

At 3 p.m. sharp she saw a slightly stooped man with thinning grey hair and weather-beaten skin step off the elevator carrying a box of sheet music. She turned to a nearby volunteer and asked him to go find Virgil.

"Welcome, Mr. Goodwin," she said. "Thank you for coming in."

They chatted as she walked him to the far side of the headquarters and stopped at a door with a sign that said "Reserved for Musical Director."

He wasn't expecting this. He had never had his own office in all his years of teaching, just a desk in a band room that was usually cluttered with instruments and permission slips, and an aging piano in the corner. He had spent a few hours in the old cramped headquarters, and he assumed that the new place would not be much of an upgrade, perhaps a larger industrial space or a rundown storefront.

Virgil came over to shake hands and Ruth slipped away to tend to the control tower, the nickname she had given to the reception desk where she liked to perch.

Douglas put the box on the desk and took some sheet music out. He had brought with him a cross section of numbers that he thought might be appropriate for a political campaign. His earliest memory of hearing a marching band as a boy was at a Fourth of July parade, and so John Philip Sousa numbers were featured prominently.

Virgil handed Douglas a printout of more than 50 volunteers who had responded to his post, indicating that they would like to join. There would be many more as the word spread, and so Virgil suggested that they just start with the local ones and not ask anyone in other parts of the country to drop everything and come out.

There were a few doubts lingering in the back of Virgil's mind. Douglas Goodwin was from a bygone era when bands played traditional marching music, and the selection of John Philip Sousa sheet music suggested that he might not understand what this band was about. Douglas and Ruth were from the same generation, and so it made sense that she would have wanted him for the job. But would the younger band members buy it?

Clowns were performers by their nature, but most did not like to be the stars themselves. Marching bands serve as a sideshow to the main attraction -- at football games and parades -- and they provided an outlet for clowns to perform without being the center of attention. Greenbeaux was unusual, in a sense, because he was willing to place himself in the limelight for his cause. But since he lived openly as a clown, he had little to lose and nothing to hide in his own version of performing.

It was a delicate subject to broach, but Virgil thought it would be a good idea to brief Douglas on the significance of marching bands in clown culture. No doubt, the old bandleader had taught dozens of clowns through the years, but he might not have realized it, and if he were to do the job he would need a primer.

This would not be like high school, where the students did what the teacher wanted. The campaign was being propped up by the Clown Underground, and the volunteers would likely have some very specific ideas about the message their candidate's marching band should convey to the world.

"Have you ever worked with clowns before?" Virgil asked.

Douglas thought this an odd question, but he supposed it was to be expected coming from a man in a clown costume. He had spent a few hours volunteering in the old headquarters, surrounded by clowns, and here he was again, albeit in a much nicer office.

"You mean, aside from on this campaign?" Douglas responded, pausing for a moment before elaborating. "When I was in the Army, I helped to put on a show for the kids on the base. I recruited a couple of guys to dress like clowns and hand out candy."

Virgil took a deep breath as he organized his thoughts. Douglas Goodwin was no different from most people who went through life oblivious to the private struggles of the clowns in their midst, but that would have to change.

"When you were teaching, did you ever notice that some of your students in the band were clowns?"

Douglas smiled. He had seen his fair share of class clowns in his 40-odd years in the school system, and he nodded affirmatively. But Virgil sensed that his question was not fully understood, and so he tried again.

"Did any of your students ever reveal that they were clowns?"

This question puzzled Douglas, and the look on his face told Virgil what he was up against. He decided to launch into a Clown 101 class to educate Douglas and prepare him for what was to come. "Okay. Let me explain. You know how Russell Greenbeaux talks about clown rights?"

Again Douglas nodded, but he didn't really understand. He had been attracted to the campaign because of his encounter with the candidate and the message in the *Des Moines Register* editorial about the morass in Washington. He had assumed that Greenbeaux and most of his supporters were professional clowns. It never dawned on him that there was any kind of a civil-rights issue at stake.

"Being a clown is not just a lifestyle choice," Virgil said. "And it's not a sexual orientation. Not normally, anyway. It is just something people are born with."

A glimmer of recognition came across Douglas' face. He understood now that Virgil must have been talking about some sort of a calling. He could relate to that. He had always felt that his life's work was in music, just as others felt they were called to the sciences or public service. But he was still one big mental leap away from grasping that there was more than a vocation involved.

"There are four basic subtypes of clowns," Virgil continued. "Happy, sad, angry, and evil."

"Got it." Douglas smiled. "And which one are you."

"Well, I am a happy clown, most of the time. You can usually tell by the way people wear their makeup. If you see someone with a smile drawn, that means they are happy. If you see a teardrop painted on or the corners of the lips tilts downward, that means they are sad. And angry clowns, well, you can usually see it in their eyes."

"And evil clowns?" Douglas asked. "How can you tell if someone is an evil clown?"

That was a fair question, Virgil thought, but not one that was easily answered. "Evil clowns don't usually look evil, despite what you might see in the movies. They try to mask their true nature. Some go for long stretches of their lives without wearing makeup or clown gear at all to avoid tipping their hand. They can appear to be happy and deceivingly charming, but you never want to have your back turned to an evil clown."

"Okay, so what type of a clown is Russell Greenbeaux?" Douglas wondered aloud.

"He's... uh. It's complicated." Virgil had wondered about this himself. The candidate's makeup didn't convey any one emotion. Greenbeaux's temperament was almost always on an even keel, but perhaps his quest was motivated by some underlying anger. It was best not to go there, and so Virgil steered the conversation back to the campaign's musical direction.

"Clowns are drawn to marching bands, and so it is quite likely -- in fact, it is almost certain -- that you had several of them in your class each year. But you probably wouldn't have known this because it wasn't safe for them to be open about it."

A moment of enlightenment was at hand. Douglas knew all about how teenagers could hide aspects of their lives. There were many reasons why: fear of social isolation, confusion about sexual identity, or to mask something else that was terribly wrong in their lives. But it had never occurred to him that being a clown was a real thing, or for that matter something to hide from others. He tried to keep a poker face, but a slight smile crept in at the idea, and he thought he should say something in acknowledgment.

"I understand. Kids can be cruel in high school, and I can see how tough it must have been for someone growing up as a clown."

Douglas was passing the empathy test, and Virgil became more relaxed as he moved on to other details that he felt the band director would need to manage the quirky army of volunteers about to come his way.

"Okay then. There are a couple of things you should know. The four subtypes of clowns are drawn to different types of instruments.   Angry clowns tend to like percussion instruments, mainly because it gives them something to beat on to get their aggression out. Happy clowns like most brass instruments, and sad clowns tend to go for woodwinds and string instruments like violins. I know this probably sounds like I am stereotyping -- and I suppose I am a bit -- but this is pretty well understood in the clown community.

This seemed interesting to Douglas, and he was starting to connect the dots with some of the angry drummers he had seen over the years. His slight smile turned broad, and he couldn't help asking the obvious question: "And what about the evil clowns? What instruments do they like to play?"

Virgil's face turned solemn. "Tubas. Evil clowns are drawn to tubas. It's a power thing."

A cold chill went through Douglas's body. Some of the most manipulative and mean-spirited band members he had ever known were tuba players. If there was any truth to what Virgil was saying, it would explain the behavior of some of his least-favorite students over the years. Clowns or not, many of his tuba players had been sociopathic to their core.

About halfway through his career as a teacher, Douglas started filming his marching band's performances. Reviewing the tapes over the years, he had noticed that a number of the students near the rear of the procession were often agitated and kept looking nervously over their shoulders. He hadn't given it much thought, but it made a lot of sense now. Something instinctively was telling these kids that it was a bad idea to have their backs turned to the tuba players marching in the last row.

"So…" Douglas resumed. "I guess we should skip the tuba section in Greenbeaux's band."

"No, I don't think we can do that. It would send a bad message to exclude some members of our community. Plus, it would be really dangerous to piss off all of the evil clowns."

Virgil sensed he was getting through to Douglas, but he still had concerns about the proposed song arrangements. The music that was popular at Clown Underground raves was unlike anything the old man would probably have opted to listen to on his own, and Virgil knew that the younger band members would view stodgy marching music as antithetical to their cause.

It might be a bit insensitive to tell the brand-new volunteer bandleader that his era had passed, but Virgil knew he had to find a way to get the message through. He settled on a tactful approach. "Over all those years that you were a teacher, you must have noticed how students' musical tastes changed."

"Oh heavens, yes," said Douglas, his face lighting up again. "I saw every fad come and go, and every generation thinks that their music was the only kind that was any good. But I told them, over and over, some day your favorite songs will only be played on oldies stations that your kids can't stand. History has a funny way of repeating itself that way."

Virgil saw his opening. "I was looking at the profiles of the people who are volunteering for the band, and there are a lot of young people. Some who probably weren't even in high school yet by the time you retired."

Douglas could see where this was going, and it didn't bother him in the least. He had been around long enough to recognize the evolutionary nature of music. Each successive generation added its own spin, and he enjoyed watching how songwriters built upon earlier sounds to deliver new variations on old themes to a fickle crop of young listeners.

He still preferred the big band and classical music of his youth, but he was not the least bit closed-minded or judgmental when he listened to popular music. Mostly he heard talented performers interpreting the work of imaginative composers, following in a tradition that had been in place since long before he was born. The songs might sound new, but in a larger sense he knew they were really based on something very old.

Over the years, he had paid careful attention to what the kids were listening to and made a game of trying to deconstruct and trace their favorite songs back to earlier influences. In the days before kids were walking around with downloaded songs on cell phones, he would ask students in his music appreciation class to bring in their favorite records and tapes. Then, he would sit at his piano in the classroom and play the songs back, interpreting them as though they belonged to another, older genre.

Students would sit transfixed as everything from hip hop to Southern rock songs they thought were brand new were dissected down to their roots, sometimes in the form of a 50-year-old song that had a nearly identical melody, rhythm and beat. This was Douglas's way of teaching students to appreciate what might have otherwise seemed old-fashioned. And it was also a way to remind himself that the music of his past lived on in new forms.

"I think we might want to lose the Sousa marches," Virgil said directly. "We need to appeal to the clowns in our base, and if the music is more contemporary than what people expect from a marching band, we can get the attention of younger voters.

"That sounds like a fun challenge. Do you have some particular songs or artists in mind?"

Virgil had to think for a minute. The music he heard at Clown Underground parties in Cleveland belonged to a younger generation than his, and he had to confess that he couldn't identify anything by name.

"Can you get me a mix tape?" Douglas asked.

Mix tape? That sounded odd coming out of the mouth of an 80-year-old man. But it gave Virgil hope that their bandleader was up to the challenge, and he promised to see what he could do. Douglas would have a few weeks to put it all together since Greenbeaux wanted to get past the C-SPAN debate and Christmas a few days later before trying to hold any rallies where the band would perform.

CHAPTER 5

After that night's pizza had been eaten and the last volunteers dispersed from Cedar Point, Greenbeaux sat down with Ruth and Virgil to start his debate preparation. They didn't want to spend the campaign's limited resources hiring a professional consultant to help, so they decided they would have to do it on their own.

Third-party candidate events don't draw the type of audience and hype that the mainstream party debates get, but the team knew that unusual candidates sometimes grabbed the media spotlight for a brief time after this type of exposure. And what was more unusual than a serious candidate dressed as a clown?

Their hope was that Greenbeaux's appearance would get the attention long enough for his common-sense message about the dysfunction in Washington to sink in. Comedy writers routinely scoured obscure political programs to find golden nuggets, and the hope was that a perfectly timed sound bite might go viral.

Ruth and Virgil wanted their message to serve as a contrast with everyone else on the stage, and they dared to imagine a pundit of some sort saying, "The clown is the only one who makes any sense." To pull that off, though, they suspected Greenbeaux would have to promote his clown credentials to flip the story around and make everyone else look silly by comparison.

This made the candidate a little nervous. He was in the race to draw attention to the plight of clowns, and he worried that becoming part of a joke would be counterproductive. But Ruth saw the hook and laid out the case.

"You are going to be the only one standing on that stage in a clown suit, and like it or not son, others will judge you to be the fool without bothering to listen to what you have to say. You have to be the foil that reflects the light back on everyone else."

Virgil agreed: "You are fighting for our right to go about our lives as clowns in public, so why not be direct about it if that's what you need to turn it around on them? Just tell them that a presidential campaign should be about the character of the people who we want to run our country. We should be judging the candidates by what is on the inside, not how they appear on the outside."

Greenbeaux recognized that as true; it was the core of the argument behind successful civil rights movements. He knew that the candidates on stage with him would be outliers, and just about anything he said was going to seem reasonable by comparison. But would playing the role of a self-deprecating clown allow his message to break through, or just make him look like a sideshow to the main attraction? He was struggling with this.

The task would be easier if the presidential race were just among third-party candidates. Those oddballs would be easy targets. But unlike candidates in mainstream party debates, he had little to gain by attacking anyone on the stage.

His real target was the status quo in Washington, and everyone else would be so wrapped up in their own limited agendas that they wouldn't even be listening to what he had to say, let alone trying to engage him in a substantive debate.

Greenbeaux had a lot to think about, and everyone was getting tired. The move to the new offices had given them an adrenaline rush that carried them through the day, but late-night marathons were for a younger breed. They agreed to divvy responsibilities for the preparation and reconvene at a more reasonable hour the next day.

Virgil was tasked with researching the other candidates who would be on the stage. Ruth was to find and review videos of previous third-party presidential debates. And Greenbeaux would organize his talking points into sound bites and zingers.

It hardly seemed possible to Virgil that just a few days earlier he was in Cleveland, being shown the door by Riley Booth. It was a different world, a different life from the exhilarating whirlwind he was now going through. He did not dread getting out of bed in the morning as he had countless times over the past year, though tonight he was anxious to some sleep.

It occurred to him that he ought to stop at the front desk and tell the night manager he would be around for a while. He had checked in with no expectations of what the next day would bring, and he still wasn't quite sure what would happen tomorrow.

His corporate career had been all about avoiding excitement. If the day was uneventful, it meant that all of the trucks had arrived as planned and nothing had caught on fire. If something went wrong, it was usually because he or someone he managed had made a mistake. Virgil had come to view boring as a good thing on the job, but there was nothing routine about being Greenbeaux's campaign manager, and he loved it.

He arrived back in his room and decided to take a quick look online at the slate of candidates scheduled to participate. What he saw unnerved him, and kept his mind racing for several hours to come.

*   *   *

The Green Party's presumptive nominee, Lydia Conner, seemed to Virgil to be the most normal of all the candidates. She was a Harvard-educated lawyer who ran an environmental advocacy group that was working to offset the effects of global warming. Her campaign website looked professional and informative, and it took some digging for Virgil to get beneath the facade and find her Achilles heel.

Lydia had led Project Pegasus, an effort to build a prototype solar car made from biodegradable materials. Her ambition was to succeed Al Gore as the leader of the environmental movement in the United States, but the project had been so fraught with delays and hiccups that it became a drag on her reputation.

The prototype car looked sleek, but it handled poorly and was severely underpowered. The engineers had secretly taken it to the Sonora Desert in Arizona the previous July for testing, hoping that the bright sunshine would provide ample energy to power the sluggish vehicle.

Unfortunately, the biggest problem with the Pegasus car was that it was absolutely delicious, or so thought a pack of wild javelinas that stumbled upon it in the middle of the night. They nibbled it down to the compressed seaweed tires, and the little bits that were left dissolved when a monsoon thunderstorm swept through the valley early the next morning.

Lydia and her team tried to keep the debacle quiet, and they might have succeeded if not for the discovery of a dozen wild boars who were found dead in the desert a few days later, poisoned by a toxic epoxy that had been hastily added to hold the otherwise organic car together.

The environmental community was embroiled in a debate about what was now being derisively called Project Piggiecide by animal-rights activists, and Lydia was running for president to restore her good name and rightful place as the up-and-coming leader of the movement.

There were also two Libertarian candidates scheduled to participate in the debate. On one end of the spectrum was Randy Druslan, a porn star who disdained any government intrusion into the bedroom, or the pool cabana, or anywhere else he happened to be filming at the time. Randy had been a dual theater and philosophy major at UCLA, where he became a follower of Objectivism and the view that seeking personal pleasure was the highest moral calling. He was such a devotee of Ayn Rand, in fact, that he had adopted the screen name Atlas Fountainhead as a tribute to her.

Druslan's website was so steeped in the language of metaphysical philosophy that Virgil found it almost incomprehensible. But the underlying political message was simple: "Leave me alone and let me do what I want." It was a self-centered rationalization to justify Druslan's hedonistic behavior, but Virgil saw the folly in trying to debate against it. After all, didn't clowns just want to be left alone to live their lives openly like everyone else?

On the other end of the Libertarian spectrum was Ed Jeter, a rancher from a rural part of Nevada who had served one term in Congress many years earlier. His belief in individualism was absolute, and the time he spent in the House of Representatives had only cemented in his mind the notion that government served no useful purpose whatsoever.

Jeter had always lived a rural existence and his two years in Washington bothered him. The people there were so different, and he found the dependencies they had -- on the government for services like trash collection and on grocery stores for food -- to be antithetical to the proper way a free man should live his life. His house was a compound built with high walls to keep other people out and his stockpile of food, guns and gold bullion in.

The design of his website was a throwback to the early days of the World Wide Web, with flashing icons and text links -- mostly dead now -- to pages about the dangers of fluoridation and the new world order. In contrast to Druslan's self-indulgent brand of Libertarianism, Jeter was advocating self-reliance at all costs. He was the master of his property, and God help the poor elk or census worker who wandered onto it.

It was easy to take a simplistic view and dismiss Jeter as just a nutcase, and Virgil did exactly that. He figured that Greenbeaux could win points with reasonable people in the audience by simply disagreeing with anything Jeter had to say, and so he saw little point in wasting his time researching him any further. Instead, he turned his attention to Agatha Cromwell, who was running for president with the Labour Party.

It was not unusual to see political candidates wrap themselves in the American flag, but Virgil had never seen someone seeking office in the United States wrap themselves in a Union Jack. Quite literally. Agatha Cromwell's website prominently featured her standing in front of the Palace of Westminster with a British flag draped over her shoulders and covering everything except her face and pregnant belly.

Agatha's biography showed that she had been born and raised in the New York, but she spent much of her adult life in London. Her platform called for Congress to be dissolved 17 days before the general election and replaced with a parliamentary form of government. Instead of a President there would be a Prime Minister, who would be selected from among the winning party's ranks.

Virgil was slightly amused by Agatha's unconventional and unconstitutional idea, but he was also concerned. The other candidates were focused on different issues, but Agatha alone was highlighting problems with Congress to support her plan for drastic reform. That was Greenbeaux's turf, and Virgil was worried that having another candidate on the debate stage saying the same thing would dilute their campaign's message.

It was highly improbable that American voters would ever be willing to do away with Congress altogether, and Greenbeaux's campaign pitch was focused on the corrosive effects of partisan politics and special-interest money instead of on scrapping the whole system as Cromwell was proposing. To draw a contrast, Greenbeaux would need to distinguish between the wisdom of the Founding Fathers who had designed the bicameral legislative system and the moral bankruptcy of leaders who were using it for selfish purposes.

Virgil slogged on with his research, coming next to a candidate from the Communist Party, Aleksandar Bolan-Svrab. Aleksandar believed that the problems of the country were rooted in the flaws of capitalism, and he wanted to turn all power and privately owned assets over to a ruling triumvirate of workers who could lead the people to a glorious future.

The 28-year-old Bolan-Svrab was seven years too young to assume the presidency, had been born in the former Yugoslavia and was not a naturalized U.S. citizen. But none of that mattered because his chances of being elected were approximately zero. Even in the unlikely event that there was a rounding error on those odds and Marx and Engels suddenly came back into vogue, he would still not be eligible to lead under his own plan because he had never held a job and, therefore, he was not technically a worker.

Under different circumstances -- in another century, or another hemisphere, or perhaps another planet -- Virgil thought that Aleksandar's youthful idealism might have served him well as a candidate for some office. But in this time and place he was an outlier, just like everybody else who would be on the stage, including Greenbeaux.

Virgil was so tired that he could have fallen asleep sitting upright in his chair, but the candidates kept getting more and more bizarre, and he could not stop himself from watching the train wreck that was slowly unfolding in front of him.

Before sitting down to do this research, he had never heard of the Interstellar Awareness Party or its candidate, Fred Spaulding. But there he was, a presidential candidate who was running to let the world know that the mother ship was coming soon, and that everyone needed to unplug their microwave ovens on Election Day to prevent the spacecraft's control panel from malfunctioning.

And then there was the Know Nothing Party, which had been resurrected from the political dead by their current presidential candidate, Orville Banks. More than a century and a half earlier, the Know Nothings had been briefly lifted by a tide of anti-immigrant sentiment before eventually fading into obscurity, though strains of the movement lived on in the form of birthers and elements of the modern-day Tea Party.

In its current incarnation, Banks had shifted the party's focus from the 19th-century fear of immigrants from Ireland and Germany to those who were coming from just about any country other than those two. But he had retained the papal conspiracy theories that were hallmarks of the original party faithful, and Virgil pegged him to be just another wing nut with a screw loose. And there were more oddballs to come.

Many of the candidates were focused on single issues that were detached from the real problems a president would face day to day, and Cannabis Party candidate, Gordie Ancona, was no exception. He was an advocate for the industrial production of hemp, and he railed against what he viewed as hysteria-driven government regulation of the plant.

But Virgil could tell from a video he found online that Gordie's policies weren't the only things that were half-baked. The candidate could be seen in a field of plants on a gorgeous sunny day in Colorado, with the rugged mountains silhouetted against the blue sky in the background. The camera followed him as he talked about plant cultivation, occasionally stopping to check on the leaves and buds on his crop.

His advocacy might have seemed quite admirable if the gentleman farmer were simply talking about the numerous commercial applications and medicinal benefits of his crop, but the spacy rambling revealed a thoroughly stoned candidate joined at the lips to his product. There was no question about whether this candidate inhaled, because he was doing so for the whole world to see in the video.

Virgil found Gordie to be somewhat of an amusing and nonthreatening character, but the last candidate on his list to research was another matter. Hill Heller, running as an Aryan Social Separatist, was a white supremacist who advocated setting up segregated communities to prevent the intermingling of people from different races.

Like Greenbeaux, Heller was banking on an underground network of supporters to spread the word of his campaign. His website didn't have links to anywhere else, but a quick search revealed that lots of unpleasant sites and message boards were linking to him.

Virgil couldn't stomach reading through all of it, but he did watch a video of the racist candidate. Heller sat in a conference surrounded by charts and maps, outlining how he would divide up the country. He would move the nation's capital to northern Idaho and establish safe zones for white populations in major cities.

Virgil was a clown and a black man, and what he was hearing was an affront on many levels. He was very proud of his ability to get along with just about anybody who was not named Riley Booth, and Heller's message was diametrically opposed to how he had been raised to treat others. Greenbeaux's campaign was about allowing clowns to step out of the shadows and integrate into society, and Virgil thought the same opportunities should be available to everyone, clown or otherwise.

It was hard to watch, but Virgil tried to look beyond the vitriolic message to find clues into Heller's personality. It wasn't that Greenbeaux needed to come up with arguments against the Aryan Social Separatist ideology -- a reasonable person would need no convincing to see the flaws -- but Virgil just hated this guy, and he wanted to pick him apart.

He could tell from looking at the video that Heller had a nervous and agitated demeanor. He appeared to be riddled with anxiety and fear, and it wouldn't have surprised Virgil if he hated clowns just as much as he hated anyone else who was different. Greenbeaux's physically imposing presence might be unsettling and intimidating to Heller, which could open the door for all sorts of psychological warfare that Virgil dreamed of unleashing.

Virgil did realize that his fantasies were neither rational nor mature, but it was cathartic to think about inflicting mental anguish on the standard-bearer of the white supremacist movement. He could not predict if the ebb and flow of the debate would allow Greenbeaux an opening to rattle Heller, but he had an idea about how to do it if the opportunity arose, and he was anxious to share it at the debate prep meeting the next day.

It was well past eleven, and the exhausted campaign manager was finally allowing himself to lie down for the night. He turned off the light, but he could not turn off his brain and stop thinking about the unusual candidates he had just researched. Heller bothered him the most, and he finally had to get up and brush his teeth again to wash away the distastefulness before he could finally fall asleep.

CHAPTER 6

Ruth allowed herself to sleep in, expecting that Virgil or her son would be there to open the headquarters first thing in the morning. But she arrived at eight fifteen to find volunteers waiting in their cars to come in and get started. She hurriedly opened the door and welcomed everyone. Then she got to work.

A full installation of phones would take a few more days, and so a volunteer had put together a virtual telecom setup that sent voice messages to e-mail. She logged in to find nearly two dozen messages waiting. Ruth listened to a handful and then assigned a volunteer the task of reviewing the rest while she turned her attention to the campaign's regular e-mail inbox to check everything else that had come in overnight.

Most of the messages were from people who wanted to join the band, and she batched all of those into a new folder that she could later send to Douglas Goodwin. She was about halfway through when she came across an e-mail from a Carrie Rollins, a reporter at the *Register,* who wanted to write a feature story about Greenbeaux and was hoping to arrange a time when they could meet that day.

Normally, Greenbeaux spent daylight hours canvassing in the field, but the team had agreed to meet and work on their debate prep at two p.m. after the lunchtime glad-handing at downtown restaurants. Ruth called the reporter back and arranged for a two-thirty meeting at Cedar Point, and texted her son to let him know.

The conference room was now presentable with basic office furniture, but it looked a bit stark with barren white walls and little ambiance. Ruth wanted to spruce it up a bit so that it would look just right for the reporter's arrival. She stopped two women dressed in garish clown regalia and matching purple bouffant wigs as they stepped off the elevator and redirected them to join her in the conference room.

On the walk over, Ruth observed how everything would look to a stranger entering the headquarters for the first time, and made notes to herself out loud about how they could stage the office for maximum impact when the reporter arrived. When they reached the conference room, she turned to the ladies and asked their opinion about how it could be decorated.

There would be no circus motif, as one of the purple-haired women proposed, and Ruth quickly went through a checklist of items that were needed to warm the space. The women seemed to get it, so Ruth had them follow her back to the control tower. She put five hundred dollars from petty cash into an envelope, handed it to them with her list of items, and sent them off to shop.

Virgil walked in shortly before nine and huddled quickly with Ruth to prioritize the day's projects. The number of volunteers showing up was increasing each day, and there were several milling around waiting for something to do. The staffing firm recruiter who had helped with the coordination earlier in the week had not been able to come in for the past two days, so Ruth had to get the workers organized on her own.

Laptop in hand, Virgil went back to his office and got to work. First, he checked the website traffic and donations, and was pleasantly surprised to see that the previous day's momentum was still going. They had received $9,000 more in donations since he had last checked, which was well beyond what they had spent the day before to get the office ready. They were building a small war chest, and he was hopeful that they would be able to start using it to make a splash before the caucuses in early January.

A few minutes later, Ruth came back to Virgil's office and he briefed her on the recent haul. They agreed they would need to be careful with their money until Christmas. The C-SPAN debate was crucial to their momentum, and they would know soon enough whether the campaign would fizzle or continue to grow.

The media coverage of the major parties was relentless, but save for Greenbeaux's editorial and a few offbeat news items, the third-party candidates were virtually invisible. Virgil had given the matter a lot of thought and was beginning to formulate a new idea that he wanted to share with Ruth.

"I want to have the band ready to go after Christmas so that we can start putting together some flash mob rallies."

Ruth had heard of flash mobs, but didn't fully understand the concept so she pressed Virgil for more details.

"The network television crews set up in a different location every day, and I want to tail them in a bus with Russell, the band, and a social media person tweeting the location to supporters who can show up for a spontaneous a rally."

Ruth's eyes brightened as she listened. The media couldn't long hope to ignore a marching band full of clowns walking by, but she was a little bit fuzzy on the details of how they would get other supporters there. "So tell me how this works. We have Russell and the band on a bus, driving around looking for camera trucks. And then?"

"We would need to get the word out through the Clown Underground that a flash mob was about to form, ideally on a Saturday when most people don't have to work and could stand by to scramble when we call the crowd together. When we find a TV crew, we tweet the location, unload the band and your son, and let them loose. If it's in a place where there are already a lot of people around, we probably wouldn't need too many of our own to make it look like a full-blown political rally."

A simple concept, it could draw plenty of attention if executed properly. Reporters might not like the idea of their live stand-ups being interrupted by Greenbeaux and his band, but Ruth suspected that it wouldn't matter what they thought. Everyone watching at home would find it entertaining, and that would be enough for the networks to start giving them airtime.

Much of the campaign was a work in progress, and Virgil and Ruth had plenty of distractions that made it hard to focus on the bigger picture. They had a beautiful headquarters, thanks to a mysterious benefactor. But the nation's attention would move on from Iowa once the caucuses were over, and they would have to figure out where to go after the media circus traveled to the next primary state.

It helped that they were under no pressure to perform well in the caucuses, an event in which supporters of the major-party candidates would gather all over the state to build consensus about who their locale was backing. Third-party candidates were largely irrelevant in that process, and Greenbeaux's operation was only there because that's where the media were camped.

Energy coming from the Clown Underground sustained the campaign for now. Money was flowing in because Greenbeaux was giving them hope, but if he fizzled in the C-SPAN debate then even that well of support would start to run dry. The nearly impossible task of getting press coverage would become more difficult, and the campaign would be close to its inevitable end.

It all came down to the debate. If he performed well, they could make plans to take the show beyond Iowa. New Hampshire, South Carolina, and Florida would soon follow with primaries, followed by a host of other states that presented a double-edged sword of opportunity and risk.

They were getting attention in one part of one state, and the clown-rights movement would greatly benefit if they could take the message to a broader audience. But they didn't have the resources the national parties enjoyed, and they would quickly spread themselves too thin if they tried to go everywhere at once.

Ruth and Virgil adjourned their impromptu meeting to tend to the pressing business at hand. She returned to the control tower, which was being inundated by a new wave of volunteers looking for direction, and he had other matters to deal with.

Members of the Clown Underground had put two and two together and identified Virgil as an important person in the campaign, and so his message threads were the most heavily trafficked on the boards. When he logged in to check on his posted request for a mix tape, he could see there were way too many responses to read through. He was not yet ready to unleash the Clown Underground on

Douglas, or vice versa, and so he postponed dealing with that until he could spend more time with his musical director later in the day.

Whenever Virgil posted on the board, his requests were straightforward requests, and he had never envisioned that they would also serve as a catalyst to spark momentum in the campaign. But Greenbeaux represented hope for the clown community, and people were looking for any clue they could find that their candidate was in the running and that the fight for their rights would soon be part of the collective American consciousness.

Virgil now recognized that his posts were at least partly responsible for the wave of donations and volunteers coming in, and he pondered whether the campaign should add a regular update to keep the enthusiasm mounting. He realized, though, that there were a couple of risks.

First, there was a natural ebb and flow to any campaign. It would be hard for them to keep manufacturing more and more good news to top what happened the previous day without being dishonest. Virgil also knew that Greenbeaux had little interest in staying in the race to the very end, and he worried about the psychological impact of artificially building expectations of a community -- his community -- when the end game was destined to be a retreat.

*   *   *

Greenbeaux came into the office shortly before two, shivering and nearly frostbitten from a bitter wind on the leading edge of a cold front. He had received his mother's message about the reporter coming to interview him, and he had spent too much time outside while organizing his thoughts and talking points

Stepping off the elevator, he noticed right away that the headquarters had been rearranged. Volunteers were manning worktables that had been moved closer to the front of the room to signal an even livelier but still orderly operation. There were tasteful wall hangings, glass vases with flowers on some tables, and large ceramic bowls filled with fresh fruit staged strategically between the control tower and the glass-walled conference room.

Ruth greeted her son and pointed out what he had already noticed about the remodeling. She grabbed a briefing packet off her desk and led him to the conference room to get warmed up and prepare.

Greenbeaux settled in and opened the envelope. Inside were copies of recent articles Carrie Rollins had written, mostly political position analysis stories and candidate biographies. There was also a copy of her bio from a professional social networking site. She had earned a master's degree in journalism from Northwestern, then worked for two years at the *Wall Street Journal* before spending the last six years at the *Register*. Also in the packet was a copy of Greenbeaux's own editorial to refresh his memory, since it was quite likely that she would use that as the starting point for her questions.

While the *Des Moines Register* was national in the scope of its political coverage and influence, it was still a local paper that needed to sell advertising to companies in the central part of the state. And so Greenbeaux had to be prepared for the local angle, if asked. He wrote down words that he associated with Iowa: friendly, common sense, mom's family, and cold. He went back and scratched out the last one, though it really was his strongest impression.

He had been welcomed to the state by an early season storm that put four inches of slushy snow on top of downed leaves that had not been fully cleared for the season. That had made the going slow at first when he was trying to get a feel for campaigning on the ground. But some of the lazier reporters just looked for an attention-grabbing sound bite and he thought better of saying anything that could be taken as a slight against Iowa.

Next, he jotted down some adjectives to describe himself: clown, tall, and entrepreneur. They all seemed obvious and not particularly revealing. Greenbeaux was a private person by nature, but he was putting himself out there publicly for the sake of the campaign. He didn't really want to delve into his childhood or rough patches in his life that would round out an interesting biographical sketch, but that was part of the game he was now playing, and he was bracing himself for some indelicate probing by the reporter.

He had proven himself to be an imperfect person many times over the course of his life, and he did fear the possibility of a picture floating around from the time of his failed marriage that could come back to haunt him. His demons and skeletons were his own -- and he really wanted to keep it that way -- but that was not always possible for a political candidate in the information age.

He imagined that the reporter had interviewed dozens of major political figures over the years, serious contenders and also-rans alike, though there was a good chance that he would be the first open clown to sit across from her. The experience would be new for her, and for him as well.

Much of the chaos around the control tower had been redirected to ensure that the right image would be projected for the reporter's arrival. Ruth tensed each time she saw the floor indicator above the elevator light up, but the appointment time came and another 15 minutes passed before the doors finally opened to reveal the reporter.

Ruth jumped out of her chair and then composed herself before walking gracefully over to the elevator with an outstretched hand to greet Carrie.

"Welcome to our headquarters," she said, smiling, and summoning as much of her old Iowa accent back into her voice as she could. "I am Ruth Greenbeaux."

"Hi, Ruth. It's a pleasure to meet you," Carrie said. "Thank you for setting this up on such short notice."

Whatever concerns Ruth had that the reporter might be out to do a hit job on her son began to evaporate under a wave of Midwestern warmth. Politics can be a dirty game, and she didn't like the idea of someone passing judgment on Russell without knowing the goodness inside his heart. He was a grown man, and he had made an informed choice to subject himself to a high level of public scrutiny. But her maternal instincts had been in a heightened state lately.

Carrie looked around with surprise at the beautiful office. The research she had seen indicated that Greenbeaux was wealthy, and she figured that he was probably bankrolling all of this himself. But as a reporter, it was her job to not assume anything.

"Wow, this place is beautiful," she told Ruth. "I've been in a lot of campaign headquarters before, and I've never seen anything quite like this in Iowa. Is this all self-financed?

Ruth's guard went back up. She was happy that the campaign could project an air of success at Cedar Point, but it hadn't occurred to her until that moment that the circumstances of their good fortune might be newsworthy. Who knew what baggage their mysterious benefactor might carry that could stain the campaign? Ruth thought that it might be wise to deflect.

"We started in much more humble accommodations, but we were swamped with volunteers, and we needed more space. We have done well with donations and offers to help since my son's editorial was published by your paper, and so we were able to upgrade a bit." All of this was true, and Ruth quickly pivoted away from the uncomfortable topic of how the office had been funded. She gently grabbed Carrie by the arm and said, "Let me give you a tour."

The two followed a path that Ruth had carefully mapped out, moving in and out of tables and past carefully selected volunteers before ending up at the conference room where Ruth introduced Carrie to her son. Greenbeaux went into campaign mode, reaching out to shake the reporter's hand and launching into friendly small talk to get the interview started.

Ruth disappeared through the door, her part of the show complete for now, and she stopped by Virgil's office. They had displaced the debate prep meeting to accommodate the reporter, and she wanted to at least catch up on what he had found out about the other candidates and share what she had seen in her review of previous third-party debates.

Virgil and Douglas had been discussing the merits of various potential band members and how many tuba players they should take on, and had just gotten to the topic of mimes when Ruth poked her head in the door. She could see by the intensity of the discussion that it would be best not to interrupt, and instead said to Virgil "debate prep in 45 minutes" before heading back to the control tower to contain the chaos.

With Ruth gone, the two men resumed their discussion. There was a lot Douglas did not know about the subculture of clowns, and he was trying to wrap his head around why Virgil so despised mimes.

"Mimes are NOT clowns," Virgil said emphatically. "We would have a real problem if one got into the band."

Douglas would form the band as Virgil wanted, but he pressed further to understand the dynamics behind the distaste he was sensing. "Forgive my ignorance, but I am curious why you don't think of mimes as clowns. We have a dozen or so volunteering to join the band, and they certainly seem more benign than tuba players."

Virgil had a mild-mannered temperament by nature, but he could feel his blood pressure rising as he struggled to explain the nuances of a clown's hierarchical view of the world. Most people did not understand their culture, and that was a big part of the struggle. But he knew that Douglas meant no disrespect.

"For starters, being a clown is more than a lifestyle choice. You are either born to be a clown, or you are not. Mimes, on the other hand, are just street performers. They feel no calling like we do, only an inclination to act like they are trapped in some invisible box that does not exist. Clowns live in the real world, and mimes live in the land of make-believe."

"But," Douglas countered for the sake of argument, "one can go to a clown college and train to be a clown without any calling whatsoever. Right?"

Virgil took a deep breath and exhaled loudly. "There are a lot of misconceptions around that. Clown colleges are really just party schools for people who want to play with balloons and have an excuse to hold tankers."

"Tankers?"

"A tanker is a party, like a kegger, but with tanks of helium instead of beer. Serious clowns go to real colleges, if they go at all. I went to Oberlin."

84

Douglas nodded affirmatively to suggest that he understood, but he really didn't see it as Virgil did. He supposed that every oppressed minority needed someone else to look down upon so that they don't have to occupy the bottom rung of the social ladder, and apparently, clowns needed mimes to be a lower caste.

*   *   *

After meeting with Carrie for 45 minutes, Greenbeaux emerged from the conference room alone and headed to the control tower in search of his mother.

"How did it go?" Ruth asked, curious why the reporter was not with him.

"It went well, I think. But she wants to talk with you."

Ruth dropped a pile of mailing label boxes on the counter and moved quickly to join the reporter. She was not quite sure why she was being summoned, but she put on a smile and her charm as she walked in and sat down, bracing herself for more questions about the headquarters.

"Your son mentioned that you are from Iowa," said Carrie.

"Oh yes, I am," Ruth said, relieved that this was not about Goldfarb or his mysterious client. "I grew up on a farm in Casey, about 50 miles west of here."

"Out of curiosity, are you any relation to Jeremiah McCaslin?"

Ruth tensed up again. Her son must have told Carrie about the family name. "Jeremiah is my cousin, but I lost touch with him many years ago."

She had no idea what he was up to these days, though given the history of the men in her family, she worried that it was no good. She hoped that the lapsed contact would provide her and Russell immunity from whatever scandal the reporter might be ready to spring on her.

"He was quite famous around here."

"Was?" Ruth said out loud. Jeremiah was her uncle Caleb's youngest son, two years older than she, and they had been played together often as children. She had long since put him out of her mind, but she was caught off guard and saddened by the thought that he may have passed.

"Yes, I'm sorry. He died last year. He started a prison ministry, and was always lobbying the legislature to get better conditions for inmates."

That struck Ruth as surprisingly noble for a McCaslin. She had managed to come out of that family with her soul intact, and perhaps Jeremiah had too. Since leaving Iowa after high school, she had used a broad brush in her mind to paint the whole family as a band of hypocritical con artists. That may have been too harsh and judgmental, but then again, maybe not.

"He ran a multilevel marketing scam that promoted an Egyptian miracle oil derived from asp venom. Then the pyramid scheme collapsed, and he went to jail. But he was a changed man when he came out, and his redemption story made him a folk hero in some circles."

Ruth suppressed the temptation to roll her eyes. Jeremiah was Caleb's son all right, and she could imagine him dramatically proclaiming "we are all sinners" to a hushed crowd as they were seduced to parting with their money in support of his cause. It was a classic McCaslin ruse, and Ruth was reminded why she had long since estranged herself from the clan.

There was a part of her that wanted to tell the reporter everything she knew about the family. Jeremiah probably had two sets of books, starting with the good book for show and then the real accounting ledger where the secrets were buried. But she was not back in Iowa to fight the ghosts of her childhood or to dispel the myth of her cousin's salvation, which might have been real for all she knew.

"I am sorry to hear that he died," Ruth said. "I hadn't seen him in more than 50 years."

Carrie wanted to know more about Ruth's roots in Iowa, and also about what it was like to be the mother of the first clown to run for president. Greenbeaux's story was unusual, but strangely compelling to a reporter's eyes. Here was a political outsider who eloquently articulated the national frustrations with Beltway insiders.

But there was more to it than that.

The reporter had done her research. She found the French news reports and footage of his campaign kick-off speech at the Lincoln Memorial, and had zeroed in on the old sound bites about clown rights that were at the core of his speeches before he started listening to the voters and evolving his message to focus on gridlock in Washington.

A cryptologist at heart, she had deciphered the code to find the Clown Underground, which was meant to be invisible from above. She drilled down into the subculture and discovered a world that few knew existed, and even fewer understood. To Carrie, Ruth was the candy inside the piñata, a lovely and seemingly normal woman who had raised and nurtured a clown. She was a bridge between two worlds who could serve as the interpreter to explain this unusual candidate to everyone else.

An hour and a half later, the two emerged from the conference room. Ruth was so proud of her son and everything he had accomplished and stood for, and she could have talked about him well into the night. She had been tempted to tell Carrie about the picture of Russell and the cowboy outfit, which was now sitting in a locked drawer at the control tower, waiting to be summoned if she needed to find inspiration.

But Ruth thought better of that idea. The picture was really about her and the courage she had found to stand up for what was right. The campaign needed this story to be about her son, and so she decided to stick to the script she was making up as she went along and refrained from pulling out the picture.

For her part, Carrie came out of the interview sensing she was on to a story that was very different than any she had written since coming to Des Moines. It was not just another political profile where she had to extract the truth, kicking and screaming, from the alternate reality that the candidate's handlers wanted the world to believe about him.

Taking the word of a candidate -- or his mother -- at face value was not a mistake she wanted to make, and so she would have a lot of fact-checking to do before she could start writing. She also had the thorny issue of the Clown Underground to contend with. There was a fine line between exposing sunlight to a hidden world, and ripping the bandage off a wound that was trying to heal itself. She would have to give more thought about what, if anything, she should write about it.

When the two walked to the elevator and said goodbye, Ruth instinctively gave her a hug, something that made Carrie a little uncomfortable. As a reporter, she needed to keep a professional distance from the subjects she interviewed. But Ruth was just about the sweetest person she had ever met, and she thought better of awkwardly pulling away after such a candid interview.

When the elevator doors closed, Ruth returned to the control tower to find a stack of messages waiting for her. Greenbeaux had left the office to go back on the trail and Virgil had stepped out to run a personal errand, and so the debate prep would have to wait. That would give her more time to review the strange footage from previous debates.

*   *   *

That night, Ruth hunkered down again to look for more clues from prior national and state debates involving third-party candidates. Her first cursory review had revealed some odd characters with unorthodox ideas, talking past each other. There had been a Bull Moose Party candidate dressed as Teddy Roosevelt who hurled epithets against Spaniards, and an array of purists who insisted that their interpretation of the Bible or the Constitution -- or both -- was the only correct one for the country to follow.

But as she watched the footage, she picked up on a theme amid the beating of dead horses. Each of the candidates, Ruth observed, occupied a place along the fringe of the political spectrum, and they formed a large circle with nobody standing in the middle.

The two main parties came closer to the center, but were so preoccupied with beating each other up that they had lost sight of this bigger picture, which now was clearly visible to Ruth. Her son had always been a moderate at heart who saw both sides of most issues. If he was to break through at the debate, he would need to be the voice of reason that respectfully defended the middle from more extreme points of view.

This was not a natural position for someone who was coming on to the political scene as a rights activist. Most of the great freedom movements in American history had started with radicals on the fringe before more-palatable mainstream leaders took up the cause to win the hearts and minds of good people in the center.

The clown-rights movement had its share of shrill voices advocating violence to draw attention to its cause, but few people in the mainstream of society knew the issue existed at all, so the more-contentious voices sounded comical to those outside of the Clown Underground. That left Greenbeaux alone as the calm moral voice of the cause.

The mere presence of a clown on the stage might perpetuate the notion that this debate of third-party candidates was a circus. But Ruth recognized that occupying the center of the spectrum would give her son a lot of space with which to move and deflect shots from the fringe. By seeming to be the most reasonable alternative, he could emerge as the winner and add a measure of respectability to both his presidential campaign and the clown-rights movement.

CHAPTER 7

A few days later, Greenbeaux was sitting on a plane to Washington going through his notes and some zingers he had prepared. He had decided to fly out the day before the debate to get ahead of a storm that was poised to bring a mix of winter weather to the mid-Atlantic States. Christmas was just a few days away, and he also didn't want to risk getting bumped from an overbooked flight without a way to get to the debate on time.

The crush of holiday travelers in the airport made it hard for him to relax and gather his thoughts. He preferred order and reasoned reflection to chaos, especially at a time when his campaign hinged on his performance in a 90-minute event. But once the fighting for overhead bin space was over and the plane was in the air, he was able to pull out his notes and concentrate.

His mother and Virgil had helped him cobble together a thorough analysis of the other third-party candidates and responses to each of their likely talking points. He still had little interest in actually being elected president, but he could clearly see a path to contention through the centrist strategy.

If he could break out first, he would be able to stake out a large swath of turf in the middle and cause a lot of headaches for the Republicans and Democrats They were preoccupied with trying to appease their respective bases in the primary season, and would not begin their scramble to the center until later when their nominations were wrapped up. That could give him a long window of opportunity to be the moderate voice in the race, and to demonstrate that clowns should be taken seriously.

One by one, he reviewed each of his rivals with an eye toward how he wanted to come across in comparison. He went through his public life wearing a clown suit, numbed to the laughter, the puzzled looks and the fear his presence sometimes triggered. But he was now very conscious of how he would appear on a national stage juxtaposed against an array of fringe candidates who would be dressed more like bankers than the sideshow freaks they really were.

Fred Spaulding was the oddest of the bunch, and the easiest to prepare for. It did not matter whether he was genuine in his belief that a spaceship was coming or if he was just faking it to get on national television. Nobody would take this guy seriously, and so there was no advantage to be gained by trying to argue with him. But still, if Greenbeaux was coerced by Spaulding or the moderator into answering questions about an impending alien invasion, he was prepared to brush it off by saying "I hope our new overlords like clowns."

Gordie Ancona was also on the easy end of the spectrum. Whatever merits there may have been to the industrial hemp movement, Ancona was hardly the best representative of the cause. He was more interested in the potent byproduct of a related cannabis plant, and he had the permanently red glassy eyes and impaired memory to prove it. Gordie posed no threat to Greenbeaux in the debate, save for the risk of conveying a contact high that might give him the munchies.

Greenbeaux had started on the campaign trail with a singular focus on clown rights, but he had figured out very early that that alone was not a winning issue for his platform. Listening to the voters, as his mother had suggested, had led him to focus on the need for politicians in Washington to find practical solutions for the common good. And he was able to articulate that frustration so well because he genuinely shared it.

Part of what made Greenbeaux such an unusual politician -- aside from the fact that he was a very tall clown -- was that he preferred to keep his political opinions to himself. His views were not a master key that unlocked the hearts of every voter, but what he was hearing from people in Iowa suggested that there was widespread support for his own closely held beliefs, and that gave him courage to come out of his shell a bit more.

The ground in the center of the political spectrum was wide open for him to take during the primary season. But to do so would mean having to explain his stance on any number of issues a president might be confronted with, from peace in the Middle East to the impending alien invasion that Fred Spaulding was predicting. And that was not a comfortable or natural thing for a man who preferred to keep his political views private.

Greenbeaux thought it odd that some otherwise intelligent people could buy into a partisan ideology wholesale. Reasonable people can disagree, but it struck him as unreasonable for people to toe a party line on every issue without divergence. His own views were all over the map. And he recognized the difficulty he would have with voters who liked 50 percent of what he said, but could not support him because they disagreed with his position on a hot-button issue that was important to them.

He would have preferred to avoid this conflict altogether by sticking to his main thesis about the dysfunction in Washington, but he knew that he could not skirt difficult issues on national television if he wanted to be considered a serious candidate. While the others were on the fringe, Greenbeaux could find both commonality and points of differentiation with many of them.

The Green Party candidate, Lydia Conner, was a good example. Project Pegasus had been a disaster, and was made trickier for her to defend because much of the funding had come from Department of Energy grants. Budget hawks and javelinas alike could agree that the failed car was hard to stomach.

Greenbeaux's years as a business owner had made him more fiscally conservative. He viewed money as a finite resource, and had experience with the types of difficult financial choices that so many in Washington were reluctant to make for fear of alienating their constituencies. He could try to establish *bona fides* as a budget hawk by attacking Lydia on the wastefulness of the whole Project Pegasus fiasco.

But that tactic was not without peril.

The environmental movement had become mainstream, and it wasn't just liberals who were putting solar panels on their houses anymore. Yes, Greenbeaux was a fiscal conservative who did not like wastefulness, but he might also be mistaken for an environmentalist. He had a technical orientation and understood the data that supported the concern about climate change. He owned a hybrid car, he had swapped out all of the incandescent light bulbs in his house, and he recycled dutifully.

Engaging the Green Party candidate on her turf would require a lot of finesse. He jotted down a sound bite calling for environmentally friendly policies to achieve energy independence in a fiscally accountable way. It was mostly jargon, but by acknowledging the worthiness of fiduciary responsibility in the quest for a smaller carbon footprint, he could capture the middle ground and still remain true to his own beliefs.

He had a similar quandary with the Libertarian candidates, particularly Randy Druslan. During the debate prep, Virgil had made a strong case for how the live-and-let-live philosophy of the porn star coalesced with the desire clowns had to be left alone to live their lives openly and in peace. But Greenbeaux saw something more that concerned him.

Virgil had opened up about how his tenure at IXM Systems had ended, and Greenbeaux could see how the lack of any legal protections for clowns had made it possible for Riley Booth to fire him without good cause. As a business owner, Greenbeaux had seen how much time and resources were wasted protecting companies from frivolous claims of discrimination. But he also saw how government regulations had served to protect employees from being fired for reasons that had nothing to do with their performance.

On some issues, Greenbeaux did have strong Libertarian leanings. But he wanted government to work better, not go away entirely, and so he couldn't buy into Randy Druslan's philosophy. Hearing the story of Virgil's firing reinforced his belief that clowns needed help to level the playing field.

Perhaps it was Druslan's status as a porn star that made Greenbeaux think of him as the poster child for narcissists who had recently come of voting age. But whatever traits might be ascribed to self-centered elements of a younger generation did not apply to Ed Jeter's bunker mentality brand of Libertarianism that had its roots in the frontier soil.

Greenbeaux did not give much thought to Jeter as a foe in the debate. He just assumed that it was pointless to try to rebut rants against fluoridation and the like that were so far outside of the mainstream. Instead, he was worried about Agatha Cromwell's Labour Party incursion onto his turf.

She was tapping into the same populist discontent with Washington that Greenbeaux had found, and that was a problem. He was not very concerned about the candidates he could research and prepare for. But Agatha had left little in the way of a digital footprint, and the lack of information made the threat feel more ominous.

He had no idea where she would put the emphasis of her message, on the switch to a parliamentary government -- which would require an unpopular constitutional overhaul -- or on the partisanship and paralysis inside the Beltway. He hoped it would be the former, and in talking it through with his mother and Virgil, he settled upon a strategy to push back on the mere suggestion that the United States should abandon the federal republic form of government.

Greenbeaux's plane hit an air pocket, and the ensuing drop and patch of rough air caused a few gasps in the cabin that broke his concentration. He nervously tapped his feet on the floor a couple of times to calm his nerves. Flying did not bother him, but the thought of crashing did, and it reminded him of his own mortality.

He had a perfectly comfortable life, with personal wealth that took basic survival worries such as food and shelter out of the equation. Running for president made him a target, and a tall one at that. He wasn't terribly worried about the possibility of staring down the barrel of an assassin's gun, but some people had an irrational hatred of clowns, and anything was possible.

Plane crashes had claimed more than a few high-profile politicians over the years. But those types of tragic events usually involved small planes traversing large rural areas, and Greenbeaux was flying on a big commercial jet between major airports. So he put it out of his mind and went back to work studying the odd assortment of people he was about to encounter.

The Communist Party candidate, Aleksandar Bolan-Svrab, had served as an unwitting source of amusement to the team during their debate preparation. Playing the role of each opposing candidate, Virgil had taken to calling Greenbeaux "comrade" when he took on the role of the 28-year-old Marxist, and the big clown started to giggle uncontrollably recalling the scene.

There were a variety of reasons why the Communist ideology had failed to take root in the United States, and Greenbeaux decided that he would not draw upon any of them in the debate if he could help it. Any candidate branded with the scarlet red letter "C" was destined to flatline in American politics, and it wasn't Greenbeaux's style to poke at roadkill for his own amusement. Particularly when there were two other candidates on the stage who were more deserving of his jabs.

Orville Banks was one of them. Seeing the struggle of his fellow clowns had made Greenbeaux more sensitive to the needs of disenfranchised minorities, and the Know Nothing Party candidate's anti-immigrant and anti-Catholic rhetoric struck him as intolerant and xenophobic.

Russell's great grandfather, Gaston Greenbeaux, had hastily emigrated from France nearly a century earlier after being tapped by his deeply religious family as the son who would become a priest. Gaston liked women. A lot. And the thought of a life of celibacy was cause enough for him to disappear in the middle of the night and try his luck in America, where, he had heard, the streets were paved with gold and all of the women were beautiful.

During a debate prep session, Ruth had to remind him to be nice and get him to tone down his rhetoric toward Banks. She did not like the idea of her son being mean to anyone, no matter how despicable the other person might seem. That included Hill Heller, the Aryan Social Separatist candidate.

Virgil had indulged his distaste for the white supremacist candidate by outlining a ploy to take him down a notch or ten during the debate. The idea, which he mentioned when Ruth had stepped out of the room during the debate prep, centered around addressing him as Hitler instead of Heller in a very deliberate way. Greenbeaux immediately seized on the concept and started practicing different vocal intonations as he pronounced the word Hitler to maximize the effect.

But when Ruth returned, she immediately put an end to the strategy. Her experience growing up in the McCaslin family may have soured her on false prophets, but it had not dampened her faith. She had wanted her son to be a living example of God's word, and had read to him passages from the Books of Luke and Matthew as a child, hoping that it would inspire him to treat others as he wished to be treated himself.

Compassion was a recurring theme in her life and how she shaped her son's character, and she suspected -- at least she hoped -- that he had been inspired to take on the fight for clown rights as a result of her efforts. She did not like Heller one bit, but she wanted Russell to act like the better man that he was when they were on the same stage.

Greenbeaux quickly acquiesced to her wishes, though there was a part of him that wanted to do what felt good rather than what his mother believed was right.

Another bump of turbulence jolted Greenbeaux again and broke his concentration. They were getting ready to land, and so he closed his notebook and put it into the bag near his feet. His campaign was at a crossroads and, in another day, he would know which direction they were going.

*   *   *

With just two weeks to go before the Iowa caucuses, the field of major party candidates was starting to take shape. It seemed like every few days a new front-runner would emerge on one side or the other, only to be shot down by a gaffe or a skeleton coming out of the closet. As Greenbeaux was flying to Washington, Democratic Senator Dominic Martelli was stepping in front of a bank of microphones to address reporters outside a food-processing plant in Manchester, New Hampshire.

The senator had cultivated a reputation as a champion of downtrodden workers, and he had gone to the factory to investigate rumors that low-paid immigrants were being forced to work 80-hour weeks in dangerous and unsanitary conditions. The event was, in reality, a photo opportunity that had been carefully choreographed by the most recent political consultant to join his team, Norm Brodie. While it was true that the plant had come under investigation by health inspectors recently, the timing of Martelli's visit was not coincidental.

Politics is a brutal sport, fought on a field with teams of imperfect men and women sitting on the sideline while the actors who still have their halos intact get to play on. The transgressions of philandering politicians were fair game in the 24-hour news cycle, but infidelity was sometimes seen as a sign of virility, and did not always disqualify candidates in the public mind in the way that signs of weakness did.

And so it came to pass that on a crisp December day, Senator Martelli emerged from a food-processing plant where onions were being chopped with what appeared to be tears in his eyes. It was Edmund Muskie all over again, and the talking heads in the news studios quickly filled in the narrative of a former front-runner who cared so much for workers that he would cry on national television. But the undertone was clear -- Martelli was too weak a man to be the leader of the free world -- and his presidential campaign effectively was coming to an end.

The political consultant, Norm Brodie, had a nickname: "Dr. Death," which some industry insiders had tagged him with for his uncanny ability to join campaigns right before they fell apart. His supporters held the opinion that he had one of the most brilliant political minds of his generation. But the fact remained that he was riding a losing streak of inglorious campaign calamities, and people were starting to notice.

For a strategist who specialized in staging optics, his clients had a habit of doing stupid things at the exact moment when the cameras started rolling. There was the congressman who showed up at a pep rally in Ann Arbor, Michigan, wearing an Ohio State sweatshirt, and a Brooklyn Borough president candidate who conspicuously ate a lobster roll and then a ham sandwich on the Sabbath in front of a shocked group of Hasidic community leaders.

The people who were in Brodie's camp were dismissive of any fault on his part, and with each successive disaster, his outsized reputation for political genius only seemed to grow. Rumors would emerge from the failed camps of the brilliant strategic and tactical moves that went unnoticed on the outside.

Norm Brodie watched on the sidelines as Senator Martelli's presidential bid unraveled in front of the cameras. There were more candidates who needed his unique services, and he would find work again. But the public nature of his losing streak was taking its toll, and now he needed a drink.

*   *   *

At Cedar Point, a crew of volunteers worked late into the night getting the word out to encourage people to watch the C-SPAN debate. The pizza was long gone and Douglas was struggling with the musical arrangement for the first band practice, which was to take place the next afternoon. He had listened to dozens of mix tapes from Clown Underground raves, and he was stumped.

There were a few common elements, a sub-Saharan clave rhythm, and a deep bass that almost never seemed to change chords. But aside from that, the music ranged from electronica to blues, depending on the region where the recording had originated. It was a puzzle, and Douglas found himself hovering among three different recordings, hoping to settle on one theme around which to build marching music for his band.

When he took off his headphones for a moment to get up for some coffee, he found that he was tapping hands on the desk in an unconscious rhythm. Suddenly, his eyes grew wide as he listened to the beat he was making and he found the motif he had been looking for.

"Bo Diddley," he said to himself, smiling, as he moved to a portable electric piano he had in the corner to start composing.

CHAPTER 8

Greenbeaux arrived a few minutes ahead of schedule at the unassuming brick building on the Virginia side of the Potomac in Shirlington. C-SPAN was renting it from a local public television station for the night while their studio was being remodeled. A set had been erected with red, white, and blue bunting covering the podiums where the candidates were to stand. The green room was built to host just a few guests for an evening news show, and so the debate participants were invited to mill about the set before the start.

Fred Spaulding and Lydia Conner were there when Greenbeaux walked in, with Ed Jeter and Aleksandar Bolan-Svrab arriving shortly afterward. Someone noticed that there were only nine podiums on the stage instead of ten, and a production assistant informed the collected group that the Labour Party candidate, Agatha Cromwell, would not be able to attend. She was eight months pregnant, and traveling from London to Washington had been ruled out by her doctor, who had ordered bed rest.

Greenbeaux was relieved knowing that the other candidate who was most likely to steal his populist anti-Congress thunder would not be there. He put on his friendliest face and moved around the stage introducing himself to the others.

He felt well-rested and professional-looking in his finest regalia. He was wearing a custom-tailored, gray wool clown suit with a green bow tie and an American flag pin on his polka-dot lapels.

An intern came around to each of the candidates and offered to apply makeup, and then paused uncomfortably when she reached Greenbeaux, who had already carefully put on his greasepaint before leaving his hotel.

"Ummmm... freshen up?" she asked tentatively. Greenbeaux smiled. "No thank you," he said, appreciatively while waving her off.

Another production assistant came onto the set and announced that the debate was being pushed back from the original eight p.m. start time. Congress was trying to wrap up its business and get out of town for the Christmas break, and so there was still a lot of activity on the hill. C-SPAN was staying with coverage of the House Postal Service Subcommittee's hearings on stamp adhesive cost overruns, and so the start of the debate would have to wait until that work was finished.

By the original appointed hour, all of the remaining participants had arrived except Orville Banks. In addition to being against immigrants and Catholics, he was also opposed to reading his e-mail, and so he knew nothing about when or where he was supposed to show up for the debate.

Greenbeaux came up to the refreshment table where Gordie Ancona was munching out on cookies and cheese cubes and reached out his hand to introduce himself.

"Oh, Dude. You're that clown," Gordie said, grinning widely and shaking his hand in return.

Gordie was everything Greenbeaux had expected: Friendly, goofy, and stoned out of his gourd. It would be a mistake to turn on him in any way, since the guy was completely benign. The same could not be said for Hill Heller, who had found a secluded corner near a pot of coffee, where he was anxiously downing cup after cup to keep himself focused.

Greenbeaux approached the white supremacist cautiously, extended his hand and introduced himself. Heller looked up and then turned away with only a sneer and a grunt in acknowledgement. Heller had a long list of the different types of people he did not like, and apparently, clowns were on it. Though to be fair, none of the other candidates who tried to be friendly to him received a reception that was any warmer.

There were times when Greenbeaux wished he didn't have to listen to his mother or his conscience, two things that had become inextricably intertwined. He really wanted to call this nervous little twit Hitler on national television, manners be damned. But he knew his mother was right, and now was not the time to ignore her sage counsel. Instead, he moved away, leaving Heller to his coffee, and struck up a conversation with Ed Jeter.

The crusty Libertarian was wearing an ill-fitting suit that was out of style when it had been cut 20 years earlier, and he had a bad toupee that was sloping off the right side of his head. But he had a surprisingly sharp intellect and sense of humor. Greenbeaux had built up an image in his mind of a crazy old man in cowboy boots carrying a shotgun to a militia meeting, but instead was surprised to find the former congressman to be quite engaging.

The other Libertarian, standing across the room and wearing a sport coat with an open-collared shirt, was busy chatting up Lydia Conner. Randy Druslan seemed more interested in casting a new leading lady than in schmoozing with the other debaters, and Greenbeaux suspected that he had wasted time preparing for the wrong Libertarian.

When the Green Party candidate finally shrugged herself free from Druslan, the porn star made his way to the college intern who was doing the makeup and inquired if she might be interested in an undress rehearsal to get ready for the show.

At nine o'clock, an announcement came from the control booth that the Postal Service Subcommittee hearings were taking much longer than expected, and that the debate start time was being pushed back by at least another hour. Gordie Ancona slipped out the back door to light up, joined by Aleksandar, the Communist Party candidate. Hill Heller poured himself yet another cup of coffee, adding more caffeine to fuel his naturally skittish and agitated personality.

Greenbeaux found a comfortable chair on the news show set in the next room and sat down to take some weight off his new white orthopedic clown shoes. It was going to be a long night, but his body clock was still stuck in the Central time zone, and so it didn't feel quite so late.

*   *   *

Norm Brodie walked into a sports bar in Manchester and asked the server if she could put C-SPAN on a television for him. The manager on duty overheard the conversation and flashed him an odd look, but grudgingly waved him over to an isolated corner where a channel was changed to accommodate him.

With the New Hampshire primary coming on the heels of the Iowa caucuses, the state faced an invasion of eggheaded policy wonks similar to the one Iowa was enduring. Every four years, the bar became home to an unusual clientele that was more interested in politics than other ruthless sports.

Norm had not quite reached his thirtieth birthday, but he had adopted the mannerisms and drinking habits of a much older and jaded campaign operative. He ordered a scotch on the rocks and sat down to brood. Out of the corner of his eye, he saw an old foe approaching, and he took a swig to steady himself.

"Hello, Dr. Death."

Norm saw that one coming, and he expected nothing less from Jessica Ketchum or anyone else who worked in opposition research. She knew how to kick a man when he was down, usually after she had already tripped him, slammed his head against the floor a couple of times and taken his wallet to see if there were any incriminating pictures inside. Their paths had crossed too many times before, usually when he was brought in to clean up a mess she had created for a candidate.

They were acquaintances in college, but had gone down different paths in life. After graduation, he became a staffer on Capitol Hill, while she had gone to work for the CIA to learn the art of espionage before joining a consulting firm that specialized in digging up the dirtiest secrets that politicians wanted to bury.

"Do you mind if I join you?"

Yes, he did. But she would have sat down anyway, and so he gestured to the chair next to him without looking up from his drink.

"So what is that, eighteen in a row?" she asked.

Norm smirked. His streak of consecutive losing campaigns was now legendary among political insiders, and had become the subject of more than a few speculative blog posts.

"Nineteen actually," he said, "but who's counting?"

"PolBlog is counting, and they think it's eighteen," she said, needling him with her razor-sharp directness. The other losses were well-documented, but she was not one to let a secret escape her clutch. If there was another implosion on his inglorious streak, she wanted to know about it.

"Nope, definitely nineteen," he said, looking back down at his drink, understanding full well that he was adding gasoline to the fire that fueled her curiosity. But he wasn't quite ready to surrender that information, and Jessica could tell, so she changed the subject.

"You know, we had a picture of your Senator Martelli at a swingers club that was about to come out."

Norm looked up from his drink again, this time directly into her eyes and stared her down with an icy glare. He knew all about the picture, in fact. It was why he had been brought onto the campaign in the first place. In a strange way, he actually owed her one for the work that had come his way. But it all was just a little too cruel. Martelli was a good man who had done something wrong, but his wife and children would also have suffered if the picture had been released.

"Well, it didn't go down that way," he said. "And so you get to keep the last remaining shard of your broken soul intact for now."

Jessica was taken aback and hurt by that. She knew that what she did was unpopular in some circles, but she rationalized it as noble because she was bringing bad things to light. Still, deep down she knew that the means she and her colleagues used were not always justified in the end.

Norm recognized right away that he had stung her, and dropped his glare. He took a sip of scotch and glanced up at her again, this time with a friendlier look, as if to say that he had only been joking. But he could see the hurt still lingering in her eyes. It was a look of vulnerability and humanity that he didn't think was possible on the face of someone who worked in opposition research.

"Number nineteen was my first campaign when I was 17 years old," he said, opening up to make amends. Her eyes met his again as he went on. "My brother was running for dogcatcher in our hometown, and I managed his campaign. He was running unopposed, but he lost anyway."

"What went wrong?" she asked, engaging again in the conversation, genuinely interested in how Norm Brodie had managed to put that rabbit back into the hat.

"There was a write-in campaign for a 98-year-old war veteran. He didn't campaign for it at all, but the sympathy vote took hold."

"People must have thought the job was an important way to honor him."

"Maybe." Norm said. "But he had been in a coma for three years and died soon after, and so he was never able to appreciate that."

"Well, someone wanted him to have the job."

Norm smiled with a hint of mischief. "My brother is the only person I know who is a bigger asshole than I am."

109

"And…"

"And I just couldn't let him win."

Jessica's face lit up for a second. It seemed that she was not the only one in the bar who practiced the dark arts. Norm had always seemed like a straight-up strategist, and in a million years she would never have thought him to be the type who could throw his own brother under the campaign bus. But then the smile was gone again and she looked away, still nursing her own pain.

Norm was starting to view Jessica in a new way. She always had her battle armor on when he saw her, tough as nails with no sign of weakness. But she looked different when she was vulnerable. Her dark hair seemed softer and her brown eyes betrayed a thoughtfulness that he had never seen in her before.

He had spent far too many years on the road, and had mastered the science of the staffer hookup, with the occasional bedding of an embedded reporter on the side. He was usually done with a campaign and off to the next so quickly that he didn't have time for relationships that lasted much longer than a couple of nights, except during the off years when he would plant himself in Washington to work on K Street projects.

Most of the people he dated worked in politics, and he rarely went about trying to meet women in bars. In addition to a common interest in politics, he also sought partners who shared his religious views. He found the hunting was best in grocery stores and gyms on Sunday mornings when his fellow lapsed Catholics and other agnostics were going on with their lives instead of attending church.

Being smart and good-looking had its advantages in politics, and Norm was not shy about going after what he wanted. And what he suddenly wanted now was Jessica. He took another drink, summoned the bartender over for a refill, and asked Jessica what she would be having.

"So now you know my darkest secret," he said.

"That is pretty big. But I have seen darker."

"Tell me, then. How exactly do you go about finding the dirt on people?" he asked.

"Simple. I go up to people who are drinking scotch and they tell me their secrets. Just like tonight."

A flash of panic came over Norm as he realized what he had revealed to an opposition researcher. That might come back to bite him someday. But for the night, his sex drive was stronger than his self-preservation instincts, and so he persisted.

"And do those guys sometimes ask you to sleep with them. Just like tonight?"

Jessica had heard some brazen lines over the years, and that one was right up there. But her time in the CIA had prepared her well to focus on her mission, which for the time being did not include sleeping with Norm.

"Sometimes they ask, but I don't get my bedfellows in politics. They always end up being too strange."

This was going to be more of a challenge than Norm was used to. Jessica was smart and disciplined, and she was savvy about how the campaign road warrior game was played. He also had to be careful not to burn a bridge that might be useful down the road. Independent opposition research firms were always peddling dirt, and campaign strategists needed to maintain open lines of communication, just in case.

The bartender brought Norm a fresh scotch and Jessica a glass of merlot. She was not above drinking hard liquor with her friends, but this was work, and she was trying her best not to let the dashing Norm Brodie turn it into play.

"So help me to understand something," Norm said, switching to a different tack. "You go out and get all of the salacious details about the love lives of historic figures. You are surrounded by all of these powerful men, but you abstain from making any history yourself?"

"Who said anything about men?" Jessica replied. She was not interested in women in that way, but still, she couldn't resist the opportunity to engage in a little psychological warfare.

"So,..." Norm said, arching his eyebrow and pointing at a passing waitress. "If we were to ask her to join us, would that make it more interesting?"

"No."

Now he was confused, which was exactly what Jessica wanted.

"Then... what would make it more interesting?"

"Interesting for whom?" she said, taking a long sip of her wine.

"For you, of course."

"Well, since you asked,..." she said, trailing off while calculating how to inflict the greatest amount of damage with the fewest possible words. "It would be a lot more interesting if I was being hit on by a political consultant with a successful track record."

He deserved that, and he could tell that he wasn't getting anywhere. But Norm was on a losing streak, and he just couldn't stop himself from taking the last of his chips and going all-in.

"I am sure my life would be a lot more interesting if my candidates won for a change," he said, making eye contact with her again. "But I am just a political hack whose only talent is for putting otherwise healthy campaigns out of their misery."

Norm caught her trying to suppress a laugh, and he suspected that was a tell. She was enjoying this. He continued:

"And so here I am, sitting in a bar in New Hampshire in the middle of winter, telling my secrets to an opposition researcher. Which -- no offense -- is like a cow telling a butcher how he wants to be cut."

"No offense taken... as long as you mean to say that the cow is you, and not I." There was no doubt that Norm was actually a very good strategist, and she could feel her defenses crumbling just a bit around the edges.

"Let me ask you something," she continued. "Why on earth would you want to spend the night with a woman who is down to the last shard of her broken soul?"

"Because," he said without missing a beat, "I love it when you talk dirty politics to me."

CHAPTER 9

The announcement came from the control room that the debate would start at eleven-thirty, just 10 minutes away. The snack food had long since been devoured by Gordie Ancona, and all of the coffee was gone as well, thanks to a now fully wired white supremacist who was about to pay for his failure to go to the bathroom before the start of the debate.

The moderator, Lee Samuels, emerged from a sound booth where he had recorded the introduction, and he walked onto the set to greet the candidates. He recognized the futility of the third-party debate, and he was looking forward to having fun with the candidates at this late hour.

The extra podium that would have belonged to the Know Nothing Party candidate was hauled away and everyone took their assigned places. The floor director gave the signal and Samuels began his welcoming comment and laid out the format and ground rules before throwing it back to the control room to play the pre-recorded intro.

> "With us in our Washington studio tonight we have former Congressman and Libertarian Party candidate Edwin Jeter. Green Party candidate and social entrepreneur Lydia Conner. Adult film actor

Randy Druslan, also a Libertarian. Aryan Social Separatist Party candidate Hill Heller. Clown-rights activist Russell Greenbeaux, who does not list an affiliation, but judging by his costume, I am guessing that he is here with the birthday party..."

It was probably a good thing that the sound was off in the studio and Greenbeaux didn't know what was being said. The moderator's wisecrack was exactly the type of stereotype about clowns that he was fighting against, and hearing it would have sent his blood pressure through the roof.

"Also with us is herbologist and Cannabis Party candidate Gordon Ancona, Junior. Interstellar Awareness Party candidate Frederick Spaulding. And Aleksandar Bolan-Svrab, the Communist Party candidate for president."

C-SPAN prided itself on being completely objective and avoided signaling a preference for any one political ideology, but at that late hour, the clown seemed like fair game in a way that joking about even a white supremacist or a Communist candidate did not.

The camera, back live in the studio, focused on Lee Samuels sitting behind a desk across from the podiums. He explained that each candidate would be given 60 seconds to make opening remarks. After that there would be a series of topical questions that had been pre-selected by the host to be asked at random. Each candidate would have the opportunity to give the first answer to a question, to be followed by five minutes of open discussion for anyone to chime in.

The candidates received these instructions in advance, and Greenbeaux had rehearsed his opening remarks. Ruth had prepared a list of current-event topics for him to study, based on questions that were being asked in the mainstream party primary debates, and he was ready with a cache of sound bites and zingers in response to what he expected others to say.

The candidates had been introduced, based on where they were assigned to stand on the stage, and Lee Samuels asked them to give their opening remarks in the same order, starting with Ed Jeter.

If the other candidates had expected the old man to talk about the topics on his outdated website, they were in for a big surprise. Jeter started by reciting the preamble to the Constitution:

> "We the people of the United States, in order to form a more perfect union, establish justice, insure domestic tranquility, provide for the common defense, promote the general welfare, and secure the blessings of liberty to ourselves and our posterity, do ordain and establish this Constitution for the United States of America."

With the remainder of his time, he explained that he was running for president because he wanted to preserve the liberty that was being eroded by an overzealous government. It was stirring theater, and Greenbeaux was caught off guard by Jeter's dramatic flair. He had not expected this, and a twinge of worry came across him as he wondered who else he might have underestimated.

Conner and Druslan were more pedestrian in their opening remarks, sticking closely to the scripts Greenbeaux had expected. The Green Party candidate spoke of environmental issues and the porn star gave a nod to free enterprise by plugging his upcoming film, "More Ass in Washington."

But when it came time for Hill Heller to give his statement, everyone could tell that something was wrong. The agitated white supremacist was now sweating heavily and doing an odd dance, shifting weight between his feet while trying to retain the contents of his overfilled bladder. He started his remarks haltingly before suddenly working himself into a furor. The visibly uncomfortable and angry man knew he was off his game, and that only increased his anxiety and made his situation worse.

Greenbeaux was trying to concentrate on what he would say in his opening statement, which was coming up next. But the spectacle unfolding beside him was so distracting that when his turn came around, he unconsciously used the first three seconds of his time to say the first thing that popped into his head.

"You might want to consider switching to decaf, Mr. Hitler."

The room erupted in laughter, but Greenbeaux was mortified and realized that he was going to have to answer to his mother for that one. He remained composed, though, and turned to face the camera, starting his prepared remarks with a straight face while the commotion was still going on.

Fifteen seconds later, Gordie Ancona, whose reaction time was a bit delayed, blurted out, "Oh dude, that clown just called you Hitler." The words stirred the room again, though more so off-camera where the tired crew heard the remark amplified over a hot microphone.

Greenbeaux went into a subconscious state while reciting his prepared speech, oblivious to Gordie's comment and the laughter around him. The delivery of the offhand comment and smooth transition to his opening remarks came across to the audience as polished and professional. But Greenbeaux didn't know that. All he knew was that he had just called another man Hitler on national television, with an intonation and emphasis on the derogatory name that he had practiced with Virgil while his mother had been out of the room.

After he concluded, he could see out of the corner of his eye that the white supremacist was seething. If Heller didn't completely hate clowns before the debate, he certainly did now. The sweaty, angry man began muttering so loudly that the control room had to cut off his mic, but not before the words "fucking clown" went out live on national television.

Hill Heller was a natural villain for people to root against, and Greenbeaux became an instant hero to the audience watching at home and those who would see replayed clips of the incident. But this sword cut both ways, and to Heller's followers, Greenbeaux was now the embodiment of their new enemy: Clowns.

In a perverse way, that was the kind of spark the clown-rights movement needed. It was hard for any class of people to become recognized as an oppressed minority if most people without an odd phobia liked them. The white supremacist movement was the gold standard for hate groups in the United States, and becoming a target of their fury could be a landmark moment in the struggle.

Greenbeaux was in the race to show that clowns could be serious people, and he feared that he was undermining his best opportunity to do that. He wrongly thought he was in trouble, and he decided to ditch his prepared zingers and focus on finding his moments to share serious political insights he had heard from voters over and over again on his sojourn through Des Moines.

As the debate moved to the question-and-answer phase, whatever congeniality had existed before the show soon evaporated, with Ed Jeter finding any opportunity he could to attack everyone else. He had come well-prepared, and was determined to use the debate platform to win the Libertarian Party's nomination.

When Lydia Conner tried to make the debate about the environment, Jeter turned it around and said, "You can do whatever the hell you want with your own money, but I don't like the idea of taxpayer dollars being used to feed pigs in the Arizona desert." Lydia gave him an icy stare, and Ed glared right back, adding for good measure: "Twelve perfectly good pigs poisoned. Now that wasn't very good for the environment, was it?"

Jeter then proceeded to tear into Aleksandar the Communist, giving him the moniker "Trotskyite Troglodyte." As nicknames go, it was only marginally less flattering than the one he dished out to Gordie Ancona: "The Stoner Anconer." Jeter was similarly dismissive of Heller, whose bad night had only gone downhill after the initial barb from Greenbeaux.

Other candidates in the debate had also taken to calling the white supremacist Hitler, and after repeated efforts to correct them, he finally screamed, "It is Heller. Hill Heller." To which Jeter quipped: "Hill Heller. Heil Hitler. What's the difference?" The loose stitching that was holding together the white supremacist's fragile ego frayed even further, and he emitted an exasperated squealing grunt to accompany the quickening of his bladder-control dance.

Even the benign Fred Spaulding, who was simply there to encourage everyone to unplug their microwave ovens on Election Day, was not immune from the abuse. Jeter loved popcorn, and he had once used his electrical engineering skills to rewire his own microwave oven so that he could cut the popping time in half. And he would be damned if he was going to let some two-bit little punk claiming to be from outer space tell him he couldn't pop a bag in November while he watched election returns.

He didn't believe in little green men from other planets, though he had seen something strange hovering above a large compost pile at what he suspected was a secret government facility on a nearby property in the Nevada valley where he lived. Some of his more paranoid neighbors in the valley thought that mind-control experiments were being conducted there. He didn't buy into that particular anti-government conspiracy theory, but he wouldn't put it past the Democrats to give something like that a try.

Jeter had done his homework on Spaulding, even going so far as to look up his birth certificate to refute the claim made in his biography that he was from the Omega Galaxy.

"You were born on March 23, 1978, in Wichita, Kansas, to Herbert and Irma Spaulding."

"Ah, you speak of my Earth parents," Spaulding replied. "My mother was impregnated by a beam of pure light from the father ship." He paused for a second, and then pointed at Greenbeaux before adding: "And his mother was too."

"That would explain a lot," Greenbeaux said under his breath, making a mental note to ask his mother about this.

Spaulding held his ground better than most against Jeter's withering blows, and Greenbeaux did as well. At one point, when the topic had turned to gridlock in Washington, he made a very strong point about the need for the parties to work together.

Jeter then jumped in: "The bureaucracy is so bloated and flawed. We have let far more bad laws and regulations in than the Founding Fathers could have ever imagined," he said, glancing over at Greenbeaux with a wry smile before adding "...and what we really need to do is send all of those clowns in Washington home."

Greenbeaux had anticipated that someone would make that tired joke with him on the stage, and he was ready with his heartfelt response. "I believe that it is unfair to tarnish the good name of clowns by associating them with the partisan bickering, obstinate gridlock, and corrupting influence that big-money contributors have on the political system."

Jeter yielded the point, mainly because he wanted to save up his breath for an attack on his real enemy. He didn't believe that any of these fringe candidates would get anywhere in the election, but Randy Druslan was another matter. The porn star stood between him and the Libertarian nomination, and he was not about to let that wretched Hollywood pervert grab the party mantle without a fight.

Druslan had been virtually shut out of the debate until that point, in large part because of Jeter's alpha male interjections. But he had also come unprepared. He was more interested in the philosophical implications of Objectivism and the possibility of an after-party where he could get laid than in engaging in a substantive debate about the political challenges facing the country.

When it was his turn to go first in the Q&A session, he had the bad luck of drawing a question about foreign relations. He had dated two Brazilian women in one of his films, but that was the extent of his knowledge on the subject. Ed Jeter was ready to pounce, starting with a rant against the United Nations, and ending with another rant about what he thought of Randy Druslan.

"You call yourself a Libertarian, but what you really are is a self-absorbed little boy who is sullying the name of my political party to justify your degenerate behavior."

Druslan was caught off-guard by the frontal assault. The best he could offer in response was a suggestion that Jeter, whose toupee had slipped two more degrees to the right during the course of the debate, should consider joining the Whig Party.

Greenbeaux had heard enough of Jeter's attacks and recognized this as an opportunity to step in to capture the middle ground.

"Now gentlemen, you are both Libertarians, and you seem to want government to do the same thing. Which, if I understand it correctly, is nothing at all. That is different from what most Americans want. Can't you just agree to disagree with everyone else?"

Greenbeaux finally felt some wind in his sails as he launched into a soliloquy comprised of his key talking points and sound bytes.

"Our founding fathers had the foresight to create a Constitution that, as Mr. Jeter so nicely quoted in his opening remarks, was intended to lay the groundwork to form a more perfect union. People disagree about what would make our union more perfect, but to me, it means that we must work together to get better as a country.

Does the government have failings? You bet. I have built a couple of companies and I have seen firsthand how oppressive regulations can bog down and hurt small businesses. But do we really want to live in a society where there are no regulations whatsoever?

I spoke with one voter who grew up in Cleveland and remembered seeing the Cuyahoga River catch on fire. I personally have seen rivers in other countries that are nothing short of toxic because the government would not impose or enforce basic pollution regulations.

What we really need is not for our government to go away, but for it to work better. Not to impose new draconian regulations in reaction to every crisis, or to gut all regulation for the sake of fulfilling some dystopian fantasy about what it means to be free. But instead to take the best ideas from different perspectives in order to find balanced and pragmatic solutions.

What we have in Washington today is a self-inflicted system of partisan gridlock, where two political parties are more interested in appeasing their base and demonizing the other side than in working together to make our union more perfect."

*   *   *

Norm and Jessica were in the throes of passion when something distracted his attention. Normally, she preferred to make love in complete darkness. But he had convinced her that some ambient light would help set the mood, and he had turned on the TV in his hotel room and discreetly set the channel to C-SPAN.

Jessica signaled to him that she sensed something was amiss, but he waved it off and turned his attention back to her. He had two great passions in life: sex and politics. Just not in that order. The sight of a clown engaged in a debate could not be ignored, and he soon looked back over at the television to catch another glimpse of the spectacle.

There was a reason Jessica preferred not to date men who worked in politics. They tended to be obsessed with all aspects of the sport: the gamesmanship, the power, the stardom, and the brutal competition where winners set the priorities for a nation and the losers retrench as the cycle starts all over again.

Norm was married to politics, and Jessica had seen too many unfaithful men in her line of work to ever knowingly become the other woman. She had not gone into the encounter with high expectations, but still, there was a little sadness knowing that even if it had worked out, he would always love politics more than her, or even himself.

She had wanted to ask Norm a question when she approached him in the bar. That was a matter of business and the night had become something else. Opposition research was a dark world of questionable tactics, but there was a line she had no intention of crossing to get information, and so she decided to wait and ask him another time.

It did not take long after they were done before she found an excuse to leave. He was interested in seeing the clown in the debate, and so he didn't fight it and ask her to stay the night. On her way out she stopped and gave him a kiss. They were similar people playing on the same field, and their paths would cross again. She wanted to stay friends, and not just because he was a useful person to know.

When the door closed, Norm lunged for the remote to unmute the television. He watched in astonishment as the debate turned into a two-man show between a clown calling for collective cooperation and an old man with a bad toupee making the case for self-reliant individualism.

*　　*　　*

It was cold outside in Washington that night, but the lights inside the studio were hot. This did not make life any easier for Hill Heller, who was now dancing around dripping in sweat. Heller thought himself to be superior to men from other races, clown or otherwise. Yet he had become the weakest person on the stage as he reached the limits of the verbal abuse and physical discomfort that he could withstand. When the end finally neared and the moderator turned to ask for his closing remarks, Heller simply said, "I have to pee" and ran off the set.

Gordie Ancona had enough as well, and he was asleep standing up at his podium. He was quiet now, but he had been snoring loudly a few minutes earlier when Aleksandar was explaining why the bourgeois should be forced to shovel horse manure on collective farms. To be fair to Gordie, though, half of the crew was on the verge of sleep as well by the time of the Communist's policy rant. It was very late, and just about everyone was ready for bed.

Greenbeaux delivered his closing statement exactly as he had rehearsed it, with just enough energy in reserve to show the power of his convictions. He was still a little dazed from his Hitler slipup, and without an audience to provide feedback he had no way to gauge how he had done.

He and Jeter had gotten into several dustups, and he was pretty sure that he had come out the loser. The Libertarian was sharp and well-prepared, and Greenbeaux felt at times that all he could do was be contrarian while Jeter danced rhetorical circles around him and the other candidates.

As the cameras cut off and the night came to a close, Greenbeaux felt a little deflated. He made the rounds to shake hands with most of his fellow candidates, almost certain that he had lost the debate. He was surprised when a couple of the others -- Fred Spaulding and Lydia Conner, in particular -- thanked him for taking on Ed Jeter. They had not appreciated being bullied, and they both made a point of telling Greenbeaux that they liked what he had to say.

It still didn't register that he might have done well or actually won the debate. But that would become evident soon enough.

*　　*　　*

Norm Brodie was stunned by what he had just seen. It was a debate performance for the ages, with two candidates perfectly articulating the case for different sides of the philosophical divide that was at the root of the country's political tensions.

In one corner was a Libertarian, skillfully advancing his thesis that the only good government was a dead government. In the other corner, a moderate who was arguing that Liberals and Conservatives in Washington were acting like children playing a high-stakes game of kick the can.

What made the interplay so compelling was that these were not the stereotypical beautiful politicians regurgitating lines that had been tested by focus groups. It was an intellectual street fight between a feisty old man with a bad toupee and a very tall clown that mixed equal parts political drama and theater of the absurd, with a cast of odd and outmatched also-rans watching helplessly from their podiums.

Norm was immediately drawn to Greenbeaux. He had heard all of the arguments about the need for bipartisanship in Washington, but rarely were they so well-articulated, and never had they come from the mouth of a man with bright green hair and a bow tie to match his name.

It was hypnotic and made all the more dramatic because clowns were supposed to be synonymous with fools. Russell Greenbeaux was many things, but he was not a fool.

In political parlance, Norm was a fixer, and one with an unusual niche at that. His nickname, Dr. Death, was well-earned and fully understood by only a few insiders. His losing streak was really a sign that he did his job well, but he couldn't go around explaining why without bringing the skeletons he had buried back to life.

Everyone had a secret in Washington, and when really bad ones were about to be exposed by Jessica Ketchum and her ilk, Norm was the guy who could euthanize a campaign to spare the candidate's family a lot of public pain. Leading contenders don't just walk away from a race to spend more time with their family without raising a lot of eyebrows, and Norm's job was to implode campaigns in a way that made sense of a quick exit.

He was handsomely rewarded for his services, but all of this secrecy was taking a toll on him. Those who knew the truth thought he was a genius, a mad scientist of sorts who created plausible deniability through willful destruction. But some pundits who were ignorant of his tradecraft had started wondering out loud how a strategist with such a lousy track record continued to find work. The talk was damaging his reputation, but more importantly, it threatened to blow his cover. Candidates might be reluctant to hire him if they thought their otherwise opaque political suicide could become transparent.

The C-SPAN debate had been a welcome distraction for Norm and fulfilled a need that even the pleasant interlude with Jessica could not. There was something intoxicating about watching Greenbeaux weave and dodge, and then counterpunch when challenged. Jeter had been devious in the way he used verbal barbs to twist the other candidates in circles before turning their own words against them to make his case. But Greenbeaux had responded to that cleverness with substance.

Norm had never heard of the clown before that night, and all he knew about him was what he had just seen on television. But he had a keen eye for potential, and he saw it in the tall man with green hair. Greenbeaux was tapping into a deep vein of populist discontent, and he spoke for many disenfranchised voters in the heartland.

It was ridiculous to think that a clown could be elected president, but that only made the notion of working for Greenbeaux more appealing. Norm had spent the better part of his career hastening the demise of doomed campaigns that seemed healthy to the outside world, and he could think of nothing more interesting than breathing life into one that everyone else would mistake for roadkill.

Norm Brodie had a lot of talents, but he also had a lot of needs. He needed to feel loved and useful. He needed to be part of a winning team, and he needed to quiet the loud whispers that were following him from one train wreck to another. For all of those reasons and more, he needed to join the Greenbeaux campaign.

What he did not need at the moment was money, and he was willing to work for free if he had to.

CHAPTER 10

Ruth had a headache again. The previous night's debate had unlocked the floodgates, bathing the campaign in much-needed attention. The e-mail inbox had nearly 600 messages waiting to be read, including media requests and several hundred automated notifications that came through whenever a donation was made online. It was nearly lunchtime, and she was falling further behind as the messages came rolling in faster than she could look at them.

Ruth, Virgil, Douglas and a handful of volunteers had watched the debate in the office, hooting and clapping every time Greenbeaux had held his ground against Jeter's onslaught. She had been a little perturbed with her son about the comment he made to Heller, but he was very contrite when she spoke with him afterward, and she had already forgiven him.

The audience that had watched the debate live was actually quite small, even by C-SPAN's standards. But the 24-hour cable news channels needed fresh information to feed their viewers, and the Hitler comment had made the entire event both entertaining and newsworthy. Clips of the verbal jousting between Greenbeaux and Jeter added substance to the occasion, and the pundits had started to buzz that it had been unusually enlightening for a third-party debate.

Virgil had been looking at numbers all morning, and was very surprised to see how the website metrics had changed. The day before, 80 percent of the traffic to the site had come through links inside the Clown Underground, but now 95 percent of the hits were from news stories or search engine results. With the spike in traffic came a surge in donations; a few dollars in many cases, a few hundred in others.

While the rest of the country was winding down for the Christmas holiday, the campaign was drowning in good fortune. Ruth and Virgil tried their best to manage all of the loose ends, but they were quickly getting overwhelmed. Greenbeaux had delayed his flight back so that he could stay in Washington to meet with reporters. He had done two live interviews so far, and had three more scheduled. With each appearance and successive replay the deluge of communication coming into the campaign became harder for the team to manage.

Ruth had assigned five volunteers to answer the phones and triage the requests. People who wanted to help with the campaign were routed to a coordinator, who was also a volunteer; media requests were steered to Ruth, who was texting her son updates about when and where to go; people wanting to contribute were directed to the website; and crank calls were quickly dismissed.

There were only a handful of those, but three of them had been disturbing, obscenity-laden rants about exterminating clowns. Different operators had answered two of the calls, and so Ruth couldn't be sure if they were from the same person who had left a nasty voice message before the office opened for the morning. The tone was more hateful and ominous than anything she could have expected, and the thought occurred to her that Russell might need security around him. But there was too much to do to dwell on that for very long, and so she moved on to manage the chaos around her.

Due to popular demand, C-SPAN was shuffling its programming schedule to rebroadcast the debate several times a day for the next week. Congress had adjourned for the year, and almost all of their program offerings were repeats anyway. They did carry a live call-in show the morning following the first rebroadcast, and all anyone phoning in to the various party lines wanted to talk about was the clown and the angry old man. A few took Jeter's side, but the overwhelming consensus was that Greenbeaux had won the debate.

All of the late-night comedy shows had taken a hiatus for the holiday, and so there would be no virtuous cycle of jokes, social media posts, reposts, tweets and retweets to benefit the campaign while the news was fresh. But Ruth and Virgil had more than they could handle now, and any extra boost might have sent them over the edge.

The attention Greenbeaux was receiving was still minor compared with what the major-party front-runners were garnering on a daily basis, but those campaigns had professional operations that were well-equipped to manage spikes in coverage on good and bad days. Ruth and Virgil knew that they needed help, and fast, but they were so caught up in the tide of the moment that they couldn't even begin to deal with that.

*   *   *

Norm Brodie had done his research, but he was having a tough time finding the right entree into Greenbeaux's operation. The world of elite political operatives was small and exclusive, and he was rarely more than two phone calls away from inside access to any major campaign.

But none of his contacts seemed to know anybody who worked at the Des Moines headquarters, and as near as he could tell, this was an amateur operation that was cut off from the normal political channels. That might be a blessing if he could be the first to put his fingerprints on it, or a curse if neophytes who wouldn't take advice were running it.

The campaign was new and didn't have any Federal Elections Committee filings on record to that point. He started making some inquiries around K Street to see if any of the lobbyists or money people had dug their roots into the campaign yet. After a dozen or so calls he finally got a hit.

*   *   *

Virgil was surprised to see a 202 area code number pop up on his cell phone. Only his family and a handful of his people in the campaign had the number, and so he thought it might be a reporter from one of the Washington bureaus trying to set up an interview. He quickly answered the call.

"Hi, this is Virgil Munsell."

"Virgil, this is Goldfarb."

It had been more than a week since his one and only conversation with the campaign's mysterious benefactor, but he immediately recognized the gruff voice on the other end. No doubt word about the debate performance had gotten around.

"Yes Mr. Gold... I mean Goldfarb. How are you?"

"I'm good. Hey, one of my colleagues heard that a top-shelf strategist wants to talk with the campaign. The guy's name is Norm Brodie. I haven't worked with him, but the word is he's one of the best."

Ruth and Greenbeaux had launched the campaign on sheer determination, and Virgil had added professional expertise to the operational side of things. They had done an admirable job of preparing for the debate and were starting to reap the fruit of their efforts, but they were quickly getting in over their heads and they needed help from a pro.

"One of the best?" Virgil said. "Well then, we would love to talk with him."

Contributions were now pouring into the campaign from small donors, but Ruth and Virgil had agreed that they still needed to be careful with their money. After the caucuses in two weeks, the campaign would need to go national to stay in the spotlight, and it would be expensive to put Greenbeaux and a marching band on the ground elsewhere. Virgil didn't know what the top consultants charged, but he suspected that it was more than they could afford.

Goldfarb gave him Norm's number to call, and then added: "I'm coming to Iowa next week after Christmas, and I'm going to bring a friend along that I want you guys to meet."

Goldfarb hung up before Virgil could learn the details of the visit. He quickly added the 202 number to his contacts and jotted it down on a yellow legal pad for good measure, making a note to follow up with Goldfarb so that they would be ready when their benefactor and his friend came calling.

Virgil went to look for Ruth so he could brief her on the call. He was a little surprised to find her in her assigned office with the door closed instead of at the control tower directing traffic. She was stretched to her limits and was anxiously trying to work out some personnel issues that would allow her to delegate more tasks and keep up with the day's deluge.

"Goldfarb called," Virgil said, interrupting her train of thought. "He's coming to town next week."

Ruth looked up, not quite sure whether she should be excited or scared by that news. "Really?"

"Yes. And he's bringing a friend along he wants us to meet."

This struck Ruth as a good sign, coming on the heels of her son's stellar debate performance. Maybe he was planning to bring along the rich guy who owned the building and liked clowns.

"Oh, and he also mentioned that some big-shot Washington political strategist is trying to get in touch with us. Goldfarb thinks we should talk with him."

Norm spent a good part of Christmas day in airports on his way to Des Moines. He didn't have much in the way of family left; just his brother, and they weren't on speaking terms. Other people might have found it sad, but it was the only life he knew, and he just accepted it as the price of his nomadic existence.

When the call finally came from Virgil, it was not unexpected. The K Street people who had shown Norm the path in were well-known for their tight control over campaigns and candidates, and it would have made sense that Greenbeaux's people would have jumped when Washington told them to. Norm appreciated having the door opened for him, but he was a little concerned about going to work for a campaign that might be subject to that kind of outside influence.

Virgil had made it clear that they didn't have the money to pay him, but Norm had already made up his mind, and he agreed to those terms. The fact that there was a tight budget suggested that the K Street people had not dug their talons too deeply into the Greenbeaux campaign yet, but one look at Cedar Point told him otherwise.

When Norm stepped off the elevator at 10:00 a.m. on December 26, Ruth was there to meet him, just as she did every invited guest who had graced the headquarters since it opened. He could hear a marching band practicing in the background as he was led to the conference room to meet with the candidate and his top advisors.

The initial boom of publicity following the debate had subsided as the networks shifted their focus back to the Democratic and Republican candidates preparing for the caucuses. They had given their top political reporters time off for Christmas, and they were coasting for now with pre-canned human-interest stories and documentaries in place of political news.

Traffic to the campaign website and online donations had dropped significantly since the day after the debate, though both measures of success were well above what they had been before Greenbeaux and Jeter squared off on C-SPAN. Most of the traffic was still coming from outside the Clown Underground, but with the news coverage drying up, the percentage of first-time visitors to the site was starting to plummet.

Norm understood the boom and bust cycles campaigns faced, and he was prepared to share his ideas about how Greenbeaux could stay in front of the press and continue to build momentum leading up to the convention season when the stakes would be higher. But first, he would have to survive Ruth's inquisition.

The candidate's mother took nothing for granted when it came to selecting the people in the campaign who would be closest to her son. She did not view herself as overprotective, nor did she want Russell to be a mama's boy. But they were now playing at a higher level, and there were more sharks in these dangerous waters.

Ruth introduced Norm to Greenbeaux and Virgil in the conference room, sat them down, and launched into her interrogation.

"Who is Goldfarb?"

"Goldfarb?" Norm had an impressive Rolodex and personally knew -- or knew of -- just about everyone in American politics who mattered. But he had never heard of anyone with that last name before.

"You know," Ruth said. "Goldfarb. The guy who sent you."

"Ah." Norm didn't know the identity of the people who had facilitated his introduction to the campaign, but that was not unusual. Sunshine doesn't reach the ground in all parts of Washington, and the lead that connected him with Cedar Point had bubbled up from a very dark place. "I don't know anyone by that name."

Ruth was puzzled, but she pressed on. "Then who sent you here?"

"I found my own way. I liked what I saw in the debate and I believe that I can help you."

Greenbeaux started to chime in, but Ruth cut him off. "Goldfarb has been very generous to our campaign, but we haven't met him or know who he works for. And now you show up willing to work for free, and I am just curious who is paying you."

"Actually, I am not being paid by anyone. I want to volunteer my services."

Virgil nodded his head. He was working for free because the cause spoke to him. They needed expert help, and he liked the idea of bringing in another person who might be a true believer.

Ruth interjected again. "We appreciate that. But I have a couple of questions. I couldn't help noticing that you worked for Senator Martelli. It's a shame how the media jumped all over him for crying on camera. And I also noticed that you worked for that poor fellow who ran for governor in Tennessee, what was his name?"

"Lowen. Miles Lowen," Greenbeaux added. Playing the setup man for his mother's line of questioning.

"Yes. That's it. Miles Lowen," Ruth said. "Nice fellow. But I didn't understand why his campaign fell apart like that. Can you explain it?"

"Okay..." Norm started, looking for the right words to avoid betraying a confidence. Lowen's problem, like so many other men in politics, was that he just loved too much. He had to find a graceful exit before a rival candidate could break the news of an illegitimate child his mistress was expecting. If that dirty laundry had aired, it would have done more than undermine his candidacy, it would have ended his marriage to an heiress and the lifestyle to which he had become accustomed.

Lowen's political downfall had been one of Norm's masterpieces. It deflected all of the attention from the candidate and placed it elsewhere. There were leaked fictional e-mails from his advisors who appeared to be plotting to secure government jobs for their family members when the election was over. Among the made-up messages released were ones from Miles Lowen making it clear that he would not tolerate unethical behavior among his staff.

Shortly after the news was broken by a reporter whom Norm had previously dated, Lowen held a press conference on the steps of the state capitol in Nashville to announce that because he believed so strongly in ethics and accountability, he would rather withdraw from the race he was leading than have the good people of Tennessee question whether their taxpayer dollars were funding nepotism.

Lowen had a cover story for exiting that enhanced -- rather than harmed -- his reputation, and Norm received a healthy consulting fee from a campaign war chest that was no longer needed for the stretch run.

"In Lowen's case, I was brought in after a crisis had been identified..." This was true. "... And I helped him write a speech that allowed for a graceful exit." Also true. "If you would like, you can call Miles as a reference."

"I did, and he said he was very pleased with the service you provided," Ruth said. "I also called Andre Fontaine."

Norm's heart skipped a beat. Everybody would gladly take at least one do-over in their lives, and the job he had done for Fontaine was the one he wanted back. Fontaine was a preacher and a political kingmaker in Houston who had decided to use his powers to get himself elected to Congress. He was running in a district where everyone who was anyone owed him. But he had a problem.

Along with political capital he had also collected a few impolitic favors, and a rival campaign acquired pharmacy records showing prescriptions in his name for penicillin. Norm was brought in to smooth things over and explain away the problem to save the campaign from the embarrassing disclosure. He carefully concocted a cover story about the good reverend contracting rheumatic fever during a recent missionary trip to a small village in the South Pacific.

Unfortunately, Norm was unfamiliar with the local media and had cozied up to a dimwitted reporter who, in his confusion, blended information that he had been provided by both Norm and the other candidate's operative. When the newsman mistakenly reported that Andre Fontaine had given gonorrhea to an entire village in Samoa, the preacher's campaign and ministry were effectively over.

Norm had always counseled his clients to tell the truth whenever possible, and so Norm decided to come clean to Ruth and tell her all of the details. Greenbeaux and Virgil were failing in their best efforts to keep from laughing as they listened to Norm's retelling of the event, and Ruth let a slight smile creep into her poker face. She had grown up in the McCaslin family, and the whole story of the less-than-holy man of the cloth sounded very familiar to her. She asked Norm: "Where is Apia?"

"Apia, I believe, is the capital of Samoa."

"Well, that explains the message Andre wanted me to relay to you."

"Oh?" Norm said, worrying about what was coming next.

"After he was done cursing your name, he asked me to tell you that if you ever set foot in Houston again, he will personally cut off your balls and put them on a slow boat to Apia."

Virgil almost fell out of his chair, unable to contain his laughter. Ruth gave him a dirty look and then continued: "Goldfarb and Miles Lowen have attested to your

139

reputation, and I guess that two out of three is good enough for us."

Norm's services were quite valuable, and he had not expected to go through this much vetting to give them away for free. But he appreciated that Ruth had done some due diligence, and that gave him some confidence that this was not a crackpot third-party campaign.

Now that he had been hired, Norm had some questions for them. "What's the deal with the band?"

Virgil stepped in to explain what Douglas was working on, including the idea of marching past live television broadcasts unannounced and having flash mob rallies. He didn't have time to get into the clown culture 101 primer before Norm's eyes lit up and he jumped in.

"That's brilliant!" he said. "But instead of just going near where they are broadcasting, I think they need to get right into the shot, march right between the camera and the reporter. People will remember that forever."

Greenbeaux and Virgil looked at each other and nodded in agreement. There had been some concern about whether they were off their rockers for putting a marching band together to pull off this kind of stunt. But having a political consultant of Norm's stature bless the idea and build upon it made them even more excited to give it a try.

Norm's real genius was for optics, and he understood how to stage events to shape the perceptions of voters watching at home. A major-party contender would never want to alienate the reporters who were riding along on the bus; they were a campaign's lifeblood, and if they turned against a candidate, the wrong information would start finding its way into living rooms around the country.

But Norm recognized that the Greenbeaux campaign needed to be about disruption. The candidate had hit a nerve in the debate with his message about breaking the cycle of dysfunction in Washington, but there was little hope that the media would continue to pay attention if the campaign didn't force the issue.

The music piping through from the band rehearsal in the background was hypnotic. To a man of Norm's generation, it sounded like Jack White. To Greenbeaux, it sounded like George Thorogood and Stevie Ray Vaughn, with a touch of the Allman Brothers. But to Douglas Goodwin, it sounded like John Lee Hooker, Elmore James, and Chuck Berry. It was not typical marching band fare, which made it all the more interesting.

Norm was becoming enchanted with the possibilities of what they could do with the band, and he asked if they could go watch the rehearsal. Ruth peeled off from the group as the other three went to the back of the office where more than six dozen clowns were playing their instruments while practicing formation marches in place. Douglas was standing on a chair shouting out directions.

Disorder broke out as some of the band members caught a glimpse of their hero candidate for the first time walking into the room. Douglas looked over his shoulder to see what was going on. He gave a quick smile, stepped down and yielded the chair for Greenbeaux to give an impromptu speech. The tall man climbed up and perched himself precariously atop the folding chair.

"Ladies and gentlemen, on behalf of myself and the entire Greenbeaux for President campaign team, I would like to thank you for coming out and volunteering your time. I understand that many of you traveled great distances and put your lives on hold to help us, and I just want you to know how deeply I appreciate your commitment to our cause."

As Greenbeaux launched into his stump speech, Norm and Virgil pulled Douglas aside to ask how everything was coming along. The bandleader explained that they were rehearsing four musical numbers, and that they would be ready to perform by New Year's Day. Everyone involved had been carefully selected from more than 200 volunteers who had come through the Clown Underground. They all had marching band experience in high school and, in many cases, college as well.

Norm saw measuring tapes on tables lining the walls, and he rightly assumed that people were being fitted for band uniforms. He had a different idea. The sight of so many clowns in one space wearing contrasting outfits was a thing of beauty to a political consultant who loved visual presentation. He thought it would be more startling for viewers to see a band filled with different-looking clowns marching toward the camera.

The room erupted in applause when Greenbeaux finished his speech. The band members were aching for their movement to take flight, and they were all thrilled to support their man and be part of it. After a few minutes, Douglas called them back to order so the rehearsal could resume. Norm and Virgil conferred, and pulled the bandleader aside before he could get started again.

The campaign advisors wanted to make sure that everyone in the band understood that the choreography was centered on the theme of disruption. They would need to learn how to master the art of precision marching through a cameraman and a reporter standing six feet apart, which might involve misdirection from their original path, if necessary.

Two days later, Cedar Point was abuzz, waiting for the arrival of Goldfarb the benefactor and his special guest. Norm had settled into his office and was preparing strategy briefs that outlined the campaign's next moves.

Before he had arrived, the plan was to appoint a press secretary as soon as possible, but Norm had convinced everyone that they first needed to build a stable of social media specialists who could broadcast the most important messages the campaign needed to relay. He loved Virgil's idea of coupling the marching band appearances with flash mobs, and he used that as an example to argue that the campaign first needed to get their channels and messengers secured.

The headquarters and base of operations would stay at Cedar Point after the caucuses, but the campaign would spend money to place Greenbeaux, the band, and a handful of operatives on the ground in key media markets around the country. New Hampshire was the next logical stop on the tour, but Northern New England was no place to send a marching band in the dead of winter. Instead, Norm wanted to put Greenbeaux on the ground with two media specialists, and then position the band in South Carolina just ahead of that state's primary.

One of the benefits of being a third-party candidate was that Greenbeaux was under no pressure to accumulate delegates to secure a convention nomination, and there was no need to get on any ballots until the general election in November. The goal was to stay relevant in the media's mind and position Greenbeaux as the sensible alternative to the status quo in Washington.

The key number Norm had identified was 15 percent. If Greenbeaux had that much support in the polls when

September rolled around, the Commission on Presidential Debates would invite him to participate in the fall debates with the Republican and Democrat candidates. And if he could get on stage with them, anything could happen.

The C-SPAN debate had given Greenbeaux a taste of what could be, and for the first time he had dared to imagine himself as a serious contender. He now thought less about the unpleasant aspects of the presidential job, and more about the historical implications of being the first clown to occupy the White House. He was not driven by the need for power, but he couldn't deny that becoming the most powerful man in the world had some appeal.

There was no longer talk in the inner circle about Greenbeaux expecting to drop out at some point, and Norm had not been briefed on that possibility. As far as he knew, the team was in it for the long haul, and his strategic briefs were based on a plan that would take them through the first Tuesday in November.

He was starting to pick up on the underlying clown rights theme that had launched the campaign in the first place, and the pressure that was coming from certain elements in the Clown Underground to make that a more prominent part of Greenbeaux's message. Over the next several days, Norm was given a primer on the historical oppression of clowns.

He had many of the same questions as Douglas. He wanted to know why mimes were not being allowed into the campaign, and he was given the same dismissive and chilly response. After he had watched the first marching band practice, he asked Virgil why the tuba section was in the front instead of the rear of the formation. He was just beginning to understand the complex world he had entered, but Norm grasped right away that there was a profound meaning behind the saying he heard several people mention: "Never turn your back on an evil clown."

CHAPTER 11

When Goldfarb and his guest showed up as planned on December 29th, they were greeted at the elevator by Ruth and shown to the conference room where Greenbeaux, Virgil, and Norm were stationed. Both visitors were clowns, but they wore regular business suits instead of full regalia.

Goldfarb was a fireplug of a man, short and stocky, with an ill-fitting blue suit that suggested to Norm he was more of a henchman than a Washington puppet master. He wore his greasepaint thin, with straight horizontal lines on the outside corners of his eyes and lips, suggesting a measure of intensity in his focus. His unkempt frizzy hair was dyed indigo blue, and reminded Ruth of the sky's color after sunset, just before it went pitch black on a moonless night.

His companion, who introduced himself as R. Johnson Shipley, appeared to be about forty years old and was wearing an immaculately tailored grey pinstripe suit. He was tall and lean, with a full mane of neatly styled dark hair. His white makeup was heavily caked, with an exaggerated smile painted on using bright red lipstick that matched his power tie, pocket handkerchief, and extra-large clown shoes.

Johnson, as he preferred to be called, had a genteel Southern drawl. Norm thought he recognized him from somewhere, but he couldn't be sure. He had never seen any men he knew in Washington wearing makeup before, and the clown look made it harder for him to place the face. When they shook hands, Norm cocked his head a little as if to say, "Have we met before?" But Johnson did not reveal any familiarity in return.

Greenbeaux, too, sensed that he knew Johnson from somewhere. He had met a lot of people over the years at Clown Underground functions, and he was almost certain that their paths had crossed. But as was the case with Norm, Johnson simply shook hands and exchanged pleasantries without signaling a glimmer of recognition.

The team had no idea what to expect from the visit. Norm had prepared three different presentations, and planned to pull up the most appropriate one depending on his gut sense from the initial interaction

The blue-sky version laid out the case for a stretch run all the way into November. The outline included every element of the strategy brief Norm had prepared, including social media tactics, grassroots organizing, budget and fundraising targets, event planning, and plans for advertising late in the summer to get them to the 15 percent poll support mark.

There were also veiled references to forming a political action committee or a Super PAC. Norm had cautioned that even if they felt comfortable enough with their benefactors to present the blue-sky option, they would still need to be vague on that point. They needed to know more about the money backing Goldfarb before they could express an interest in partnering to that extent.

The second scenario, which Norm nicknamed partly cloudy, revealed much of the same information, but was more opaque about the campaign's strategic plans. It went into detail about what had been done to date, and hinted at the strategy to put Greenbeaux and the marching band on the ground in primary states. But it omitted any mention of money or staffing needs beyond the core leadership team and other volunteers.

They would give the partly cloudy presentation if there were hints that their benefactors might have ulterior motives, or if there was any lingering doubt about either of the men visiting Cedar Point.

The third option carried the code name dark skies. Their benefactors had revealed almost nothing to them aside from their access to deep pockets, and the team knew that there was no such thing as a free lunch in Washington. Every candidate needs big money, and everyone who has big money to give needs something in return.

For all they knew, someone in the Clown Underground was filthy rich and wanted to help the campaign anonymously, but Norm and Ruth both felt strongly that they couldn't take that for granted.

The dark skies presentation option would give the visitors nothing of value; no insight into what the campaign was planning and no promises whatsoever. It was to be invoked if anyone felt that they were going to be pressured to compromise their principles in any way. They had started from humble beginnings in the outbuilding of an industrial supply company, and they could hand back the keys to Cedar Point and start over somewhere new if they had to.

Norm had been impressed that the candidate, his mother, and his campaign manager were so committed to maintaining their integrity. That was indicative of novices who had yet to encounter the hard, grey-area choices that big-stage political campaigns inevitably face. But still, it was refreshing, and it reminded him of when he first arrived on Capitol Hill, determined to change the world without compromising.

Virgil and Greenbeaux liked their visitors very much, and they were pleased to see that they were both clowns who were there to support the movement. They were confident they were among friends, and they were expecting Norm to give the blue-sky presentation.

Ruth wasn't so sure. Goldfarb seemed nice enough, but there was something about Johnson that bothered her. His mannerisms were just a little too polished and the smile painted on his face seemed a touch too broad. There was nothing in their friendly conversation to suggest that they were going to ask for anything untoward, but her gut told her to proceed cautiously.

"I hope you don't mind our Iowa weather too much," she told her visitors while catching Norm's eye. "Most days this time of year are cold and partly cloudy."

Norm nodded in agreement, and opened his computer to pull up the second presentation deck.

*　　*　　*

That night, Norm's phone buzzed and he looked down to see that a text had come in from a number with a 303 area code. Jessica was originally from Denver, and so he thought it might be from her.

"What did that poor clown ever do to deserve a visit from Dr. Death?"

Yep, it was definitely from her. He didn't recall giving her his phone number, but tracking people down was what she did for a living. He secretly enjoyed her friendly abuse, and he was glad that she had found him.

Word was spreading that the venerable Norm Brodie had joined the campaign staff of a clown, and those who understood his secret talent were puzzled. Third-party candidates lead a marginal existence in the realm of American politics, and they were free to come and go from a race without the need to create an expensive mythology surrounding their exit.

Those who did not understand Norm's business method saw this move as a sign that the hapless consultant on a losing streak was hitting bottom. But Jessica knew better. It was her job to figure out what everyone in politics was up to, and Norm's secret identity was old news to her. But still, she was as confused by this move as everyone else who appreciated his genius.

"I've run off to join the circus," Norm texted back.

"Did they need you to euthanize some animals?" she asked, teasing again.

"No, the only thing I am killing is time," he answered. "I found work as an animal trainer."

It bothered her that she couldn't figure out what was going on in his mind. Had she broken his heart and sent him off on a journey to find himself? Not likely. She guessed the only thing Norm needed to find was another bottle of scotch.

She tried another approach, probing for clues about why the man had jumped into the abyss of third-party politics. "I thought you only knew how to train donkeys and elephants."

He was now fonder of Jessica than he would ever admit, but she worked in opposition research, and he wasn't about to let his guard down. If he told her the real reasons he had joined Team Greenbeaux -- or that he was working for free -- he risked telling the whole world. And nothing about that was good for business.

"They have a couple of old dogs here that I am teaching new tricks," he replied cryptically.

"What type of circus is it?" she texted back. Hoping that he would give her something, anything. But he wasn't biting.

"One with lots of clowns in it."

This man was going to drive her mad. She needed to figure him out, and he just wouldn't give an inch. The only new thing she had learned that night in New Hampshire was that he couldn't let his brother win. Deep down, she knew that he was the wrong type of man for her long-term happiness. But there was something endearing about him that she was having a hard time getting over, and she needed to stop thinking about him.

*   *   *

Carrie Rollins was trying to fall asleep on New Year's Eve. Rather than partying on into the night, she had stayed home with her husband and two-year-old daughter, hoping to get a good night's sleep before a big day ahead. Her story about the Greenbeaux campaign was set to run in the morning edition, and she had a gut feeling that all hell was about to break loose.

Exploring the world of the Clown Underground online had become her secret obsession. She had decided not to include anything about it in the story because it was a form of intelligence and insight, and she wanted to stay one step ahead of other reporters on what she suspected was going to become a big story.

She had discovered that there was going to be a massive invasion of clowns in Des Moines, descending in a flash mob for a surprise rally shortly after noon at a secret location. From what she could tell on the message boards, there were busloads of people coming from other cities, and all of this was invisible to everyone outside the clown culture. Except for her.

Her editors had not planned to run her story about Greenbeaux until mid-January, saving the prime newsprint space for coverage of the main-party candidates until the caucuses were over. But Carrie had convinced them that a newsworthy event was going to take place on New Year's Day, and they had yielded front-page space below the fold that morning to get ahead of the story.

She did not hint at the impending spectacle in the article, fearing that she might ruin the element of surprise and scare off the clowns from holding their event. She preferred to write only about that which was known or certain to happen, and it would be a setback if she published information about an event that never materialized.

Carrie tried to go to sleep shortly after she had her daughter in bed at eight-thirty, but she was fixated on the big day ahead and couldn't shut off her mind. She was still awake when she heard neighbors counting down, then cheers and the sound of gunfire and fireworks far off in the distance. Tomorrow and the next year were here and she was still too excited to sleep.

CHAPTER 12

At precisely 12:03 p.m., Douglas Goodwin gave the signal and the first of two buses filled with clowns and their musical instruments was unloaded two blocks east of the Polk County Courthouse. The major networks had set up their coverage for the day using the impressive-looking building as their backdrop, and so it was decided that would be the location of their flash mob rally.

Norm typically had a cameo role near the candidate at each of his staged events, but today he had chosen to station himself at Cedar Point. Newly installed televisions lined a wall in the break room that he had converted into a fully functioning war room.

Norm was watching live feeds intently to make sure that the staging he had blocked out with Douglas and Virgil was still going to work.

Fox News was set up far off to the right of the courthouse, and MSNBC was located on the left, though they were now showing a program about life in a prison that most Republicans who flipped past the channel assumed housed only hardened Democrats. CNN was positioned right down the middle, and Norm could see the optics taking shape along the parade route as he had planned. The reporter he wanted to target, Naomi Winston, was standing in front of the camera in her favorite red outfit, and all of the wheels were now in motion.

Norm was not a vengeful person by nature, but he was an opportunist, and it seemed only fitting that Naomi should be the one standing in the way of the band's march forward. The two had a May-June romance in Washington the previous year, which ended when her publicist made a convincing argument that it would be better for her career to be seen on the arm of a Redskins linebacker who had just filmed a shoe commercial.

Naomi had batted her long eyelashes and twirled her luscious blond hair to leach information from him that she turned into a series of exclusive reports. There wasn't anything he revealed that harmed any of his clients, but when it was all over he realized that he had been used. The whole relationship had been a one-way street, though there was one valuable piece of information that he had learned from her that he was about to use to his benefit.

On one fateful night, shortly before the relationship ended, they stopped by a carnival they saw from the road in Silver Spring. After riding the Ferris wheel, the two walked down the makeshift midway, past the barkers, to a place where the sideshows were taking place. He could sense that she was tensing up and then panicking as they neared a man making balloon animals, and he soon realized that she was terrified of clowns. It seemed innocuous to Norm at the time, but with a marching band full of clowns at his command, he now had a mark to make the optics just a little more interesting.

At 12:06, the clowns were standing in formation waiting for the signal from Cedar Point, the buses shielding their presence from the reporters and bystanders who were out and about enjoying a sunny and mild January day. The

154

network anchor in Atlanta was still talking through the top-of-the-hour news and playing prerecorded stories, and after a commercial break he would cut to a live update on the caucuses from Naomi.

Two minutes later, the band began marching silently on their three-minute walk to approach at an angle from behind the cameraman. Their instruments were set to be raised when they were ten paces away; the tubas would lead the procession with a deep bass opening chord that was designed to announce their entrance in a distinctive way.

At 12:10, Norm sent out the tweet to call the flash mob forth:

#clownsontheground 12:30@Polk County Courthouse.

Carrie Rollins was in the newsroom with the *Register's* live blogger, waiting to break the news of the event before anyone else. When she saw the tweet come across with the expected #clownsontheground hashtag, she tapped the blogger on the shoulder and called out the time and location. Within seconds, the news was published.

> "We have just received word of a big rally for the Greenbeaux campaign at the Polk County Courthouse starting at 12:30."

She grabbed her coat and was on her way to get down to the courthouse when she noticed something interesting on a TV in the newsroom. A reporter on the television stopped midsentence, her eyes grew wide, and then she started screaming in terror live on the air. Above the din, a marching band was playing a song that sounded vaguely like *Where the River Flows,* Carrie's favorite song by Collective Soul.

Carrie stopped briefly in her tracks, watching as the backs of the band members appeared in the shot, marching right past the crazed reporter on their way to the courthouse. The network quickly sent the feed back to the surprised anchor in Atlanta, who was trying to remain calm and make sense of the situation as the director shouted through his earpiece.

Televisions in the *Register* newsroom that were tuned to other networks suddenly showed a flurry of activity. The Fox News camera that had been broadcasting a live report panned over to show a marching band filled with clowns wearing green bow ties playing the blues while they went past. The frantic scene on CNN had also caught MSNBC's attention. They cut away from the prison documentary and were live and focused on the procession while their reporter scrambled to get into place and explain what was going on.

By that time, Carrie was already out the door, followed closely by a photojournalist and two other reporters who were clued in that something unusual was happening.

The pace of activity around the courthouse was picking up as Greenbeaux's supporters began to descend for the rally. Buses filled with clowns from Chicago, Omaha, Fargo, Kansas City, St. Louis, Minneapolis and other faraway places that had been circling Des Moines awaiting the tweet suddenly moved in, as did hundreds of local supporters who were poised and ready to go.

Greenbeaux had been waiting calmly out of sight with Virgil and three other volunteers, who were carrying a microphone and several Bluetooth amplifiers as well as a step stool that would serve as the tall clown's makeshift stage. They could hear the band playing in the distance, and heard Norm yell "Go, go, go" over a cell phone to a different ground crew on the other side of the courthouse.

156

Carrie's article that morning had captured a lot of attention locally, and the combination of the live blog message and the breaking network news coverage was stirring up a frenzy in Des Moines. People on the street and in shops were watching as an army of clowns moved in from all directions. Many bystanders dropped what they were doing to follow along to see what was happening.

Ruth joined Norm in the war room to watch the scene unfold. The televisions on the wall were all focusing on the marching band, which was now circling the courthouse. The *Register* blog post had revealed that a Greenbeaux rally was the focal point of the activity, and one by one the networks started announcing that they were awaiting remarks from the candidate to the gathering crowd.

As breaking news went, the political rally of an unknown contender was small potatoes barely worth the airtime it might get at off hours. But to viewers who had seen Naomi Winston's freak-out broadcast live, this was a riveting drama. The Twitterverse exploded with comments and six-second videos of the episode, and people flocked to the news networks to see what was happening.

CNN was hesitant to replay their reporter's moment of terror, and so they kept their cameras trained on the marching band. Winston had locked herself in the truck and wasn't coming out, and so the play-by-play commentary that viewers heard had to come from the studios in Atlanta and Washington.

Ruth was new to the excitement of live political events, and she was silent as she watched in awe as all the major news networks began coverage of her son's rally. Norm was used to the big stage, and he was trying to play it cool, as though this was just another day at work. But he was elated, and he knew that he was witnessing a scene that would forever be prominently featured on his highlight reel.

Greenbeaux was stepping back into the spotlight on New Year's Day, and people everywhere were clamoring to know more. The *Register* story that had run in the morning was now trending online as people searched to make sense of what they were seeing on the television. Carrie had focused on Ruth and Greenbeaux's origins, and she had not leaned too heavily on the clown rights struggle that had motivated the campaign.

There were still many questions to be answered. Greenbeaux's fame from the debate performance had been fleeting, and most people who saw him were puzzled because they had no idea that clowns could be anything more than horror-movie villains or children's entertainers.

There was a disconnect that needed to be reconciled; the man who so perfectly articulated the frustrations of Americans living outside the Beltway was wearing greasepaint and a clown suit.

Reporters on the scene at the courthouse and talking heads in the studio scrambled to find more information to fill the airtime as they waited for the candidate to speak. Details of the *Register* story began to emerge about a successful businessman who was running to give clowns a voice. The camera crews on the ground were capturing the excitement of his loyal followers, many of whom held white placards with the image of a green bow tie that Norm had commissioned for the event. Others carried homemade signs with slogans like "Go Green" and "I'm Down With The Clown."

At precisely 12:30, the prompt came from Norm in the war room at Cedar Point. Greenbeaux emerged from the shadows and walked into the collected throng that now numbered in the thousands. He stood tall with a shock of green hair that rose above the crowd, and the excitement grew as his supporters spotted him. Volunteers cleared a small circle and placed the step stool on the ground, and when he climbed up, there was no doubt about who the man of the hour was.

"Welcome my friends. Welcome to a new era in politics, when the powers that control Washington will now have to listen to We The People. An era when those of you who want more than just Republicans and Democrats in Washington will have a third choice."

Greenbeaux was whipping the crowd into a frenzy, and the networks chose not to cut away for a commercial break. The first of January was supposed to be a slow news day, a time when people were more interested in watching bowl games than in following a political rally. Even in a presidential election year, with the Iowa caucuses just days away, this type of spectacle was unusual.

Campaigns craved media attention, and they bent over backwards to keep the press informed of their every move, and yet the Greenbeaux campaign had done no such thing. They had kept the whole thing a secret until the band marched right into Naomi Winston's worst nightmare and the crowd was summoned to descend.

The age of the mass flash mob political rally had arrived, and the suddenness of it all had shocked the networks. The backroom people were watching this trending on social media, and they realized that some sort of cultural phenomenon was unfolding before their eyes.

* * *

Shortly after the rally was over, Cedar Point was overflowing with activity. Busloads of people who had come in from other cities came by to see the headquarters and ask what they could do. Ruth didn't have a quick answer, and so she started stuffing people in the open space in the back where the band had practiced until Virgil returned and they could figure it out together.

Norm was tied up trying to field all of the requests from media outlets that wanted to speak with the candidate. He was now seriously regretting his decision to forestall hiring a press secretary. He suspected that the campaign was just seeing another bump like the one they had experienced after the debate, but if they had more days like this one, Greenbeaux might enter the collective American consciousness, and the media demands would become too intense for them to handle with the staff they had in place.

Ruth could see that he was overwhelmed and, on a whim, she went to the back room where the new volunteers were being directed. She grabbed a chair, climbed up, and called for everyone's attention.

"Please raise your hand if you have experience as a journalist or in public relations."

Three hands went up. Ruth stepped down and asked them to follow her to the conference room where she quickly conducted a group interview. One, a retired English teacher, had been a faculty sponsor for the school's student newspaper. That was not exactly what Ruth was looking for. A second had done an internship with a public relations firm when he was in college thirty years earlier. Still not right.

The third one, however, seemed like a much better fit to throw into the fire. She was a former newspaper reporter who worked in corporate communication for a large chain of retail stores. That would have to do, and so Ruth conscripted her to be press secretary for the day and handed her off to Norm.

*   *   *

Late that night, after all of the volunteers had gone home, Virgil and Norm went to a bar to have a drink and unwind before heading back to their respective hotels. They had pulled off a nearly impossible task: they had broken the major party stranglehold on media coverage just days before the caucuses.

Traffic to the Greenbeaux for President site during the rally had reached a level that was nearly eight times higher than what they had seen during the peak of the post-debate coverage. The numbers continued to spike throughout the day as Greenbeaux appeared in live interviews on various programs, and news stories were posted about how the unique rally had caught the networks off-guard.

The focal point of the whole affair was Naomi Winston's shocked reaction to seeing a wall of terrifying clowns coming toward her in the form of a marching band, and the deer-in-the-headlights look of the anchor who suddenly had the camera back on him in Atlanta.

Norm did feel a twinge of remorse for what he had put Naomi through, but that did not last very long. She was seriously disliked by others in the political community who had been similarly used, abused and left for dead while she climbed the ladder, and Norm had received more than a few congratulatory messages from his fellow politicos who were celebrating her comeuppance.

Virgil had also received some nice messages. His daughter left him a voicemail to let him know that his cat was doing well, and that she was very proud of him for his work on the Greenbeaux campaign. He also received an interesting e-mail from Milton Kobeck, a former co-worker at IXM Systems.

Milton said that he had really wanted to talk with Virgil after he showed up in his clown gear, and he felt bad that he had not done so. Milton was also a clown, but he was close to retirement and he was too scared to make the approach at work before the firing. "You are a hero for standing up for your principles at IXM," he said. "And I also want to thank you for what you are doing for the Greenbeaux campaign."

It had been a good day for Virgil. His idea for the flash mob rally had worked better than anyone could have imagined, thanks in large part to Douglas' perfectly timed marching band and Norm's finishing touches on the strategy and execution. He was feeling useful and fulfilled in his new job, and thanks to the kind note from Milton, just a touch heroic as well.

*　　*　　*

Norm awoke to find that text messages had come in overnight from Jessica. "Best takedown of an ex-girlfriend. Ever." The second one read: "You nearly scared the devil out of her."

It was no secret that Norm and Naomi had once dated, and political tongues were wagging. One theory now circulating was that the reason Norm had joined the Greenbeaux campaign was to fulfill an elaborate revenge fantasy against possibly the most hated woman in the media. What other reason could there possibly be? Even Jessica wondered about this, and it worried her just a little.

Norm answered. "It was just a happy coincidence."

A reply quickly came back: "Happy? Yes. Coincidence? Not so sure about that." After a few minutes without hearing back, Jessica added: "Don't you ever dare think of taking revenge on me like that :-)"

Norm looked at his phone and laughed before replying. "Never, my dear."

He enjoyed the banter, and he started to type out a question: "RU going to be in Iowa any time soon?" But he thought better of it and hit backspace until the message was gone. He really liked Jessica, but the campaign was just heating up and he didn't think he would be able to spare the time and attention she deserved.

CHAPTER 13

George Sommer was sitting in the Republican National Committee headquarters in Washington trying to solve a lot of problems simultaneously. The Republican Party was under siege in California, and he was talking his team in Sacramento through yet another major crisis. As far as he was concerned, Democrats were only good at two things: slathering liberal bumper stickers on their cars and rallying people to protest. And, yet, they had somehow gained the upper hand in technology, captured the hearts and minds of the majority of young voters, and were now poised to completely take over the home state of Ronald Reagan and Richard Nixon.

Over the crackle of the ham radio they were using to communicate, he could hear the panic of his people on the ground. They were safe for now inside their headquarters in Sacramento, but they were not sure how long their provisions would hold out. The fear in the room was palpable, and George overheard the sounds of protesters in the distance and a strange humming noise that he couldn't quite identify.

"Tell me what you see," George said in a calm voice.

"There are… there are hundreds of them," came the frantic reply. "They are all waving protest signs and singing. *Cumbaya*, I think."

George had seen this play out before. It was Vermont all over again, and he wanted to avoid a repeat of what happened there before the Golden State and its 55 electoral votes were lost forever.

"Have you called 911 and asked them to send people over to protect the building?" he asked.

"Yes. Yes we did. Though I don't think they are sending anyone to help. The operator said she would forward our request to the police union, but they don't like our position on pension reform."

Above the crackles, George could hear the ominous humming sound in the background getting louder "What is that…" he asked, "what is that noise?"

"The Democrats have a guy in some kind of a hovercraft circling above us. It smells really bad and there are flies buzzing around it. I think they might be using chemical warfare on us."

George had heard enough. "If he is threatening you, you can shoot him down."

"We can't do that," came the response

"Why not?" George asked. "Are you out of ammunition?"

"No. We still have 20,000 rounds."

George was getting frustrated with the scared little wimps at the headquarters in Sacramento. "Well, then, why can't you shoot him down?"

"California doesn't have a Stand Your Ground law," came the reply.

Dammit, George thought, nothing was easy today. "Okay, go to the bunker and unseal the red packet, then stand by for further instructions." He threw down the microphone in disgust and turned to Skip Bancroft, his other big problem at the moment.

"You are from California, right?"

"Sort of. I went to college there, sir."

George opened a folder on the table and reviewed Skip's resumé. They had hired him straight out of UC Berkeley the previous summer, but there had been an incident. Earlier in the week, he had been seen driving his sister's Prius that had a troublesome combination of bumper stickers on the back end.

Back in the day, when the Republican Party still owned the technological and financial advantage over Democrats, they had invested heavily in psychographic research in an attempt decode the odd pattern of messages that many liberals were inclined to put on their cars.

Among the findings was that people with five or more different types of stickers were benign, mainly because they lacked focus and couldn't get others to follow them. Another personality type that emerged from the research was dubbed "Volcano." These were angry people who vented their frustration and rage by proclaiming their grievances against conservatives on their bumpers, typically without too much rational thought about the underlying reason why they were mad in the first place.

But there was one personality type in particular that had the Republican researchers worried. Individuals with bumper stickers about poverty, peace, or tolerance were

166

problematic for the party if they were plastered in combination with some type of religious symbol on the car.

The study revealed that these were people who had read the Bible and concluded that Jesus loved the poor and was not fond of moneychangers infringing on what they thought should remain sacred. That interpretation didn't settle well with some of the Republican Party's wealthiest donors, who wanted to cut social programs to pay for upper-income tax cuts.

It was also bothersome to many in their evangelical base who had read the same book but concluded that it wasn't the responsibility of government to help the poor. Instead, they thought the party needed to focus on winning the culture war. They were alarmed at what was now deemed socially acceptable, and they were desperate to steer the country back to the idyllic times of the 1950's. The war on Christmas was the final assault against their religious liberty, and they were no longer willing to stand idly by while a good Christian shopping mall elf could be fired for refusing to say "seasons greetings."

The Prius that Skip was seen driving had a fish and a dove on it, along with stickers about co-existing and random acts of kindness. The incident was brought to the attention of the brass upstairs, and George needed to get Skip out of the building before anyone saw it happen again.

"It says here that you were president of the College Republicans at Berkeley, and that you more than doubled the club's membership during your time there."

"Yes sir," said Skip. "We had five members when I was a freshman, and I was able to increase that to eleven by the time I graduated."

As a percentage of the 35,000 students on campus, the membership was small. But still, getting the number of openly Republican students up to double digits was an impressive accomplishment in a hostile environment like Berkeley.

"Skip, our people in California are having some trouble, and I'm sending you there to help."

"Oh no, sir. Please don't make me go back to California. You don't know what it's like for Republicans over there." His voice trembled as he continued. "One time, they pelted us with their Birkenstocks when we tried to stage a counter-protest at their nonviolence rally."

George let out a heavy sigh. He couldn't send the poor boy back against his will, and he needed to think of another plan.

The ham radio was crackling again. This time he could hear the troops in the bunker reading off a pre-apocalypse checklist they had found among the papers in the red packet. They reviewed each of the seven signs to see if the end was imminent, and they were now convinced that six had already happened. They were excited, wondering aloud if the lawlessness outside their headquarters was the final indication that they were about to be raptured.

The team in Sacramento would have to wait for further instructions until George could figure out what to do with the kid. He glanced at a television on the wall and saw Greenbeaux being interviewed by Fox News. Clips were shown of the large, spontaneous rally that had caught everyone off guard and thrown the third-party candidate into the public eye. That gave him an idea.

"Skip, how would you like to be part of a covert operation?"

*   *   *

Virgil stared at the numbers on his computer screen in amazement. The traffic to the campaign's site had actually increased from the day before, not dropped. The Clown Underground was abuzz, but the vast majority of visitors to the website were not coming from there. One after another, stories about Greenbeaux and the campaign were popping up on the news feeds, indicating that the media wasn't letting go of the story.

Norm had cautioned them that interest was likely to drop as time wore on, just as it had following the initial spike after the debate. But it wasn't abating. The office was flooded with volunteers looking to help, and Ruth was having trouble figuring out what to do with all of them.

The caucuses were coming up on Saturday, and while the format was ill-suited for a third-party candidate to fare well in the voting, the team had decided to fan volunteers out over the most-populated areas of the state to have a presence. Ruth was working on getting the walk-ins organized to help with that.

It was an uphill battle. Caucusgoers had to be registered in one of the two main parties to participate, and that would prevent disenfranchised voters who were registered as Independents from taking part. But if they could get some registered Democrats and Republicans to caucus for Greenbeaux, it would send a strong signal that there was discontent within the parties themselves.

Along with the boom in web traffic had come a huge influx of donations, and they were now sitting on more than a half million dollars at their disposal. Ruth was the de facto treasurer and had the final word over how and when money was to be spent. Campaign finance laws were complex, and she was grateful to now have some professional guidance above and beyond what the early campaign volunteers with legal and financial training had provided.

Norm had pointed her in the direction of a consultant who quickly reviewed the books and confirmed that everything was in compliance. It had not cost a lot of money, and the piece of mind it gave her was well worth the investment. With the windfall of donations coming in, Ruth recognized it was time to ease up on the purse strings and compensate those who had devoted themselves to the campaign.

When she came to a stopping point in her volunteer organizing, she called Douglas to the conference room and handed him an envelope with a check in it. She explained that the money was a consulting fee for his services. Douglas had played a key role in the previous day's success, and she let him know that he deserved to be rewarded.

The music he had composed was spot on, and the precision timing and marching he orchestrated had turned the surprise into a spectacle. The campaign was planning to take the band on the road, and the money was a token to pay Douglas for his time and professional expertise, above and beyond his expenses.

As he left the room, he took a sneak peek in the envelope. The $7,000 check seemed like a small fortune to a retired teacher living on a fixed income, and he felt like dancing on the way back to his office.

Ruth called Norm in next and presented him with a check for $10,000. She apologized in advance, knowing that it was much smaller than he was used to getting. He smiled. It was indeed the smallest paycheck he had seen in years, but he realized that he was getting something far more valuable out of this.

His phone had been ringing and beeping with texts steadily over the last 24 hours. The people who thought he had gone off the deep end for joining a clown's third-party campaign were now contacting him and asking to work on Greenbeaux's staff. His reputation as a brilliant strategist was even stronger, though he knew he was getting far more credit than he deserved for what had happened outside the Polk County Courthouse.

The marching band had been Greenbeaux's idea, and Virgil had envisioned using a flash mob for the rally, which was now being talked about 24/7 as the political stunt of the future. Norm had contributed his knowledge of Naomi Winston's secret fear, and some finishing touches that allowed the whole thing to come together. And my, how it had all come together.

He would come out on top, if he chose to walk away now. His losing streak would be over, and nobody would count it against his record if -- and most likely when -- Greenbeaux eventually bowed out of the race. Flash mobs had been used on a small scale for protests and political purposes before, but never in this way, and Norm Brodie would forever be remembered as the strategist who brought the practice to the big leagues.

There was a part of him that just wanted to leave and go hang out with Jessica for a while. He enjoyed the banter and the odd intellectual dance between them. It made him think that maybe, just maybe, the relationship could last for a while. He wouldn't mind that. He was tired of the treadmill of short-term hookups, and he wanted to see if this one could work.

Norm's relationships with campaigns always followed the same trajectory as the ones he had with women. He would arrive on the scene, work his magic, and get out when he was needed elsewhere. There were a lot of good reasons

171

for him to walk away from Cedar Point, but something was compelling him to stay, at least for the time being.

He thanked Ruth for the check and went back to his office.

Next, she called Virgil into the office, closed the door and presented him with a check for $12,000. Virgil had no reason to expect that he would be paid anything at all, but Ruth felt that it was only right. He was the campaign manager, and he deserved to get the biggest check.

Virgil was aware that the donations coming in now were sufficient to allow them to start paying some staff. But he wasn't doing this for the money. He believed in the cause, and more importantly, he loved the work. He looked at the envelope and his eyes started to mist up.

"This is too much," he said.

"No, it's not enough," Ruth replied. "What you have brought to this campaign cannot be measured in dollars. Without you, we wouldn't have anything. The headquarters. The way Russell was prepared for the debate. The flash mob that drew coverage from the networks. You did that."

Virgil couldn't stop himself from getting emotional as he thanked Ruth. "My spirit was a bit broken when I left Cleveland to drive here, but you took me in, you entrusted me with an important job, and you always made me feel like I was needed. You helped me heal."

Ruth started to choke up as well. She and Virgil had formed a strong bond. They were always in sync, and she completely trusted him to make decisions for the campaign that were in her son's best interest. Even the suggestion he made that Greenbeaux call Heller Hitler -- which she still didn't like -- had worked to their advantage. They had known each other for less than a month, but it felt like they had been friends their whole lives.

She thanked Virgil again, and they both went back to work.

*   *   *

Over at the *Register*, Carrie Rollins was putting the finishing touches on a follow-up piece to the feature about Greenbeaux that had run the day before. The editor of the paper had stopped by to personally congratulate her on the coup, and encouraged her to continue working on coverage of the clown's campaign.

"How did you know that something so big was about to happen?" he asked.

She responded in as coy a manner as she thought she could get away with: "A good reporter never reveals her sources." She then added the kind of smile that let the big boss know that this secret was covered by journalistic privilege, and she couldn't be pressed to tell.

Carrie could sense from the euphoric reaction in the Clown Underground that everyone believed a major breakthrough had occurred within the movement. There were a few voices upset that Greenbeaux had used the platform on national television to talk about the problems in Washington instead of the discrimination faced by clowns, but those people were heavily outnumbered.

She had also sensed that people outside of the clown community who were discovering Greenbeaux for the first time were confused. Here was a politician who spoke so eloquently about their concerns, but he was dressed as a clown. Why? They couldn't figure it out.

Her follow-up piece would use the courthouse rally as a starting point, and then work backward to explain how

Greenbeaux had gotten to that point. It would delve even further into his relationship with his mother and the trigger points that led him to run for President, particularly the clown rights issues that she had downplayed in her first story. She wouldn't reveal any secrets of the Clown Underground, but anyone who read the article would walk away with a clear understanding that there was far more to being a clown than they had ever imagined.

CHAPTER 14

The young man who presented himself to Ruth at the control tower was clean-cut and courteous. He was deferential and answered her questions with a polite "Yes ma'am." He seemed to be a little stumped when she asked why he wanted to volunteer with the campaign; he didn't say anything about the rally or the buzz in the air like the other non-clown workers did. But he had come to help, and so Ruth spared him further grilling and steered him to the coordinator who was managing the envelope stuffers.

Skip Bancroft worked his way to the tables that had been positioned in the middle of the open room where the band had been practicing. He took off his tweed sport coat, sat down at an empty chair, and started stuffing. He was a policy wonk who had studied political science, and he had envisioned a glamorous life working for the Republican National Committee, vanquishing foes of the free markets and limited government.

But from day one, all he had been asked to do was get coffee, make copies, and dust the shrine to Ronald Reagan that adorned the men's room on the third floor. And now, he was sitting in an office in Des Moines, surrounded by clowns, and stuffing envelopes for a candidate he had never heard of the week before. But, it was all in the name of gathering intelligence about a rebel movement, and he supposed that it was a promotion of sorts.

He had grown up in a very large and politically engaged family outside of DC. His mother and all of his sisters were Democrats, while he, his brothers and father were not. Elections were big events for the family, and everyone was expected to pick a side and work for a candidate. On the evening when the results came in, they would tally precinct-by-precinct votes on big pieces of poster board in the living room. For the Bancroft family, it was all one big strategy game drawn out with X's moving to the left and the Y chromosomes moving in lockstep to the right.

His mother had encouraged Skip to go to Berkeley, and not just because it was a fine public ivy university. She was well aware of its reputation as a bastion of liberal ideology, and she hoped that some of it might rub off on the most thoughtful of her children. He was naturally empathetic, and of all her sons she thought he might just be the one who would take up the cause of the downtrodden and disenfranchised.

But Republicans were the only oppressed minority group on the Berkeley campus, and Skip saw it as his calling to lead them out of the wilderness.

*   *   *

It was Friday, the day before the caucuses, and Greenbeaux had wanted to be in New Hampshire by this time to establish a foothold before the media arrived from Iowa in full force. Unlike the major party candidates, he had no operation on the ground whatsoever, and he needed to get a feel for the territory and shake some hands to get started.

But he was so tied up with interview requests that he couldn't break away, which he realized was not a bad problem to have. The rally had turned him into a social media sensation, and there were memes going around depicting him as The Most Interesting Clown in the World. One variation showed Naomi Winston screaming in horror as she was engulfed by clowns, with the caption, "I don't always use marching bands to make my point, but when I do, it is terrifying."

That buzz was keeping the otherwise fickle political press interested in his story. Even CNN, which had seen one of their rising stars fall apart in a sea of clowns, sent a crew over to Cedar Point for an interview with Greenbeaux. They had to bring in a reporter from Washington to interview him and cover the rest of the caucuses, though, because Naomi Winston had checked herself into a facility.

The treatment program was in Florida, which was as far away from Iowa as she could hope to get while still being available to jump back into election coverage when the clowns were gone. With time for calmer reflection, she pieced together what had happened. She had been doing her live stand-up in front of the courthouse, reporting on the activities of various candidates before Saturday's caucuses.

Suddenly, there was a loud blast of music, and a wall of evil-looking clowns with tubas emerged from behind the cameraman and started advancing toward her. They were followed by sad-looking clowns with clarinets and piccolos, and happy clowns with flutes and trumpets and trombones. And then, finally, after what seemed like an eternity, she found herself surrounded by some very angry-looking clowns pounding violently on drums as they marched past.

The whole incident triggered a bad memory from her childhood, a movie she had seen about a clown who chopped up dozens of people in a bloody rampage at an abandoned amusement park. It may have been a low-budget summer horror movie to everyone else, but to Naomi Winston it felt like a documentary, and clowns were forever imprinted on her mind as the most feared and reviled creatures on earth.

After the incident in Des Moines, she learned that the band was from the campaign of a clown who was running for president, and that the strategist behind the stunt was an ex-boyfriend.

She might be cold and manipulative, but she was not one to take on a grudge impulsively without serious forethought and calculation. She had lots of time to think as the hours and then days passed in a place with soft, pastel-colored walls and lots of calm, soothing voices. There was no question in her mind about what must happen now, and Naomi vowed that she would take down that son of a bitch Norm Brodie if it was the last thing she ever did.

*　　*　　*

The phones at Cedar Point were ringing off the hook; more equipment was brought in and volunteers were trained to answer them. Most of the calls coming in were from people in other parts of the country asking if they could help organize Greenbeaux's efforts elsewhere, but there were occasionally some very disturbing ones mixed in as well.

The angry and threatening calls that first came in after Greenbeaux's exchange with Heller had died down when the post-debate bounce subsided, but they were back once again with renewed intensity.

The campaign received word from an organization that tracked extremist groups that they might want to beef up security around the candidate and headquarters. There was no specific threat that had been identified, but there was a lot of chatter among white supremacists who were now angry with clowns in general and Greenbeaux in particular.

The candidate was busy with interviews, but Ruth huddled the other leaders together in her office when word of the threat came in. Norm had by far the most political campaign experience among the team, but he had never encountered anything like this.

Virgil suggested they hire a security guard to stand outside the building as a deterrent. If a specific threat was later identified, he reasoned, they could inform the Secret Service and let them deal with an investigation and protection. They agreed to Virgil's plan, and turned their focus again on all of the details that were overwhelming them.

Norm went back to his office to triage the media requests. It had been nice to have a volunteer with corporate communication expertise to help him right after the rally, but she was from out of town and could only help for that one day. He was used to seeing staff turnover on campaigns, but it seemed much harder to maintain continuity with an all-volunteer army instead of paid workers.

There wasn't much time, but he was determined to finish putting a PR team together. Local colleges were on winter break, and he hoped that he could pick up a couple of savvy social media interns before the semester started again.

Virgil had a whiteboard in his office and was diagramming all of the logistical moves they would need to make for the push in to other states. Greenbeaux was going to leave for New Hampshire soon, and then he would go on to South Carolina, where Douglas and the band would join him for another rally.

A good number of the band members who were local would not be able to put their lives on hold long enough to go on an extended road trip, and Douglas was working on a system to recruit, train, and integrate new band members as the campaign moved on. There were buses, meals, and lodging to coordinate, along with all of the other operational details that were happening on a much larger scale than anything Douglas had ever needed to arrange for his high school students. Fortunately, this was Virgil's strong suit, and he was able to step in to help prepare project plans and Gantt charts to get it all organized.

For her part, Ruth was happiest at the control tower, where she could serve as greeter, concierge, master of ceremonies, and final arbiter to make order out of the chaos. It was not unlike how it had been after the editorial first appeared in the *Register* and people started flocking to the outbuilding that served as their original headquarters. But now, instead of managing the flow of a few dozen people throughout a day, she was dealing with hundreds of them, including camera crews and other journalists who were arriving to get a piece of her son's time.

*   *   *

Rachel Montoya was looking at her watch. It wasn't an ordinary timepiece, or even one of those camera phone wrist gadgets that everyone else seemed to think was so cool and advanced. This one was far more special. Without any visual or digital prompts, it sent information to her mind about time, temperature and anything else that might be important for a person to know. It also allowed her to transmit to other devices without needing to touch, dial or even speak a command.

It was just one of many tools the Democratic Party had developed in its state-of-the-art laboratories, staffed with the best and brightest minds the scientific community had to offer. They licensed many of their less-proprietary technologies to the NSA, which provided all of the funding they needed to build and operate their top-secret 42-acre underground research laboratory and data center in the middle of the Nevada desert, where Rachel was stationed.

The site was invisible from the view of satellites above, save for a small, run-down barn that housed one solitary donkey, which the interns took turns going above ground to feed. All vehicle traffic came in through a tunnel entrance a half-mile away that had been disguised to look like an abandoned gold mine from above.

No sunlight came into the facility, which made the mundane laboratory work a little drearier for those toiling below. Even the more senior scientists had started asking the interns if they could take a shift on donkey duty so that they could get some fresh air.

The technological advantage the Democratic Party now held over its rival was staggering, but it had not always been that way. Before 2005, Republicans were running circles around them with their data-driven get-out-the-vote efforts. And then one day, while looking at an unusual pattern in donor trends, a junior Democratic staffer at the committee had an epiphany: The vast majority of people who lived and worked in Silicon Valley were Democrats, and if the party could tap into that collective brainpower, it might hope to catch up and perhaps surpass the GOP.

What followed was a massive ramp-up as the Democratic Party methodically hired brilliant programmers and physicists, who developed technologies that allowed them to dominate the voter-turnout battles in the next two presidential elections. They were just getting started on a strategy that would have surpassed anything that even George Orwell's vivid imagination could have envisioned.

They were working on a plan to end the culture war for good and reshape society by using their brainwave technology to implant perceptual messaging in new Hollywood releases and streaming videos. So far it was only a one-channel process, but they were hoping to soon receive data from subjects without the use of an affixed wrist transmitter. This would enable them to gather more accurate polling information and better allocate their resources on the ground.

Rachel was watching a three-dimensional holographic data presentation about how they had used multiple regression analysis to crack the code Republicans employed when communicating with their field operatives. The code, it turned out, was a simple transnumeration of chapter and verse combinations in the Book of Revelation. They would have broken it earlier, but the Republicans had masked their code by using only portions of certain sections -- not whole verses verbatim -- and by using different published versions of the Bible to indicate verb tense.

It was during this presentation that a message came through her watch telling her she needed to stay afterward and learn about a special assignment.

She had graduated from MIT two years earlier with a degree in physics, and had immediately been put to work on a project to design and build an environmentally friendly, compost-powered hovercraft that could be deployed to provide air cover at protests Democrats were organizing. After that was rolled out, she was assigned to a project that would enable precinct captains to communicate telepathically with each other using the wrist devices.

The work was interesting from a scientific perspective, but she really wanted to get out of the lab more. Rachel told her supervisor of this desire, and she was hoping that the message meant she was about to get her chance. She mentally processed the presentation takeaways and stored them in her watch, and then got up to meet with her boss, Alex, who was standing near the front of the room.

"Are you familiar with Russell Greenbeaux?" he asked.

Rachel was not. She had been working late nights in the lab, and hadn't had time to catch up on the outside world. Alex briefed her on Greenbeaux's rally and the social media storm that followed.

"We have been tracking Republican chatter since we cracked their code a few weeks ago," said Alex. "Earlier today we intercepted a message indicating that they have placed an operative inside the Greenbeaux campaign. His code name is Berkeley."

Rachel listened intently. The distinction between right and wrong had gotten a little blurry at work recently, and she hoped that they didn't want her to go out and kill someone. Even MIT graduates have lines they are not willing to cross.

Alex continued: "We want you to go to Iowa, embed yourself in the campaign, identify the target, and..."

Here it comes. She was expecting to hear the words "terminate him" next.

"... And we want you to observe and report back what you find out about him."

Rachel was relieved. Her mind had been playing tricks on her lately, and she wasn't sure if it was caused by the long hours in the lab or a side effect of the technology that had been scanning her brain waves. Of course they didn't want her to kill someone for political purposes. They weren't that evil. Were they? No, she thought. They were simply giving her the chance to go into the field, as she had requested.

"Got it," she said.

"We will brief you tonight, and you will leave in the morning," he continued. "Oh, and one more thing. NSA phone-tracking records indicate that a strategist on Greenbeaux's staff is connected to an opposition researcher. We can't risk having word of this technology get out yet, so you will have to leave the watch here."

CHAPTER 15

Caucus day had arrived in Iowa, and the clamor at Cedar Point had died down considerably. The media were turning their attention back to the two main parties for the day, and many of the volunteers who had clogged the office were now dispersed around the state. Anyone new who walked in to help was sent back out to a caucus site with a packet of leaflets and a loose set of talking points to follow.

Ruth appreciated the relative calm and the opportunity it afforded to think through the crucial next steps with Virgil and Norm. Iowa was in the middle of a veritable heat wave, with mild temperatures in the 50's, but Greenbeaux was on a plane with a social media intern and a press handler -- also an intern -- headed to New Hampshire where the thermometer was hovering around zero.

The plan was for them to drive from the airport in Manchester to a mall and then a diner while the social media person live-tweeted the events. The day's schedule had been leaked in advance to the Clown Underground to ensure that there would be some swarming around him. To make the crowd look more spontaneous, people were instructed to wait for the secret #clownsontheground hashtag message to go out ten minutes before his arrival.

Carrie Rollins could see all of this from her perch in Iowa, and she was able to tip off news of Greenbeaux's expected movements to a friend at the Associated Press who was stationed in New Hampshire. She kept the Clown Underground and hashtag information to herself as a trade secret, but she was happy to share the wealth with a select few colleagues who could send her back details in return.

Norm was finally out from under the crush of media requests, and he went to the conference room to join Ruth and Virgil to discuss planning and assess the day's events. There were reports from around the state that volunteers were getting a mostly positive reaction from caucus-goers.

There had been some quizzical looks from people who didn't understand why there were clowns hanging out at caucus locations where they were trying to perform their solemn civic duty. But for the most part, people were aware of Greenbeaux and were friendly to his volunteers. Many of the caucus-goers around the state had even asked to have their pictures taken with the clowns.

It was a measure of how far the campaign had come in the weeks since Greenbeaux started his efforts in Iowa. Gone was the sense of aversion that many had felt toward the candidate and the message of clown rights he was harping on when he first started knocking on doors. There was still a lot of puzzlement about him being a clown, but his thoughts on Washington were resonating and people were starting to take him seriously.

Douglas Goodwin was a registered Republican, and he had left to caucus in his precinct for Greenbeaux. He had long since become disenchanted with his party, but he couldn't bring himself to register as a Democrat. He enjoyed going to caucuses every four years, and he wouldn't be able to do that anymore if he listed his affiliation as Independent. And so a Republican he would stay, though in name only.

Virgil had been a Democrat all of his adult life, but he had become disillusioned with the partisan rancor and blamed everyone equally for the divisiveness in the country. The campaign's message of fixing what was broken had really spoken to him, and he would have voted for Greenbeaux even if he had been a Republican. He would never tell that to his own 83-year-old mother, though. The thought of her son voting for a Republican would probably kill her.

Norm was an opportunist, and his affiliation was only to the candidate who happened to need his services at the time. Politics was a game to him, and he didn't care whether he had the red checkers or the black, just so long as he could jump people and be a kingmaker. Or as was more his custom, to take the crowns off of others at their own request.

The office was almost empty as their meeting wound down. Ruth had left the control tower in the hands of the clean-cut young man who came back for a second day, and as she returned, she found him flirting with a pretty young woman in an MIT sweatshirt who had come by to volunteer. Ruth was about to grab a packet and send the woman out to a caucus site when Virgil walked by and spotted her.

"Did you go to MIT?" Virgil asked.

"Yes."

"Then you must be good with math," he said.

Rachel Montoya laughed. "Sometimes I dream in numbers."

"Perfect. I have a job for you," Virgil said, leading her to a small whiteboard in the war room where he was working on a structural equation model for the campaign's operations.

Lester Pulcinella needed a new issue, and he needed one fast. The senator was likely to finish no better than sixth among the Republican candidates in Iowa, where he had put all of his resources, and the internal polling showed him with low single-digit numbers in New Hampshire.

He had bolted out to a strong second-place finish in the past summer's straw poll, but his campaign had tanked because of lackluster debate performances and a gaffe where he called an old lady in a wheelchair a leech for wanting a cost-of-living adjustment in her Social Security check. He was having a hard time raising money, and if something didn't change quickly, his dream of becoming president would be over in a week.

He didn't have as much personal wealth as many of his colleagues in the Senate did to bankroll a campaign, and he had already told his paid staff that Sunday would probably be their last day. He would have to go it alone, without the professional strategists and entourage that seemed like a necessity, but who had not served him particularly well.

He was a scrappy street brawler by nature, and he was going to have to come out swinging on some new issue and rile up enough voters if he wanted to keep his hopes alive. He didn't have a signature legislative accomplishment to hang his hat on, and the one bill he had sponsored -- an effort to rename Washington's professional baseball team the Reagan Nationals -- never got out of committee. He tried to make passing no laws whatsoever sound like a good thing for Congress to do, but voters weren't buying it, and he needed some fresh red meat to feed to the base.

He went through his checklist of hot-button issues and nothing seemed to fit. He couldn't go back to attacking Social Security -- he had already been electrocuted once on that third rail -- and most of the core conservative issues were either taken by other candidates or so unpalatable to Independents that they would render him unelectable if he decided to run for president again in four years.

As he prepared to leave his hotel room, something caught his interest on the television. Greenbeaux was being mobbed by hundreds of people at a mall in New Hampshire. Interesting, he thought. There were a lot of people who seemed to really like the guy and his anti-Washington rhetoric. Being a senator had privileges, but running on a platform against partisan insiders wasn't one of them, especially when he would need to fire up the right-wing base to survive in the primaries.

But Greenbeaux had a flaw. And perhaps, Pulcinella thought, he might be able to find his own voice railing against someone who was dressing as a clown and making a mockery of the serious business of running the greatest country on Earth. It was a long shot, but it was the only shot he had.

*   *   *

That night, Norm was sitting in his hotel room watching coverage of the Iowa results. It had been another good day for Greenbeaux, despite not being much of a factor in either the Democrat or Republican caucuses. The networks reported scattered cases of people caucusing for him, but even that small show of support surpassed everyone's expectations. He had already moved on, and the networks were now showing footage that a Boston station had shot of him being engulfed by a crowd at the mall earlier that day in New Hampshire.

Looking carefully at the clip, Norm focused in on one very interesting detail: It appeared that the majority of people around him at the mall were not clowns. The heads-up had only gone out to the Clown Underground, and they had anticipated that the crowd would be almost entirely composed of his followers.

But if other people were excited to see him, it meant that the campaign was breaking through. The Internet memes were turning him into a national figure, which was a positive development. Norm hoped that people were flocking to Greenbeaux because they liked his ideas and wanted his leadership, and not just because he was now a celebrity.

There were some good people working behind the scenes at Cedar Point, and they were doing an exceptionally good job for political novices. Norm liked them on a personal level as well, but he had to roll up his sleeves a little more than he normally did on a campaign to get things done, and he was feeling the absence of a paid professional staff. He was also missing companionship, and that wasn't making the job any easier.

Norm had hoped that Jessica would text him again, but he hadn't heard from her in a while. He picked his phone up to type out a text and then, on a whim, dialed her number instead. He surprised himself with this move, and as he heard it ring, he quickly thought about what he would say on her voicemail if she didn't pick up.

On the third ring, a familiar voice came across.

"Well, if it isn't Doctor Death."

"Hello, Jessica," he said. He was less in the mood for the back-and-forth sparring, and just wanted to hear her voice. "How are you?"

She thought that this was an unusually friendly way for him to start a conversation, and wondered what he wanted. "I'm doing well considering."

"Considering what?"

"I am stuck in Boston on a big dig for inside information, and it's cold as hell outside," she said.

"You ought to come out to Iowa and see me. It is much warmer here." He didn't want to let his guard down too much around her, but he wanted to see her, and he didn't mind if she knew that.

Jessica was both surprised and pleased to hear him say it. She couldn't figure this guy out, and this was a clue. There were a million different possible ways to respond, but she decided to just be honest: "You know, I wish I could. That sounds a lot nicer than what I'm doing."

Norm could feel himself starting to relax. This was the closest thing that he had to an intimate relationship in his life. He had been thinking about her a lot, and he was grateful to hear some warmth in her voice.

Jessica continued: "It sounds like you have had a much more interesting week than I have."

"It has indeed been that. This is a very different type of project for me, but it has been a nice change of pace."

"So tell me," she said. "How did you pull off the New Years Day stunt?"

There weren't really many trade secrets involved, and so he opened up and gave her an abridged version of the behind-the-scenes story. He explained that the marching band was already in the works when he arrived, and that the campaign manager had come up with the flash mob idea. He left out the details about the Clown Underground, though, since that was the key ingredient that had allowed them to pull together such a large crowd without anyone else knowing about it in advance.

"And Naomi Winston?" she asked, curious to know how he had managed to expertly choreograph his ex-girlfriend's worst nightmare.

"You know, that was really just a coincidence," he lied. Norm could tell by the text she had sent earlier that his takedown of Naomi had triggered a bit of fear on her end. They were both powerful people in their own right, but with that came vulnerability. He would be safer if she had his back, and she needed to know that he wouldn't harm her.

He continued: "We knew that the courthouse was one of the locations the news crews were likely to go on New Year's Day when we had the rally planned. CNN set up on our preferred route, near where we wanted to park the buses, so we marched the band past their cameras."

Jessica was almost convinced, but one thing didn't make sense.

"So the band gets off the bus," she said, "and they start marching toward the courthouse. But they didn't just go straight down the street. They swerved onto the sidewalk where Naomi was standing, and then swerved back onto the street after they went by her."

"Oh that," Norm said, realizing that there were some cracks in his cover story. He tried followed his own advice to infuse as much honesty into the story as possible. "You have to understand something about the tuba section that was leading the way."

Jessica laughed. She wasn't an expert on marching bands, but she had picked up on comments floating around about how unusual it was that Greenbeaux's band had an inverted formation, with the tubas in the front and the drummers in the rear.

Norm had learned so many interesting and unusual things about clowns that week, and he proceeded to share much of it with Jessica. The most fascinating insights of all were about evil clowns. Tuba-playing evil clowns were not above steering the band right into the path of a camera crew to get attention. It fit the story and it was also true, although he left out the part about how he and Douglas had coached the band to take the meandering path that they did.

He went on to elaborate about the different things he had learned from Virgil's tutorial; how the sad clowns use their makeup to reveal their nature with the downward tilt of their lips, and the happy ones do the same with a smile. How none of them can stand mimes, and don't want to acknowledge them as being part of their culture. But it was the evil clowns that had captured his imagination.

"Everyone keeps warning me, 'Never turn your back on an evil clown,' and I'm beginning to wonder what kind of damage these guys can do when you're not looking."

He felt a little odd opening up to someone who worked in opposition research, but there was nothing Norm told Jessica that could be used against Greenbeaux or himself if one of her clients needed information. It had been such an unusual week, and he found it cathartic to share his adventure with a confidante outside the campaign. That shoulder to share the burden had been missing in his life, and he appreciated having it, even it was only over the phone.

Jessica found the whole conversation fascinating, and she loved hearing directly from the source about how the biggest political spectacle of the New Year had come together. Catching Norm in a more candid state with his guard lowered was also helping her to piece the puzzle together.

She hadn't considered before that it might be possible to find lasting happiness with a political man, but there was something different about Norm Brodie. In a business filled with self-promoters, where power was taken by taking credit, he was humble and deferential. He could have claimed responsibility for the whole stunt at the courthouse, but he didn't. Everyone always talked about how brilliant he was, but he never said that about himself or overstated his own importance.

They were very much the same person, driven political animals that loved the hunt and the kill. But they were also both inquisitive and more thoughtful than others imagined them to be. Studying him was a form of introspection. It wasn't always a comfortable thing to do, but with each peek under Norm's hood, Jessica learned more about herself.

CHAPTER 16

By Tuesday, the campaign was seeing the first tangible data to suggest that Greenbeaux had indeed broken through. Two different national polls released that day showed him with high single-digit numbers when lumped in with candidates from the other parties. That was unusual for a third-party candidate and a very positive sign. But something was still holding him back.

Norm didn't want to overplay the element of surprise that had worked so well in the previous week. They had proven their ability to summon people out of the woodwork when they chose, and he didn't want the trick to seem stale if they really needed it again later.

He decided that they should hold off on sending out advance notice of appearances to the Clown Underground. What he was thinking -- but did not want to say out loud lest he offend -- was that Greenbeaux should be seen more with normal people around him at rallies to send a signal across the country that he had mainstream appeal.

Carrie Rollins had taken notice of the lack of new information coming through the message boards from the campaign, and she was beginning to suspect that they were holding back after discovering that she was trolling the

Clown Underground for inside information. Her article, which had run in Sunday's paper, contained information that could only have been culled from that source. She also thought that the *Register's* blogging about the courthouse rally moments after the location announcement at #clownsontheground must have tipped off the campaign to what she was up to.

The Greenbeaux campaign had not made those connections, but they had seen the article, and were impressed that the reporter was tuned in to the clown-rights issues that had launched the campaign in the first place. Norm saw in it an opportunity to pivot. Voters who were oblivious to the struggles clowns faced didn't take Greenbeaux seriously. But if the campaign could get other people to make it an issue while Greenbeaux was addressing the partisanship problem, voters would then begin to understand that he was not engaging in a farce.

The next logical step for the campaign was to get proxies to bring the clown-rights issue to the forefront. Norm thought that Virgil's background and his firing from his job for being a clown would make him a good poster child for the cause. But Virgil didn't want to make himself the focal point, and so Norm would need to find another way to get that message out.

*   *   *

Skip Bancroft was starting to insinuate himself into the campaign. He was having the opportunity to do a lot of different things and was getting a lesson in grassroots politics that had been out of his reach at the stuffy Republican headquarters. He liked the energy that came with people working together to make things happen on the ground.

Before he left DC, he had been given strict instructions he was expected to follow to avoid being tied back to the Republican Party. He was to use his real name and address information, in case he was asked to show identification, but he would have to change other details of his background story to prevent detection.

He would have no work history; instead, he was to say that he had just graduated from college and had time to volunteer because he had not found a job yet. His past at UC Berkeley was now gone, replaced with a degree from the University of Maryland, a campus near his parents' home that was familiar to him. Instead of being president of the College Republicans, he now was to claim membership in the debate club.

In his few days on the Greenbeaux campaign, he had not found any intelligence of real value. The people were friendly and passionate about helping their candidate, and the only thing unusual was that most of them were clowns. He was planning to report back to headquarters that the campaign's marching band was getting ready to leave for South Carolina, and that the candidate was going to join them after the New Hampshire primary.

There was one other piece of information that was important to him: He had met a girl that he really liked, and he was trying to work up the courage to ask her out. But he was not about to put that into the message to headquarters.

He was almost ready to submit his report, but he was having trouble with the secret code, and needed to take one more look at the Gideon's Bible in his hotel room to double-check some chapter and verse numbers. Unlike many of his counterparts in the field, he had not memorized the entire Book of Revelation in preparation for the apocalypse before he came to work for the Republican Party, and certain parts of the chapter and verse combinations were giving him problems. In particular, he kept mixing up the code for the letters P and Q.

This was to be his first report back, and he wanted to make a good impression. After he was finally satisfied that he had given it his best shot, he left the room in search of a copy store where he could fax the report back to headquarters.

* * *

Lester Pulcinella stood in a living room in Keene, New Hampshire, preparing for a performance in front of a small group of supporters who were strategically arranged to look like a much larger crowd. When a video camera whirred to life, the senator began a carefully crafted speech loaded with sound bites about America, the Founding Fathers, and the shameful display of people dressing up as clowns to mock the greatest constitutional democracy on Earth.

"It may make for good political comedy to send musicians crashing into a reporter a candidate doesn't like, but our country is not a circus, and we should not allow an unfunny clown to distract us from the serious problems we need to address as a nation."

After two hours of taping variations on the theme from different angles, Pulcinella retired to a back room where he and a video editor began piecing together footage of what would eventually look like a large-scale rally where multiple film crews had been deployed.

Fox News had been under a lot of pressure from their shadow governance committee at the RNC to start undermining the clown, whom they now recognized as a serious threat to keeping their base focused on real challenges, like suppressing minority voter turnout and purging the remaining moderates from the party ranks. It was true that Greenbeaux had benefitted from one-sided coverage over the past week, and so when they received Pulcinella's tape they decided that the fair and balanced thing to do was to run portions of it every hour for three straight days.

CNN picked up the tape and played excerpts a few times, but MSNBC was not favorably inclined to air anything the conservative firebrand had to say. Instead, they chose to stick with their regularly scheduled lineup of liberal talking points and prison documentaries.

When Norm saw the clip he just rolled his eyes. Two years earlier, when Pulcinella was running for re-election, the strategist had been contacted by the senator's camp inquiring if he might want to take on a double-agent assignment.

Pulcinella's idea was to have Norm manufacture some incriminating evidence against his opponent, the state's lieutenant governor. Then, they would arrange for Norm to be recommended to the other camp, in the hopes that he would be hired to bring a dignified death to the other campaign before the falsified evidence had to be released and the opponent was actually slandered.

Norm wanted no part of that plan and impolitely declined to participate. That didn't stop the Pulcinella campaign from summoning a consultant from the dark side to do the first half of the job. An audio recording was edited to sound like the lieutenant governor had disparaged handicapped military veterans. It was released three days before the election. The damage was done before the recording could be debunked and Pulcinella won a narrow victory and return passage back to Washington.

When Virgil saw the clip of Pulcinella railing against Greenbeaux and other clowns, he had a hard time controlling his anger. But Norm had seen it all before. This current stunt was a minor infraction compared to what the senator was capable of, and so he encouraged Virgil not to take it personally. If Greenbeaux remained in contention all the way up to November, he would face much harsher treatment than the senator's current bombardment.

As angry as he was with Pulcinella, Virgil was too busy with campaign management to spend much time dwelling on it. He and Douglas were trying to get the band on the bus to South Carolina by Friday afternoon and keep the campaign under control as it was flung farther away from Cedar Point.

The new volunteer from MIT was a real quant jock, and she quickly picked up the logistics concepts Virgil was teaching her. Virgil and Douglas were planning to send her on the bus so she could manage the event operations on the road.

Greenbeaux was contacted in New Hampshire and given the heads-up when the Pulcinella clip first surfaced. Reporters were now stopping him to talk as he worked the pavement, and the team at Cedar Point wanted to make sure that he wasn't caught off-guard. If there was anything worse than getting cornered with a gotcha question, it was falling apart on a softball you should have known to expect.

The news of the strong poll numbers had buoyed everyone's already high spirits, and the adrenaline rush was carrying him through the long, cold days in New Hampshire. Greenbeaux laughed off the comments aimed against him by Pulcinella. It was all politics, and he didn't take it personally.

He had spent some time during his debate preparation working on zingers to deflect any barbs against clowns, and he was ready with a response when the time came that a reporter finally asked him about Pulcinella's comments:

"The senator must understand that he has contributed greatly to the very problem I have been discussing. Voters are telling me that they are tired of the hyper-partisanship and the ideologically driven obstinacy coming out of Washington. If all he can see is that the messenger is a clown, then clearly, he has not understood the message."

Greenbeaux was on his game. The debate had prepared him well for the type of questions he was getting from the press, and he was pleased that his talking points -- which were starting to sound a little cliché to his own ear -- were met with nods and positive feedback when other people heard them for the first time.

He was not alone in feeling good about the week's developments.

Lester Pulcinella was also enjoying a bounce. He didn't need to worry about showing that he could reach across the aisle or make nice with Independents at this stage of the election. All he needed was to appeal to the base and pick off enough conservative voters in the New Hampshire primary to bring him back into contention.

The 24/7 Fox News coverage was helping him to reach these very people, and a new poll showed him in a tie for third place among the Republicans in the upcoming primary. New Hampshire voters tended to be more moderate than those in the next set of primary states, and if he could emerge on his feet, he would be able to raise some money and be a strong contender again for the nomination.

The strategy was working, and so he decided to double down on the anti-clown rhetoric.

*   *   *

Rachel didn't mind the idea of a road trip with the band. She had spent nearly two years in an underground facility with only intermittent breaks, and being out in the world again had done wonders for her spirit.

She also found the projects Virgil gave her to be very interesting. Rachel had always thought of herself as a scientist first and a Democrat second, and she had expected to go back to school at some point for her Ph.D. rather than continue working in politics. But what she was learning about supply chain management, logistics and operations was interesting, and she had started to entertain thoughts of following that career path later.

She had met a lot of interesting and unusual people in the office, but she hadn't yet been able to detect who the Republican operative was. She continued to wear her MIT sweatshirt, since it served as a conversation starter and opened the door to ask others where they had gone to college.

She knew that the Republican operative had been given the codename Berkeley, and so she strongly suspected that he was connected in some way to the University of California. The educated people she had spoken with on the campaign had all gone to college in the Midwest, except for one really cute guy who told her he had graduated from the University of Maryland.

CHAPTER 17

The core leadership team was in the office before 8:00 a.m. on Friday, preparing for the band's departure in the late afternoon. They were also busy battling renewed attacks from Pulcinella, who was now accusing Greenbeaux of being a Communist sympathizer who was organizing subversives to undermine the United States government and hasten the rise of a totalitarian new world order.

The attack was loaded with dog-whistle words that only people on the far-right responded favorably to, and Norm saw it as a transparent attempt to draw a contrast with the less-extreme Republican candidates who were ahead of him in the polls. More and more, Norm found himself serving as a soothing voice to calm the army of clown volunteers cycling through Cedar Point who were incensed about anyone attacking their hero candidate.

There was too much to do, but everything had to be dropped when some unexpected visitors stepped off the elevator. Goldfarb and R. Johnson Shipley were there, along with three new henchmen. Ruth quickly channeled them all to the conference room, then rounded up Virgil and Norm.

When everyone had assembled, Goldfarb started by congratulating the campaign on its success, and went around the room to introduce his new colleagues who had joined him. Virgil immediately had a bad feeling about the three, a sense that was confirmed when he heard their names: Puck, Pluck, and Tuck.

Their exaggerated red ball noses and the bicycle horns affixed to their belts suggested to Virgil that this was a team of circus clowns, and the coordinated stage names confirmed what he had feared. He had been the victim of profiling himself, and he did not like to stereotype. But as far as he was concerned, dimwitted circus clowns were only one small step above mimes in the greater hierarchy.

Circus clowns perpetuated all of the negative stereotypes that Greenbeaux loathed and was working to overcome. Virgil would not have been surprised to see these guys and twenty more like them piling out of a small car, and he was nervous about having them affiliated with the campaign.

Goldfarb announced that they were prepared to put more resources behind the campaign, and that Johnson would be leading a Super PAC that had been formed to provide additional support. The last time they were at Cedar Point, it had been Greenbeaux's team that was anxious to present its strategy. But now it was the team from Washington's turn.

Johnson stood up and moved with grace and swagger toward the end of the table. He turned to the collected group, and in a Southern drawl, he began his pitch.

"Lady and gentlemen. A month ago, we became aware that Russell Greenbeaux had launched a campaign to become the president of the United States of America. There are many people who aspire to that noble office, but very few who have the wherewithal to make the dream come true.

And while we cannot back every horse in the race, we do like to put our money on winners when we see them."

Norm noticed that Puck, Pluck and Tuck were hanging on his every word. He had charisma, style, and an immaculately pressed suit, and they were soaking it all in as Johnson continued.

"As you can see by the folks we have assembled here today, we are all fellow clowns and we too would like to see Mr. Greenbeaux do well for our people."

The circus clowns were shaking their heads and most of their bodies in wholehearted agreement. One of them honked his horn to show approval.

"Our wealthy clients share our sympathies, and with the success of the past week, we have been able to convince them to increase their support."

Norm had seen this in the past, and wanted more details before he let the campaign get much further entwined with these people. "Who are your backers?" he inquired.

"Well, Mr. Brodie, you are aware that the world we all inhabit requires a certain amount of discretion, and that it would not be proper for us to disclose their names. But since you asked, I can share that our clientele includes a couple of very, very wealthy brothers."

All three circus clowns gasped and looked at each other with excitement. They had been instructed not to speak in the meeting, but Pluck couldn't contain himself and asked cautiously: "Is it… is it the Ringling Brothers?"

Johnson shot him a look suggesting that he had either revealed too much information or said something stupid. Johnson continued, but while he was talking, Norm received a text that caught his attention. His eyes grew wide as he looked at the phone, then excused himself to make a call.

The visitors knew that Norm was a key person they needed to get bought in, and Johnson decided to put the pitch on hold until he returned.

Outside the conference room, Norm was staring at his phone as he moved hurriedly toward his office and shut the door so that he could call Jessica. She answered right away.

"You might want to bring in a pest-control company to do something about that mole problem," she said.

Norm was amazed at her resourcefulness, and grateful that she had uncovered and shared a photograph of Skip Bancroft's Republican National Committee employee identification card.

"How did you find that?" Norm asked, knowing full well that she would never reveal her methods or sources.

"The Republicans have antiquated technology and communication tools," she said, "and they do a sloppy job with their security. They were using an encrypted string, but suffice it to say that the Dixie Cups on both ends were unsecured."

Norm thanked her, and quickly got off the phone so that he could return to the meeting. He settled back down in his chair and tried to refocus, but Ruth and Virgil could tell that something was wrong. When Johnson tried to restart, Norm stopped him and asked if they could take a 15-minute break so that his team could attend to urgent business.

As they adjourned, Norm signaled Ruth and Virgil over to his office and shared the photo of Skip's employee ID that was now on his phone.

"That kid from Maryland is a spy," he said. "The Republicans must be getting nervous because they sent him here to infiltrate our campaign."

Virgil and Ruth looked at each other in surprise. She felt a little betrayed, but there was so much she still had to learn about presidential politics, and spying was a part of that.

Norm asked: "Did he have access to the shared drive, or any computers or devices around the office?"

"I don't think so," said Ruth. "He's mostly been doing odd jobs, collating and packet stuffing, stapling yard signs, things like that. Right now he's answering phones at a table near the control tower."

Virgil was not new to this -- he had dealt with an issue of corporate espionage a few years earlier -- but he was still shocked. "We need to get him out of the campaign right now," he said, "and let him know that what he did was not appreciated."

"I wouldn't do that," Norm said.

Ruth and Virgil stared back at him with puzzled expressions. "Why?" they asked simultaneously.

Norm continued: "If we kick him out, the Republicans are just going to send another operative back in, and we might not be lucky enough to find out who that is next time. We need to be friendly to our volunteers without seeming paranoid, and we can't do that if we're looking at each of them as a potential traitor."

"Well, we can't let him gain access to any inside information," Ruth said, "and so I don't think we can have him hanging around Cedar Point anymore."

"Maybe we should put him on a slow boat to Apia," quipped Virgil, giving a Norm a look.

"Or…" said Norm, ignoring the comment. "…We could put him on a bus to South Carolina."

They all agreed that sending Skip away with the band would solve the problem temporarily. They weren't planning any surprise rallies for a while, and even if they had been, that information and anything else that would happen on the road in Greenbeaux's campaign was of little value to the major political parties.

The only risk in having the band's movements known would be if protest rallies were being planned against Greenbeaux. But that approach was more in the milieu of the Democrats, and the campaign didn't need to worry about Skip giving information to them.

Ruth had the most interaction with Skip on a daily basis, and so it fell to her to give him the news that he was being transferred to the Palmetto State. Norm and Virgil went back over to the conference room to meet with their guests, though they were both trying to sneak a peek through the glass wall at the conversation that was about to take place near the control tower.

Ruth put on her game face and approached Skip carefully.

"Hi, Skip. Do you have a minute?"

He put down his headset and looked up at her smiling face. "Sure. What can I do?"

"Skip, as you know we're getting ready to send the band on a bus to South Carolina. We are going to need an extra set of hands there to help with the operation, and we have noticed the good work you are doing here, so we thought of you."

Skip beamed a broad smile back. He had learned all that he could about answering phones and stuffing envelopes, and he was excited to be invited onto a campaign bus. There wasn't much intelligence of value to find in Cedar Point anyway, and he thought it might be fun to go. This would give him something new to report back to headquarters, and he thought his boss might be impressed that he had been entrusted to join the crew that was meeting the candidate on the road.

Most importantly, though, he knew that Rachel was going to be on the trip, and it made him happy to think that he would remain close to her and could continue his pursuit.

"Yes, I would love to go! Thank you for thinking of me."

Ruth smiled again: "That's great. I think we have enough volunteers here to hold down the fort for the day. You go right away and get packed. Take care of any errands you might need to run and maybe do a little sightseeing. The bus will leave at 4:30 sharp, so meet us back here at 4:00 this afternoon."

After she saw him safely onto the elevator and looked out the window to make sure he was leaving the parking lot, she returned to the conference room. Norm apologized to their guests and explained that they were getting ready to send a crew on the road, and there had been a problem with one of their volunteers. He thanked them for their patience and invited Johnson to resume.

"Yes, thank you," said the dapper clown, smiling and expertly masking his resentment at having the spotlight taken away briefly.

"To better support your efforts, we are forming a political action committee, a Super PAC in fact, that I will be heading. "Again, the three circus clowns nodded their heads and honked their horns in agreement.

This raised a red flag for Norm. Usually, PACs tied to a specific candidate were initiated by the campaigns to attract outside donors, not the other way around, and so he decided to probe a little deeper.

"Where will the PAC be located?"

Johnson knew that Norm didn't need a lesson about the murky world of soft money, but there were others in the room he needed to bring along, and so he began to thread a needle for the audience.

"As you know, Mr. Brodie, there has to be a wall of separation between campaigns and their political action committees. However, there is additional space here on the second floor of this building that needs only very minor finishing to be ready. We will have a work crew come in over the weekend to put in a door through the wall by the elevator and make other minor modifications. I will be ready to move in on Monday."

This made Norm uncomfortable, but these were the campaign's largest donors so far. It was their building, and if they wanted to put in another office on the floor, he was in no position to object.

"And in terms of coordination?" Norm asking a leading question he already knew the answer to.

"Again, as you know," Johnson continued, "PACs must remain independent of the campaigns they are supporting, and there cannot be the appearance of prearranged coordination between them. But that doesn't mean we can't help you. In fact, we brought you a couple of experts on clown rights to work here in the headquarters and help advise the campaign."

He pointed to Puck, Pluck and Tuck, who looked at each other, slightly confused. They were far from being experts on anything, other than the proper way to throw a pie into someone's face. All they were told was that they had won a trip to Iowa to meet Greenbeaux and hang out with the campaign for a while. But they had already earned Johnson's wrath for speaking up once, so they thought they had better keep their mouths shut.

Virgil didn't like these honking circus freaks, and he certainly didn't want them hanging around the headquarters. He decided to speak up. "So... they are our volunteers, correct?"

"Yes," said Johnson. "They are your volunteers, and you may assign them to do whatever tasks you choose without any prior consultation from us."

"Okay, then," Virgil said. "I think we could use their help on the bus. What do you think, Ruth?"

She was not impressed with the three clowns Goldfarb and Johnson had brought along, and the honking had tipped her off that they were prone to the type of stereotypical behavior that her son abhorred. "Oh yes, Virgil. I do believe that we have room for three more on the bus."

Now Puck, Pluck and Tuck were really confused. But they were keeping their mouths shut, and would ask Goldfarb what all this meant later.

"One more question," Norm inquired. "What are you going to call the political action committee?"

"It will be called Clowns United."

*   *   *

Two buses pulled out of the Cedar Point parking lot shortly after four-thirty that afternoon, and headed east on Interstate 80 for an 18-hour drive. Buses with marching bands on them can be lively places, and these two were no exceptions. Douglas, Rachel and Skip were the only ones aside from the relief driver on board bus two who were not clowns, and they clustered together near the front.

Skip was the first one on board, and he was secretly thrilled when Rachel asked if the seat next to him was taken when she got on.

There was laughter, music and singing for the first few hours, but most people wanted a more relaxed atmosphere after their dinner stop. Unfortunately, Puck, Pluck and Tuck were aboard bus two, and their persistent honking was driving others to distraction. They were also running up and down the aisles throwing confetti they had smuggled aboard.

Finally, one of the tuba players had enough. He snuck up behind Tuck when his back was turned, grabbed him in a headlock and announced in a voice loud enough for the other two circus performers to hear: "I am going to rip your spleen out through your nostrils and use it to clean the valves on my tuba if you don't settle down and sit quietly in your seat right now, you little circus freak."

The bus was serenely quiet after that. Skip and Rachel talked softly into the night, sharing stories about their lives. He had to fictionalize his college experience, but he spoke warmly of his family, and without revealing his partisan leanings, he shared how he became interested in politics.

She made only vague references to what she did for a living, mentioning lab research and physics concepts that she assumed would go over his head. If he understood the statistical structure of electromagnetic wave transition, he did not let on, and she was cryptic enough that he would never figure out that she was really working on tools of political domination to ensure that each successive generation would be more progressive than the last.

Rachel was getting comfortable with Skip, and he with her. Life in an underground lab with a bunch of older scientists and mathematicians did not lend itself to human intimacy. The few people her age were all interns who were training to be political hacks, and were mostly concerned with feeding the donkey.

Rachel was enjoying Skip's company. She was still focused on her mission, but she was stuck on a bus for 18 hours, and she doubted that the Republican infiltrator was one of the clowns onboard. As the night wore on, she grew tired, and when she finally fell asleep, her head was leaning on the shoulder of a man she was beginning to trust.

CHAPTER 18

Greenbeaux was in his hotel room, taking a quick break to rest his tired feet before going back out to shake hands during the dinnertime rush at local diners. A film crew from a Canadian network had shadowed him during his sojourn earlier in the day, catching him as he worked the crowds and asking questions during lulls when voters didn't surround him.

He had noticed a significant shift in how people were reacting to him. A month earlier, some people had run away when he approached, and most others simply laughed when he told them he was running for president. But after the big rally, people had started seeking him out. So much so that it was getting harder for him to get from point A to point B without needing his young handlers to jump in to clear the way.

He was also aware that almost all those mobbing around him were ordinary-looking people, and were not wearing greasepaint or regalia. There had been a few clowns dressed in street clothes who had approached him and thanked him for what he was doing, but now his following included far more people who liked him solely for his message of healing the corrosive partisan divide.

As he looked out the window of his hotel in the fading light of the winter afternoon, something caught his eye that encapsulated exactly how far he and his people had come. Outside was a man walking alone down the street in clown regalia. Two others passing in the opposite direction gave him a thumbs-up as they went by.

Greenbeaux had no way of knowing if the lone clown was familiar with the other two, but he didn't think so. It was rare to see a clown walking out in public, and he doubted that the man would have dared to wear his regalia and greasepaint on the street before the campaign's big rally had suddenly made being a clown more acceptable. He watched as the man walked out of sight, and then sat back down to rest his tired feet.

It was surreal for him to think that nearly 10 percent of the voting public polled was saying that he -- Russell Greenbeaux -- was their first choice to become the next President of the United States. It inspired feelings that were equal parts awesome, humbling and frightening. What if he really did pull this off and was elected?

He would have a thankless job, and would only get the hard problems that needed a no-win decision. He would have the country's nuclear codes at his fingertips, and might make a misstep that led to the end of humankind. He would have to deal with a Congress comprised almost entirely of senators and representatives who had no partisan allegiance to him whatsoever, and then government might really stop working altogether.

All of this would be on his shoulders. Twenty-four hours a day, seven days a week, fifty-two weeks a year, for four years. Possibly eight years if he went completely insane and decided to run for a second term. It was indeed frightening, and it was made more vivid and real because he was doing surprisingly well in the race. Certainly much better than he could have ever imagined when he first dreamed this up as a publicity stunt on behalf of clown rights.

At times like these, Greenbeaux pulled back from the edge by reminding himself that he had not been elected to anything yet. Even if he wanted the job -- which he was starting to come around to, despite small moments of terror -- he still had the impossible task of being elected as a third-party candidate.

All of these conflicting emotions wore on him. But, in the space of a month, he had accomplished far more for clowns than he had previously thought possible. Clowns were now feeling more secure in their own skin, and Exhibit A of that case had just walked down the street past the hotel. He was no longer a sideshow freak in the presidential election; he was quickly becoming a main attraction, and his people were the beneficiaries.

*   *   *

With the band well on its way to South Carolina and much of the chaos around the office dying down, Virgil wanted to spend his Saturday doing some advance planning. Greenbeaux wouldn't be on any ballots during the primary season, but Norm still wanted him to have a timely presence in key states, where the media would be planted.

The campaign also needed to think about getting teams in place to collect signatures in all 50 states and make sure that people could vote for him without having to write in his name come Election Day in November. This was no small task, but the Clown Underground was a huge asset that could be deployed. They still had plenty of time left for that.

Virgil wanted to chart out the route maps that the band would take for the next several weeks. Norm and Ruth would be needed for this process, and Virgil wanted to have his ideas neatly organized when that meeting came.

They had received a request from the Professional Rodeo Clowns Association to have Greenbeaux appear at an event in Arizona the following month. La Fiesta de los Vaqueros was one of the most important weeks of the year in Tucson, and the organizers of the annual rodeo and parade events were eager to draw big names to town.

The festivities were to be held after the Arizona primary, which was scheduled earlier than normal in the cycle so the state could have more influence over the election process. But there were still very good reasons for the campaign to come out in full force. Rodeo clowns were the alpha males of the clown world, and being associated with them would send a signal of strength to Greenbeaux's base.

It was also good for the campaign to start thinking about establishing a presence in the West. There were several states in the region that were not solidly red or blue, and if Greenbeaux was still in the race in November, he would need to be competitive in those swing states in order to have any chance of victory whatsoever.

The coast had some large markets like Los Angeles, San Francisco, and Seattle that would be good places to go. Their goal was to have their poll numbers at or above 15 percent by the end of summer, and getting media attention in large population centers was an important step in that direction. But Norm cautioned them against putting too much emphasis on states like California that were on either tail end of the partisan curve, since their electoral votes would remain unwinnable.

Virgil tried to tune out the sounds of a distasteful Lester Pulcinella interview being replayed on a TV in the war room. He asked a volunteer to get him a map of the United States, and some pins and yarn so he could start visually charting out route options.

*   *   *

Naomi Winston was feeling a little better. She had checked herself out of the facility in Florida to continue convalescing at her condo in the Buckhead neighborhood of Atlanta, and was focusing all of her mental energy on options for revenge. The fire of hatred burned strong in her soul, bringing with it warmth and light to an otherwise cold, dark and desolate place.

Hell would freeze over before she would let a band of clowns walk all over her again, and it would be a righteous day when Norm Brodie felt the wrath of what she had planned. Naomi had thought about killing him -- slowly and painfully -- but if she did that, she would go to jail, and beautiful women like her tended not to do very well behind bars. At least, that's what she had gathered from watching a show about prison life on MSNBC.

She had considered hiring someone else to do the job, but that also involved the very real possibility of getting caught and being incarcerated. For a while, she settled on a plan to kill him and make it look like an accident. But in a calmer and more rational moment of reflection, she realized that there was a risk that he would die instantly without suffering and, above all else, she wanted him to suffer.

No, she thought, cold-blooded murder was too good for Norman Herbert Walker Brodie. Instead, she decided to kill something more important to him than life itself: his career. She would trap him in a way that so badly tainted his name and reputation that it would be political suicide for any candidate to hire him again. This thought gave her joy for a few fleeting hours, until she realized that political suicide was precisely the service most of his clients hired him to provide, and her idea might actually be of some benefit to him.

Finally, she concocted a plan of action. With surgical precision, she would gut him from the inside out. She would inflict psychological wounds so deep that he would forever lose his love for politics, and with that, the only joy he had in life.

Naomi would need help, but she knew just the guy in Washington to call. He was a former infomercial pitchman whose moral compass pointed due South, and he owed her a favor.

As it turned out, Naomi was not the only one who was angry.

Hill Heller had been stewing ever since the C-SPAN debate. That night was supposed to be his coming-out party, when all corners of the nation would hear his grand plan to separate the races. It was he -- not Greenbeaux -- who was to have been interviewed the next day by all the networks, allowing him to unify white people and change the course of the country forever.

But that stupid tall clown man had ruined it all by calling him Hitler, causing him to lose his poise and confidence. Then the other fools in the debate had followed that lead, disparaging him and his cause. The followers who were watching had seen Heller at the lowest moment of his life, and the one thing he could not afford was to be seen as weak by the strong men in his army.

The Aryan Social Separatist Party had reassessed the danger posed by clowns, increasing the threat level from non-existent to code black, the highest level that could be assigned to the inferiors who populated their long and comprehensive enemies list. Heller had sent a message to his people after the debate to show that he was still strong and in charge, and he vowed to lead them into battle against their clown enemies, foreign and domestic.

He had calmed down a little after Christmas when Greenbeaux was no longer appearing on the news. But the flood of coverage that ensued with the New Year's Day rally had twisted the knife lodged in his heart. They needed to stop that man in the clown suit and send a message to everyone else in that degenerate, makeup-wearing race. And so his call to arms was renewed.

CHAPTER 19

The call came in from the Secret Service shortly after 8:00 on Monday morning. A specific threat had been identified, and they were sending a field agent over to Cedar Point to brief the campaign.

Ruth had become increasingly worried. The angry phone calls threatening Greenbeaux had resumed, and the security service they had hired to protect the building kept sending over guards who were more interested in sitting in their cars to stay warm than in guarding the front door. Ruth could have placed a guard at the control tower, but then she wouldn't have been able to use that space, and the campaign would lose the deterrent of having protection stationed outside.

Virgil came dashing into the office, followed by Norm less than a minute behind. Ruth had included the words "Secret Service" and "Specific Threat" in messages to them. They gathered in the conference room, and Ruth shared what she had learned from the call.

They speculated about the possibilities, but Norm calmed them by explaining that it was not at all uncommon for presidential candidates to receive threats. They decided to disperse until the agent arrived for the briefing. It took a while, but finally, at nine-thirty, two men in dark suits stepped off the elevator and asked for Ruth.

They had expected to see only one agent, and the gravity of the situation became magnified in their minds when they saw a second, who identified himself at the door as being from the FBI. The team assembled again in the conference room, and the visitors introduced themselves to start.

"I am Agent Donald Baker from the Secret Service, and this is Special Agent Michael Watanabe from the FBI."

This was serious business, and Ruth and Virgil both found themselves tensing up involuntarily. They were listening intently as Watanabe took the lead.

"I am assigned to a unit that monitors the chatter of domestic terror threats, and we have been tracking some unusual activity over the weekend. It came from a group that was not previously on our radar screen, but we thought it was serious enough that we should bring it to your attention."

Ruth shared the information about the hate calls that had been coming in. She described the messages in detail, and provided as much information as she could. The agents nodded their heads in acknowledgement.

"Those types of calls are not uncommon for campaign offices to receive, " Watanabe said. "That could be important information, given the timing of the threat we identified. But it could also be unrelated. The group we are monitoring seems to prefer electronic communication. We did intercept a couple of phone calls between members of the cell, but there was no verbal communication that we could detect."

Ruth interjected again. "What type of threat are we talking about?"

222

"We are not sure exactly," said Watanabe, "but we do know that they are focusing on an event planned in Charleston."

Ruth, Virgil and Norm all let out audible sighs. Rather than holding another surprise event, they had decided to publicize a rally with Greenbeaux the next day. The band was going to march down the street leading up to a park, where the candidate would be waiting to give remarks on a formal stage.

This was a big production, and they had worked with the city to make arrangements for traffic control and to block off streets. They had publicized the event through the Clown Underground, but had also sent out press releases and were receiving a lot of local media coverage.

Norm spoke up. "Do you think we should cancel the event?"

"That is up to you," said Baker. "But this type of situation is not that unusual. It is not coming from a known group, and there was no specific mention of violence."

"So, you think it would be safe for us to continue with the rally?" Norm asked.

"Safe is a relative term," said Baker. "If everything was completely safe, there would be no need for the Secret Service, and I would be out of a job. We will have a strong presence there and protection around the candidate. We have also been in touch with the Charleston Police Department to make them aware of the situation and coordinate our efforts."

Ruth and Virgil looked visibly relieved, but Norm pressed on: "Can you tell us anything else about the group or what they are planning?"

"The best indication we have is that they're looking to disrupt the event in some way," said Watanabe. "The group calls itself the Silent Majority, and the chatter indicates that they hoped to put a lot of other white faces in the crowd."

*   *   *

Ruth was able to reach her son on the phone just after he finished a live interview at a radio station in New Hampshire. She told him about the visit from the agents, and that Virgil and Norm agreed that they should go ahead with the rally. They thought that there might be some hecklers to contend with, but they were comfortable that the law enforcement presence was going to make the situation safe for everyone.

Security had been weighing heavily on Greenbeaux's mind lately. It wasn't just the hateful phone calls that had been pouring into the office. As awareness built for the campaign, so did the size of the crowds that wanted his attention. He was now officially a major political figure, and he had a nagging fear he could become a target of some plot or crazed individual.

But he agreed that they should proceed. The New Hampshire primary was the next day and, as was becoming his custom, he would plan to leave there before the voting was fully under way and arrive on the ground in the next state ahead of the other candidates.

The marching band had arrived in South Carolina on Saturday, and was hunkered down in Sumter, where they were acclimating new members and practicing for the rally. Word from the road was that everything was going fairly smoothly, though there had been a few glitches along the way, particularly with the three circus clowns.

When the band first arrived, it was too early for them to check into the hotel, and they met the new members at a park and started practicing. This would have been fine, except that Puck and Tuck started chasing each other and honking their horns. The commotion did not settle well with a family of swans trying to relax in a nearby pond.

The swans unleashed a torrent of pecking and feather-ruffling fury that impressed even the angriest clowns in the drum line. When the mauling was done, the horn-honking circus clowns were left to tend to their wounds without any sympathy or medical attention from the band.

Despite this minor distraction, Douglas was confident the band would be ready for the rally on Tuesday. The candidate would be there, and that was a source of great excitement among the new clowns who had joined the band.

Greenbeaux was still holding steady in the polls, and there was reason to believe that he would get a strong write-in vote from Independents in New Hampshire, who were allowed to participate using a ballot of their choice from one of the two major parties. The campaign had recruited volunteers from the Clown Underground to stand at the polls around the state and hand out printed leaflets that had a picture of a green bow tie and the words "write-in" underneath.

Everything was falling into place. The campaign now had a map with pins and yarn showing the path the candidate and band would take next. From South Carolina the entire entourage would travel together to the swing state of Florida, where they would hold similar rallies in Jacksonville, Orlando, and Miami, before heading up the Gulf Coast to Tampa and Tallahassee.

The cost of the road trip was not cheap, with food, lodging and transportation for the band and everyone else to cover, as well as significant costs for security, rentals, stage setup, and decorations at each event site. But the donations kept coming in online, and they now had close to two million dollars in the bank.

No single front-runner was emerging from the Democrat or Republican packs, and Norm saw a narrow window of opportunity to seize the optics. The marching band had become a social media sensation in its own right, and the campaign was banking on its popularity to help lure crowds to see the candidate. With divided loyalties reducing the size of rallies held by the major-party contenders, there was a good chance Greenbeaux could outdraw everyone else in the race and look like a front-runner himself.

Rachel was working furiously to stay one step ahead of the logistics on the ground, and she had deputized Skip to help. This was just fine with him, since he hadn't been assigned a specific job when he left Iowa. People were noticing that the two were spending a lot of time together, even when they weren't working on campaign tasks.

There was a general suspicion among band members that they had become an item, and that seemed to grow stronger when Rachel took Skip with her when she left for Charleston on Monday to do advance work for the rally. These rumors were a concern back in Cedar Point because, if they were true, the campaign would not be able to entrust the newly indispensable Rachel with as much inside information for fear that Skip might get his hands on it and report it to the Republicans.

Ruth routinely reviewed the online statement of campaign expense reports that were linked to credit cards issued to a few key staffers. One look at Rachel's bill told Ruth everything she needed to know; there was a charge for only one hotel room in Charleston on Monday night.

*   *   *

The familiar-looking R. Johnson Shipley had settled into the office of Clowns United, which was now open for business behind a newly installed door near the elevator. He was making his presence known, and he frequently walked around the Greenbeaux headquarters, stopping to talk with staff and volunteers. Mostly, he was trying to charm everyone with his Southern drawl and a folksy manner, but Norm was not taken in.

He had worked with many K Street people over the years, and Johnson seemed to fit the mold of a particularly insidious type. He was so finely polished that his surface flaws were invisible to the outside world. But everyone has imperfections, and it struck Norm that the people who tried the hardest to hide them had the deepest cracks in their interior.

He doubted that Johnson worked for Goldfarb, and suspected it was the other way around. There was a wall between the Greenbeaux campaign and the people paying for their accommodations at Cedar Point, and Johnson was likely the connection that tied it all together. Money gets what money wants, and eventually the benefactors would let the campaign know what was expected in return.

Toward the end of the day, Johnson stopped by Norm's office for a chat, and after a brief exchange of pleasantries, he got down to business.

"Now, Mr. Brodie, I know that you are only just becoming familiar with the peculiarities of the clown culture, and I have no doubt that you have many questions about why we behave the way we do sometimes."

Norm smiled and nodded politely as Johnson continued talking.

"... And as one who has only recently allowed myself to be seen publicly as a clown, I can attest to the strain of trying to conform to a world that has very fixed ideas of who we are. But we are a good and loving people, and we have a strong affection for all of God's creatures."

Johnson pivoted and sat on Norm's desk, leaning in close enough to drop his voice barely above a whisper.

"There is a bill that will be introduced shortly in Congress, that I -- and the financial backers who are so generously supporting the Greenbeaux for President campaign -- support. This bill will help animals, and not just any animals mind you, but circus animals, who are vital to the economic interests of many working clowns."

Norm maintained the smile on his face, but he knew exactly what was coming next.

"It is called the Circus Animals Protection Act, or CAPA for short. And we do not doubt that Mr. Greenbeaux will share our enthusiasm for this humanitarian bill that protects so many of the Great Almighty's most helpless creatures."

Johnson gave a sly smile, stepped away from the desk, and started to head out of the room before turning back to face Norm and said, "I will draw up some talking points that Mr. Greenbeaux can use in his speeches to show his support for the cause."

After Johnson had left his office, Norm went down the hall and found a social media intern.

"We might want to feature Clowns United on our blog," he said. "When you have the chance, please take a picture of Mr. Shipley and send it to me."

CHAPTER 20

A man who used the alias Pete stood on Broad Street in Charleston, watching the crowd gather along the route where the band was about to march past. He was a musician, and his long, flowing black hair made him look like the rock star he aspired to be. He still performed, though not in front of large crowds of beautiful screaming women, as he had once dreamed. Many people didn't understand his artistry, and he often felt frustrated that his talent wasn't more widely recognized.

Pete considered himself to be one of the leaders of his people, standing up against a tyranny that was denying them their rightful place atop the hierarchy. He had come to detest Greenbeaux, and was heeding the call to take a stand. The candidate and his campaign had sent their signal, making it clear what they thought of his kind. There had been one vile insult after another, bringing shame and embarrassment to a proud people.

The slight was to be redressed this day in front of all of these folks in Charleston and the world watching on television. Pete could hear Greenbeaux's band now less than one block away, playing as they marched toward him. He looked for the signal and braced himself for that one dramatic act that would bring glory to him and revenge for his people.

He kept his eyes fixed on his fellow insurgent across the street, and when the black beret was tossed in the air, he stepped off the curb and walked calmly to the middle of the street to commence.

Pete was now squarely in front of the band and he started wailing on his air guitar to the beat of the rocking blues melody cutting through the air.

The tuba players in the front were the first to notice the mime with the white painted face who had just stepped in front of them. A few stopped playing in confusion, trying to sort out the scene unfolding in front of them, while the right side of the front line continued moving forward as they prepared to use their heavy brass instruments as bludgeons against the intruder.

More white-faced mimes streamed out of the crowd, positioning themselves for a showdown with the band from which they had been excluded. It had been a dark day when Virgil's post came across the Clown Underground message board, asking for volunteers to serve in Greenbeaux's band. Mimes were clowns too, and they were fighting to be recognized among their brethren.

They had superior showmanship to all other clowns, and used their entire bodies to entertain, unlike those birthday party bozos who only moved their fingers to make balloon animals and honk their stupid horns. The mime's underappreciated art form was silent and elegant, telling the story of a humanity yearning to break free from the invisible box in which it was trapped.

They had wanted to join the campaign, to stand in solidarity with all other clowns and proclaim that society should accept them for who they are. But the message from the Greenbeaux campaign had been very clear. "No Mimes." Several of their people had tried to join anyway, only to be rebuffed without so much as the courtesy of a rejection note in reply. And now, they were descending on the street for a showdown with the band that they could not join.

At first, the crowd roared with laughter. They did not understand the tensions between mimes and clowns, and thought the air guitarist and invasion of street performers with black berets was all a part of the show. But when the violence erupted, they realized that something very different was going on. Americans might not have fully embraced hockey and its glorious bench-clearing slugfests like their neighbors to the North, but they did appreciate a good fight when they saw one, and the crowd suddenly became ringside cheerleaders at an epic brawl.

But the fight was not a fair one. It was the first-responding evil clowns on the front line against a wiry man who was switching technique from air guitar to shadow boxing. It did not take the rest of the band long to figure out what the disruption was all about and join the fight against all of the mimes who were blocking their path.

Angry clowns in the rear threw down their drums and raced forward, looking for something to hit, while the sad clowns, utterly disheartened that their performance had been ruined, started to cry. Some of the happy clowns tried to console them, but they too were turning into sad clowns as everything fell apart around them.

The alarm went out over the police radios, and uniformed officers began running to the scene. Most had been stationed in Seaside Park where the rally was to take place, and they had several blocks to cover before they could get to the fight and break it up. The Secret Service agents on the scene did not join them; they were well-trained to ignore what might be a diversion and stayed focused on protecting the candidate.

Repeated shouts of "Not Funny," the code name the Secret Service had assigned to Greenbeaux, were relayed over their radios, and men in dark blue suits with plastic earpieces moved in to whisk the candidate away from danger.

As all of this played out, the cameramen from local news stations, who were shooting footage of the event for their evening broadcast, suddenly found themselves on the scene of a breaking national story. Within moments, the news networks were cutting away from analysis of the New Hampshire primary voting to carry the story of a major incident.

The first pictures to come through were from a helicopter above, and the aerial footage seemed to suggest that there was some type of assault on the band, with militiamen in black berets attacking from the sidewalks. The images from the street took longer to come in, and it was several minutes before the talking heads in the news studios figured out that someone in the tuba section had thrown the first punch.

Once again, the nation's attention was riveted on Greenbeaux's band, though not in the way the campaign had planned. There was to be no rally on this day. But the networks couldn't have been happier; they had gotten a far more dramatic story to cover, with intrigue, drama, and lots of ratings-boosting violence.

The subdued Yankees in New Hampshire continued going to the polls in an orderly fashion, only mildly annoyed that the news from down South had taken away a little of the attention on their state's big day. This calmness was not universal throughout the Granite State, though, and one man who stood in front of the cameras in Portsmouth appeared to be more than a little outraged.

"Government spending is out of control, threatening to turn us into just another province of the Communist Chinese who hold our debt," said Lester Pulcinella. "But a clown fight is what the mainstream media believes is the most important political issue on the day when the good people of New Hampshire are going to the polls to select the Republican who will become the next president of the United States of America. Am I the only one who can see that this is a problem?"

The campaign war room was in a frenzy as the team scrambled to get reports from the ground in Charleston. Greenbeaux was at a safe location two miles away from Seaside Park. Rachel was shepherding the band members she could find back to the buses, while Douglas was looking after the clowns who were being treated in a medical triage unit that had been set up. Skip was busy talking with the police, using the debate skills that he had allegedly picked up at the University of Maryland to negotiate the release of several members of Greenbeaux's band and entourage so they could get everyone out of the state as quickly as possible.

Ruth was tallying the head count on a whiteboard, trying to keep track of who was accounted for and who was still missing. She was being helped by an intern who was shouting out names to her as band members called in asking where to go.

Norm was monitoring press reports of the incident while Johnson stood over his shoulder, smiling and howling with laughter as each close-up punch delivered by a band member to the jaw of a mime was broadcast again and again by the networks.

Reporters were calling, looking for the candidate to interview and trying to get a comment from the campaign about the incident. Finally, Norm locked himself in his office and typed out a generic "thoughts and prayers" release that he shared with Ruth and Virgil before sending it out to the media.

Virgil was now listening to Rachel on a speakerphone, and working through whether the ground team in South Carolina needed to stay in Charleston for the night, or if they could keep moving on toward Florida. Finally, when Rachel signaled to Cedar Point that they had everyone on the buses that they were going to get, Virgil gave the approval for them to pull out of town. Douglas and Skip were also on board, but Greenbeaux and his media interns were not. They would stay in Charleston for a day to avoid signaling a retreat, and then would figure out the next moves from there.

Ruth, Virgil, and Norm went to the conference room, away from Johnson and the chaos elsewhere at Cedar Point, to take stock of the situation. Most of the band was intact, with only a few minor injuries that did not require hospitalization, but three tuba players and two drummers were being detained on assault charges.

The bus was heading west on Route 17 when the call came to Rachel from Virgil. Instead of turning south toward Florida when they reached Interstate 95, they were to turn north and head back to Iowa. The team needed time to regroup, and all agreed they shouldn't risk putting the band back out there if there was even a remote possibility another ambush might be waiting.

The band had not been out in the public eye every day, so the campaign didn't have to worry about sending a bad signal if the musical attraction disappeared from the scene for a week or two. Perhaps the campaign could conduct

235

some psychological testing to weed out the members with antisocial and violent tendencies. That might mean fewer people playing tuba and drums, but five of those band members were sitting in a South Carolina jail anyway, so the attrition had already started.

In the heat of the moment, the team developed tunnel vision while focusing so intently on getting everyone out of Charleston. They became oblivious to the vote tallying that was being reported from New Hampshire. If they had been paying attention, they would have surely noted that their candidate was the story of the night.

By Wednesday morning, when the counting was done and all of the write-ins had been accounted for, Greenbeaux had received a full 15 percent of the vote on both the Republican and Democrat ballots. Volunteers at the polls had noticed an uptick in positive reactions to the leaflets they were handing out in the latter part of the afternoon after word of the melee had gotten out.

The band had already established a bit of a badass reputation because of the incident at the Polk County Courthouse on New Year's Day, and people seemed to like the scrappy spirit Greenbeaux now represented. They were sick of what was happening inside the Beltway, and they wanted someone who was going to fight for them.

*　　*　　*

Riley Booth stood in the hallway outside the same conference room at IXM Systems where he had fired Virgil a month earlier, and again found himself talking with Sharon from Human Resources. Normally, firing people was his favorite part of the job, but he was under a lot of stress. The holidays had not been good to him, and he had spent much of his time off driving around Cleveland trying to catch his wife in the act of cheating on him.

Milton Kobeck was sitting nervously inside the conference room. He understood the consequences that Virgil had faced when he came to work dressed as a clown, but he had reached the point where he could not sit idly by without taking a stand. Virgil was now his hero, so he summoned his courage, put on his greasepaint and clown suit, and came to work dressed as himself.

Outside the room, Sharon was laying out the rules for Riley. Everyone in the head office was well aware that Virgil had gone on to become Greenbeaux's campaign manager after he was fired. They also recognized that clowns had come into vogue and that their rights were now part of the national dialogue.

The company did not want to become a test case for a discrimination lawsuit about clown rights, and there was some concern that Virgil's post-firing success had put them at risk for a public relations disaster if things were not handled properly.

Riley could fire Milton if he so chose, which was his prerogative as the boss, and it was acceptable for him to use the dress-code violation as the grounds for termination. But that would have to be the sole reason, and under no circumstances was Riley to mention that this was happening because Milton was a clown.

Sharon hoped she had gotten this message through the man's thick skull, and she crossed her fingers as they entered the room where Milton Kobeck was nervously fidgeting. Riley sat down and wasted little time getting started.

"Milton, we are going to have to fire you."

The wounded man's heart nearly leapt out of his chest. He knew this might happen when he had decided to follow

Virgil's heroic lead, but after 29 years of service, it was still a complete jolt to his system.

"Why," he asked, fighting back the tears he could feel coming. "Is it because I am a clown?"

"No, it is not because you are a clown," Riley replied smugly. "It is because you are old."

Sharon shrieked. It was the kind of involuntary yelp that comes when a woman realizes that six months of her professional life and a half-million dollars of the company's money was about to get sucked into the legal vortex of an age discrimination lawsuit. She yanked back the separation packet she had discreetly slipped across the table moments earlier when Riley Booth started talking.

"No!" she shouted. "No, Mr. Kobeck, you are not fired. He was only kidding. Go back to work. Everything is fine."

A confused but relieved Milton Kobeck excused himself from the room, while Sharon stared down Riley with an icy glare.

The dense man in the room had a bad habit of making lawyers very wealthy. Sharon didn't know what was more shocking, that Riley Booth didn't get that it was illegal to fire people for being old, or that he had not learned from his past mistakes.

For his part, Riley Booth was not sure what had just happened, and he was thinking that he might have to visit the head of Human Resources and tell her to fire Sharon.

CHAPTER 21

After a few brief appearances around Charleston on Wednesday morning, Greenbeaux and the interns caught a plane to Iowa so the team could regroup. He wanted to be there to welcome back the band when it arrived at Cedar Point.

The drivers and their backups were not well-enough rested to handle an 18-hour drive straight through to Des Moines, so the buses stopped for the night in Knoxville, near the University of Tennessee. The battered and bruised clowns caused a stir when they checked in for the night.

Other guests recognized the celebrities from the endless coverage of the fight on television, and the hotel demanded a large deposit as security against the expectation of rock-star caliber damage to the rooms. This was a precaution the management took only in extreme situations, such as when hooligans from the University of Kentucky were in town for a game.

The buses were back on the road after breakfast, and Greenbeaux was there to shake everyone's hand when they arrived in Des Moines that night. The exhaustion from the trip was such that Puck, Pluck and Tuck were too zonked to honk, and just about everyone made a quick exit homeward.

Ruth and Virgil were also there waiting. They were impressed by the work everyone in the crew had done in Charleston, including Skip. He had safely negotiated the release of several band members who should have been locked up for life, plus the three circus clowns who came off the curb to join the battle. Feelings toward the mole had softened a bit. He would be let back into the offices the next day, but plans were made to keep him preoccupied and away from any sensitive information on the computer network.

On Friday, Rachel and Skip would be deployed to Florida to do some work in advance of Greenbeaux's trip to the state. There would be no big rallies as earlier planned, just meet and greets in public places where the news cameras could see the popular candidate being mobbed again. The advance team would scout locations and map out all of the ground movements. This would serve the candidate well, but the team also hoped that it would keep their superstar Rachel happy.

It was just starting to sink in to everyone how good Tuesday's New Hampshire primary results had been, and the campaign was preparing volunteers from the Clown Underground to carry out a repeat performance of the leaflet distribution in a large number of states with primaries slated over the next two weeks. In New Hampshire, they had reached the 15 percent mark in the vote tally, and so the goal of having that level of national support in the polls by the end of summer now seemed quite possible.

But whatever elation they felt was always tempered by the realities of a grinding political campaign. By morning, everyone on the staff was back at Cedar Point, looking ahead to the next round of primaries and trying to put the events in Charleston behind them.

The marching band was a point of pride for the clown community, but there were risks inherent in putting it out there with evil tuba players on the front line. Nobody had been seriously hurt in the melee, but Greenbeaux's marching band was now a target, and the campaign seemed to have a lot of enemies milling about.

Greenbeaux, Ruth, Virgil, and Norm settled into the conference room to make some decisions about their next moves. The marching band was trending on social media, but Ruth in particular felt they needed time to let the risks abate before bringing them back. She was a peacemaker by nature who didn't understand the tension that had led to violence between clowns and mimes in the same intuitive way that her son and Virgil did.

She didn't take the mimes side, *per se*, but she saw parallels between their plight and the campaign's mission: They were an aggrieved group fighting for recognition from a similarly downtrodden people, who were not fully accepted by the larger society. Ruth thought that Norm might be inclined to share that perspective since he wasn't a clown, but convincing others in the campaign would be a tough sell.

Her son didn't have to go out and proclaim his love of mimes to the world, but as always, she wanted him to have empathy and compassion. Ruth found the resolve to raise the issue, but in her usual roundabout way.

"You know, I was reading the Bible yesterday," she said.

Norm looked away disinterested, but her son and Virgil met her gaze. Greenbeaux knew that his mother only quoted that book when she wanted to make a point that ended with him feeling guilty, and he braced himself as she continued.

"I was looking for strength, because, as you know, I am opposed to violence in any form."

Greenbeaux saw what was coming, and he dismissed it with a pre-emptive strike: "They attacked us first."

"That may be," Ruth said. "But I am reminded of the verses that speak of treating others as you would like to be treated yourself."

Virgil did not care for theological arguments being used against his most strongly held positions, and so he jumped in.

"How about an eye-for-an-eye. That's in the Bible too. We could find a marching band full of mimes and pick a fight to disrupt their performance."

Ruth stared right through him and replied. "Is that how you wanted our band to be treated in Charleston?"

"No," he said, chastened. "It is not." He looked down, recognizing that he had helped her to make her case.

She continued: "I think we need to take the high road. You two might not like mimes, but we should treat them with the same dignity and respect that we want the rest of the country to treat clowns."

Virgil felt the guilt Ruth had intended for her son, as he had whenever his own mother had lectured him about the golden rule. Greenbeaux was absorbing a larger dose of it. The point had been made, but he needed some time to reconcile his deep-seated prejudice with what his mother believed in her heart to be right.

Norm had endured enough of the biblical clown guilt, and he decided to steer the conversation back to the business at hand.

"What are we going to do with the band?" he asked.

Virgil had already taken Florida off the map, and he had been looking for a natural point to insert the band again. They needed time to reform the group with more emotionally stable tuba and drum sections, and he wanted to give Douglas and the rest of the crew a chance to recharge.

"There is a rodeo festival in Tucson in February," Virgil said. "That's when I think we should bring the band back."

*   *   *

Pete's real name was Pierre St. Pierre, but he had been using the Anglicized version ever since the start of the Iraq war when disdain for anything French had swept the nation. Those had been dark days for mimes, but things were different now, and he was almost ready to take back his name. But first, he had some unfinished business.

Things in Charleston did not go as planned. The confrontation had been intended to spark acceptance, but instead, it had led to violence and a further deterioration in a relationship he had wanted to salvage.

His injuries were painful, and he was not very comfortable on the flight to Des Moines, but he had a mission and he was not to be deterred. It was difficult to put on his white face makeup with a dislocated left shoulder, and his swollen mouth throbbed as he applied the black lipstick that completed his look. But when he was done putting on his armor, he felt properly dressed for the battle that was to come.

He had assembled a small battalion, nearly four dozen of his own kind, wearing the black and white striped uniform of the Silent Majority army. They assembled in a grocery store parking lot, notified the press, and then descended on Cedar Point.

Pete was media savvy and knew how to draw attention. In his day job, he was a mime language interpreter, and was well-known to others of his kind as the man in the lower corner of the screen describing tragic news in a way that they could understand. If miners were trapped below ground, he would using his entire body to communicate the horror of being stuck in an enclosed space, and then would pull on an imaginary rope to describe the heroic efforts to rescue them.

It was the middle of the afternoon when the call of trouble came in to the front desk. The security guard who had been sleeping in his car outside the Cedar Point offices awoke to find protesters near the entrance wearing black and white. They were carrying large signs made of blank white poster board without words on them and chanting a slogan that only they could hear.

There was a commotion in the office as people ran to the window to get a glimpse of what was going on. The yell of "Mimes!" went out among the clowns, and Ruth had to block the elevators to prevent some of the volunteers from running out to use yard sign stakes as deadly weapons.

One after another, vans with satellite dishes on top and news crews inside screeched to a halt in the parking lot. Reporters and cameramen jumped out and began their rain dance, fighting for the best camera angles to film the end of the political drought that began in the state when the caucuses ended.

Rachel was watching the scene unfold from a window near the control tower when Skip came up and put a hand on her shoulder. He squinted his eyes and then refocused, slowly taking in the scene outside. Then a look of disgust came over his face.

"Damn Democrats. They will protest anything."

Rachel didn't think her party was involved in this. There was no telltale smell of compost or swarm of flies that would signal the presence of one of their environmentally friendly hovercraft. But as she processed the comment, a realization came over her and she turned to look at him. All of the inconsistencies in his University of Maryland cover story now made sense.

"Wow," she said. "When you say things like that, it makes me think that you could not have possibly graduated from a liberal school like UC Berkeley."

Skip froze, the look on his face betraying the truth. He had been so careful. What had he done wrong? Had he talked in his sleep? She certainly did. Those odd mathematical equation dreams she had were endearing, though it had frightened him a little when she awoke one night shouting, "Carry the one, dammit. Carry the one!"

Rachel knew she had caught him, but it didn't really matter to her. She had long since decided that she wasn't going back to Nevada, and she liked him too much to rat him out.

"That's okay, Skip," she said. "We all have our little secrets."

Greenbeaux had now made his way to the window, and he could see Pete leading the protesters in what appeared to be a silent chorus of *We Shall Overcome*. He looked at his mother and announced, "I'm going out to talk with them."

Virgil tried to stop him. "Don't. They might try to kill you!"

"I guess I will just have to take that chance," Greenbeaux said.

Ruth stepped aside from the elevator door and let him pass. She was also afraid for his safety, but she had raised him to make his own decisions, and she would not stand in his way.

Greenbeaux could feel the eyes of the nation on him as the cameras focused on his walk from the front door to the area where the protesters were gathered near the edge of the parking lot thirty feet away.

The mimes stopped, surprised that their efforts had lured Russell Greenbeaux out of the safety of his plush offices. Cautiously, Pete stepped forward to square off with the much taller man. He began slowly, explaining with gestures and movements the grievances of mimes. Greenbeaux stood there, nodding his head with a serious expression that conveyed concern as Pete worked his way up to describing the fight.

It was a hard conversation for the mime to have; his aching shoulder made it painful to describe the physicality of the fight. But this was the most important moment of his adult life, and he was going to sacrifice his body if he had to, just as mimes had done throughout history.

When Pete calmed down, Greenbeaux said a few words and then extended his arm and shook hands with Pete.

Greenbeaux had just violated a cardinal rule of politics: Never anger your base. The clowns who were watching from the office and on television -- the same people who had given life to his campaign -- now felt like a dagger had been thrust into their backs. But Ruth looked down, beaming with the pride that only a mother can feel when she sees her child doing something very nice for someone else.

He waved to the press but did not respond to any of their questions, choosing instead to walk back into the building.

Without the candidate to comment, the reporters rushed forward to get the next best thing. They swarmed around the leader of the mimes, thrusting their microphones in his face. One person asked who he was.

The man raised his chin proudly, looked squarely into the cameras and spoke. "My name is Pierre."

*   *   *

Jessica was staring at her phone, trying to figure out how she knew the familiar-looking man in the picture Norm had sent to her. The name R. Johnson Shipley wasn't ringing any bells, but she had seen him somewhere before.

She ran the image through the facial recognition software used to identify politicians who appeared on hidden cameras at a swingers club her firm owned near Capitol Hill, but that didn't turn up anything. Then she searched the proprietary database that kept track of every embarrassing high school yearbook photo that had been published in the United States since 1953. Still no hits. No criminal record, no offshore bank accounts, no court-ordered support payments for a secret love child. None of the usual tools worked.

There was one more thing she could try, but it was dangerous. The NSA had a database that she knew how to access. It was where they tracked every visit to every porn site that had ever been made by a U.S. citizen. But the Democratic Party had designed the underlying software, and if she accessed it, she risked opening up a trap door on her own computer. It was a gamble, but her curiosity was getting the better of her, so she decided to go for it.

The system took about 10 seconds to run her query, and then a very curious message popped up: "Subject not found." That was highly unusual. Less than one percent of all male American citizens over the age of 18 did not have their private desires stored there, and most of those had either been incapacitated or incarcerated since the days before dial-up modems hit the market.

This told Jessica one of three things: He was asexual, he was using an alias, or he was a foreign national. Or perhaps it was some combination of those possibilities.

On a hunch, she typed the words R. Johnson Shipley Canadian into a search engine and Bingo! Up popped a picture of one Robert J. Shipley. He was not wearing clown makeup, and he looked several years younger than the picture on her phone, but now it all made sense.

Jessica knew exactly why he seemed so familiar, and she quickly typed a two-word reply to Norm:

"Bear Aware."

CHAPTER 22

Norm came into the office early the next day, anxious to share what his friend in opposition research had uncovered. He crowded everyone into his office and locked the door. On his computer was a video of an old but famous infomercial, and when he hit play, everyone in the small room collectively said "Ah!" Now they all remembered why the man looked so familiar.

Ten seconds in, Johnson's face appeared on the screen and he began to speak. Instead of the folksy Southern drawl, they heard a woodsy Pacific Northwest dialect that sounded vaguely Canadian.

"I'm Robert Shipley for Bear Aware, and tonight I'm going to show you an amazing new product that will keep bears out of your campground for good. And to prove to you just how safe and reliable it is, I'm going to spend the night in that tent! Just me, a can of Bear Aware, and this .38 caliber revolver, which I am bringing along to prove a point."

The camera panned down to reveal a small tent in the middle of an enclosure with five very unhappy grizzlies milling about, and then cut to a scene of the enclosure emptied of bears. Shipley was seen applying a pungent tonic to the outside of the tent. He winced a little and shook his head before turning to the camera and saying: "The smell tells you it's working."

Greenbeaux and his leadership team glanced at each other knowingly. The man in the perfect suit who had insinuated himself into the office was something other than the Southern gentleman he portrayed himself to be. He was a pitchman, married not to the cause of clown rights, but to himself and whatever product he happened to be selling.

As the infomercial went on, Johnson entered the tent and the bears were led back into the enclosure. The middle section of the program showed him talking about the product's benefits while the bears could be heard roaring outside.

"The secret formula of coyote pheromone and other special ingredients keeps the bears at bay. Bear Aware releases a nontoxic neurochemical that blocks their olfactory system. They temporarily lose their sense of smell and their appetite, and become too lethargic to hunt."

Near the end, Johnson could be seen emerging from the tent and triumphantly proclaiming, "It's morning, I'm still alive, and look, all six bullets are still in the cylinder."

It was a convincing argument that sold peace of mind, but nothing more. The brown bottles contained a worthless mixture of vinegar, ammonia and another chemical that caused some men who came in contact with it to grow excessive amounts of unwanted hair on their shoulders and back.

The mixture actually did more to agitate bears than repel them. There were lawsuits filed by several mauling victims, and in later versions of the infomercial, disclaimers were added in small print that provided a long list of different types of bears the product did not work on. Which, not coincidentally, included every single species.

The bad publicity caused sales to plummet. The marketers found it necessary to add the incentive of a second bottle of the potion with every order, which they said was valued at $49.99. And there was a bonus gift for those lucky few who called within the first ten minutes each time the program was shown around the clock: A box of .38-caliber bullets packaged as "Bear Arms," which came with its own set of disclaimers in order to comply with laws governing the interstate sale of ammunition.

Robert Shipley's reputation became so entwined with the defective product that nobody else would hire him to pitch their wares. Facing an involuntary retirement from the industry, he went on a quest to reinvent himself. Through a series of coincidences, and a favor he was expected to pay back when the time was right, he ended up as a lobbyist on K Street in Washington.

That was the one place where a dishonest man could make an honest living doing questionable things without being questioned. It was a bit tricky being a foreign national in a city where politicians were always wrapping themselves in the red, white, and blue. But he was good at finding the green, and so he carved a successful niche for himself as a chameleon that was invisible in sunlight.

He transformed himself from the notorious infomercial pitchman Robert Shipley to a more refined Southern gentleman who preferred to go by his middle name. Gone was the Alberta accent, replaced instead with a genteel drawl that a linguist might trace back to a wealthy family in Mississippi.

He was good at what he did, and had a knack for being in the right office at the right time. Which helped to explain why he was standing outside Norm's door when the impromptu video session adjourned. The sight of the lobbyist clown waiting outside startled the four as they emerged, but if Johnson had overheard their conversation, he did not let on.

Instead, he greeted them with his overdrawn smile and said, "Mr. Greenbeaux and Miss Ruth, I am so happy to see you this morning. I was wondering if I could trouble y'all for a brief meeting with Mr. Munsell and Mr. Brodie."

Ruth and Virgil concocted reasons to excuse themselves, but the candidate and Norm followed Johnson into the conference room where Puck, Pluck and Tuck were waiting. Greenbeaux was worried when he saw the circus clowns in the room. Had they reported something they saw on the road back to Johnson? He couldn't be sure, but he would let the President and Chief Executive Officer of Clowns United have his say first before jumping to a conclusion.

Johnson closed the door and began.

"I have asked Misters Puck, Pluck and Tuck to join us this morning because I wanted to speak to you about something that is near and dear to the hearts of working clowns like my friends here. Now, Mr. Brodie may recall our earlier conversation in which I mentioned to him that CAPA -- the Circus Animals Protection Act -- is about to be introduced before Congress. This is a very important bill, not just for me and my clients mind you, but even more so for people who work in the circus industry."

Johnson looked over and nodded to the three men he had brought into the room. They then honked their horns in approval as they had been coached to do.

"I do believe that you, Mr. Greenbeaux, will find CAPA to be a particularly strong issue to appeal to the clowns who have supported you, especially in light of yesterday's incident that has so upset many of your followers."

The message boards in the Clown Underground were boiling over with rage following the handshake with Pierre, and the early reports were that volunteers who had been slated to work the polls in upcoming primaries were defecting in droves.

But Norm wasn't too worried about that.

The handshake with a former adversary had played very well on the networks, with one pundit even calling it "presidential." The strategist had been trying to steer the campaign to this moment, when Greenbeaux's appeal would reach beyond the base that had launched him and into the mainstream of the voting population. Perhaps CAPA would be a good thing to appeal to clowns and other voters alike, but Norm did not have high hopes, and he decided to try a diversion before Johnson could continue with the pitch.

"If you wouldn't mind, Johnson," Norm started, "before we get into discussions of legislation that none of us have yet had the opportunity to read, I wanted to ask a few questions.

"Why of course, Mr. Brodie," replied Johnson, his wide smile overcompensating for the intense dislike he was feeling toward Norm. "Please proceed."

"Thank you. As you know, I am the only one in the room here who is not a clown, and so I am at a bit of a disadvantage when it comes to understanding the culture. Whenever I can, I like to learn more about everyone who is drawn to our candidate. This helps me to do a better job of implementing a strategy that will reach the hearts of our core audience."

Based on what Norm had seen in the Bear Aware video, he wasn't one hundred percent convinced that Johnson was really a clown, and he wanted to go down a line of questioning to see if he would make a mistake that the other clowns in the room would be able to catch.

"I am curious about you, Johnson. When did you first realize that you were a clown?"

"Me?" Johnson said. "I was born a clown, and I realized at a very early age that it was part of my identity."

"I have heard that from a lot of people around here," said Norm. "Tell me, when did you first reveal to your friends that you are a clown."

Johnson laughed. He didn't mind being the center of attention and was starting to warm up to the questions. "Well, like so many other clowns, I was not always open and honest with others about who I was, and it was not until recently, very recently in fact, that I decided it was safe to share this information with the rest of the world."

"What made you finally decide to go public?" Norm probed.

"I suppose the environment has become a lot more friendly for clowns nowadays, thanks to Mr. Greenbeaux over there. But there are other reasons."

"Such as?" inquired Norm.

"Well, if I may be blunt, women are attracted to clowns, and that was a strong incentive," Johnson said. There were knowing laughs from the three circus clowns, who honked their horns in approval.

"Really?" said Norm, trying to sound sincere and not flippant. "This is very interesting. Please tell me more."

"You see, Mr. Brodie," said Johnson, leaning back and putting his feet on the table, "when a woman selects a mate, she looks for certain attributes, specific clues in their physical appearance to signal virility. Perhaps a strong jawline or a muscular physique."

Norm didn't know where Johnson was going with this, but he truly was intrigued.

"And when a woman sees the size of a clown's shoes, she just naturally assumes that he has a large..."

"Johnson!" Greenbeaux shouted. The abrupt interruption surprised everyone in the room. "I have worked tirelessly throughout my entire adult life to dispel stereotypes about clowns. And there are a lot of them; from the one about us liking to all pack into tiny cars to theories about anatomical abnormalities that are implied because of our large shoes. I do not want anyone associated with this campaign perpetuating these myths that are holding our people back."

"I understand that, Mr. Greenbeaux, but that particular impression helps us, not hurts us," said Johnson, trying to maintain his composure over a rage that was bubbling to the surface. "And you would do well to understand that you are on thin ice after yesterday's incident with the handshake. If the word got out that you want everyone in the world to stop believing that there is a deeper meaning behind the size of our shoes, then I assure you, every man in the Clown Underground will abandon your campaign."

Norm was getting a rare glimpse into the dynamics of a world he knew little about, but it was becoming a little too intense, even for his political gladiator tastes. He needed to steer this meeting to a conclusion quickly, and so he brought the topic back to CAPA.

"Okay, Johnson. I think I understand your perspective about clowns. Let's switch back to the Circus Animals Protection Act."

Almost instantaneously, Johnson composed himself and started dripping the faux Southern charm again.

"Why yes, Mr. Brodie, of course. CAPA provides protections for circus animals in areas like transportation and the environment. Whatever our differences are on issues that have no consequence to the political future of our country, I am sure that we can all agree on the merits of this bill. I mentioned when we spoke that I would put some talking points together, and I have. They were sent to you earlier this morning by way of electronic mail."

"Very well," said Norm. "We will have staff members review the bill and then figure out the best way to proceed."

"Oh, I understand Mr. Brodie," said Johnson. "But it is a very long bill. I wouldn't want to put a member of your staff through the tedious experience of reading every page, and so I took the liberty of composing an executive summary to make the process easier for you."

"How long is the whole bill?" Norm asked.

"Nine hundred fifty-three pages," said Johnson bluntly.

Norm should have seen this coming. A 953-page bill to protect circus animals? He knew a Trojan horse when he saw one, and a bill this size was bound to be loaded with all sorts of unpleasant things that a lobbyist like Johnson would want to keep hidden from daylight. But the campaign needed to review the bill on its own merits before making a policy decision one way or another, and Norm wanted to get this meeting over with.

"Fair enough, Johnson," he said. "We will take a look at your talking points and skim the bill, and then we can decide if the Greenbeaux campaign will take a position one way or another."

That was as much of a concession as Johnson knew he could get after this difficult discussion, and so he smiled and shook hands around the table -- including with Greenbeaux -- and went back to his office on the other side of the elevator.

Norm walked to his desk and typed out an e-mail to Rachel, who was in the air at the moment flying to Orlando with Skip. It was brief and to the point: "Please research the Circus Animals Protection Act and report back."

*   *   *

Greenbeaux was scheduled to leave for Florida in a few hours, and he wanted to wrap up loose ends. He was sitting in his office trying to concentrate, but he was finding it very difficult with a Linkin Park song blaring on an infinite loop right outside the door. The circus clowns were dancing and quite literally bouncing off the walls with bicycle horns blaring away.

The reaction from the Clown Underground was weighing heavily on him. The message boards were continuing to overflow with fury at what was being characterized as a grand betrayal and the ultimate sellout, and he could tell that there were fewer volunteers hanging around the office that morning.

The more he thought about it, the more Greenbeaux came to see his mother's wisdom. In his heart, he knew that he had done the right thing, but he was now alienating the very people he had joined the race to fight for.

But Norm was happy, and saw the optics taking shape to position Greenbeaux as a man who really could bring some civility back to the national discourse. With one diplomatic handshake, he had demonstrated that he was the type who could put aside petty differences for the sake of the country.

Virgil wasn't so sure. He had listened to Ruth's morality lecture and understood why Greenbeaux had extended his hand, but it was causing all kinds of new headaches for him. The Professional Rodeo Clowns Association had withdrawn its invitation and asked the campaign not to come to Tucson, and thus they had lost the signature event that was to mark the marching band's triumphant return.

He was also concerned about the volunteer base they were losing. Yes, the campaign's message was resonating with mainstream voters. But much of the New Hampshire success was the result of an army of clowns standing outside in very cold weather handing out leaflets and asking voters to write in Greenbeaux's name.

The onslaught of primaries and a few caucuses was about to begin, and Virgil didn't see how he could get enough volunteers to convince people to write in a name instead of pulling a lever or filling in a bubble for someone not listed on the ballot.

All of these competing voices and the blaring music made it difficult for Greenbeaux to think, so he decided to take a walk. Dodging the bouncing clowns and confetti flying through the air, he made his way down to Norm's office, where it was more quiet. He closed the door behind him to talk strategy in private.

"These honking clowns are driving me crazy," said Greenbeaux.

"I know, but they came as part of the package with Johnson," Norm said. "We can't send them on the road again; that was a disaster. There's a video clip making the rounds on YouTube showing them among eight clowns coming out of a tiny port-a-potty together in Charleston. And that is really bad optics if you want to dispel the stereotype of clowns packing themselves together in tiny spaces."

"I hate these circus clowns," Greenbeaux said. "I want to get them out of my campaign altogether."

"Don't worry, I'll take care of making them disappear," said Norm. "By the time you get back from Florida they will be gone."

Greenbeaux nodded his head in approval and gratitude. "Thanks. Now, if we could only find a way to make Johnson disappear as well."

"That reminds me," Norm said. "There's something I have been wondering about, and you would know more about this than me, so I thought I would ask. Do you think Johnson is a real clown?"

"Oh yes, he definitely is," Greenbeaux said. "But I think we should all be careful not to turn our back on him."

*   *   *

Ruth found herself staring at the cowboy picture again, looking for a deep reservoir of inner strength that the image always helped her find. She was proud of her son for the handshake with the mime, but she could now see that the aftermath was taking a toll on him and the campaign.

She had raised Russell to do the right thing, and he had. But there was a part of her that wondered if she was imposing her own righteousness to her son's detriment. Growing up in the McCaslin family had taught her a thing or two about preachiness, and she didn't always like what she saw when her own tendencies were reflected back to her.

The picture of herself comforting the young cowboy had become a crutch for her, and she wondered if it was symptomatic of her own problems. The picture wasn't about her son, it was about her. And therein lay the problem. Ruth wondered whether the careful sculpting of her son's moral character was really an attempt to compensate for something that was wrong in her own life.

She knew that she was imperfect in the eyes of God, and that when the time for her judgment came, she would have some answering to do. But there was still work to finish on Earth, to help herself, her son, and the rest of the world.

Ruth said a silent prayer, laid the cowboy picture down on the counter, and turned her back to the desk as she got up to greet some visitors arriving on the elevator.

CHAPTER 23

Rachel and Skip greeted Greenbeaux when he arrived in Orlando, pointed him in the right direction, and hopped in the car for the long drive down to Miami to do the advance work for the next stop. She had located and downloaded a copy of the proposed Circus Animals Protection Act, and read random sections aloud as they traveled down the road.

Their political differences were becoming apparent as they discussed the merits of what was being proposed, but one thing was not up for debate: CAPA had nothing to do with circus animals. Perhaps the authors thought that it would be inhumane for any creature to live in a country with any Wall Street oversight or environmental regulation whatsoever, but even that tortured explanation could not account for the disconnect between the bill's public title and the reality that lurked within its pages.

The two were only able to cover a small portion of the massive bill's sections on the four-hour drive, but by the time they arrived at their hotel, they had a good idea about what they should report back to the campaign. Norm had also relayed Johnson's talking points and executive summary, and they could tell that nothing aligned between what the lobbyist wanted them to believe and what was actually in the bill.

There were things in CAPA that Rachel and Skip both detested, albeit for different reasons. But what displeased them most was the blatant misrepresentation of what the Circus Animals Protection Act's name implied. The only animals being protected were the sharks that swam around with very crafty lobbyists on their payroll.

It would take them time to read the entire bill and make sure they weren't missing something, but their summary review revealed a wholesale gutting of financial regulations, along with some budget-busting giveaways and tax incentives for the producers of coal and other fossil fuels. Rachel sent a note to Norm confirming what he suspected about the Trojan horse that was CAPA. In turn, he forwarded that note to Greenbeaux, along with another interesting piece of information he had received earlier.

A text had come in from Jessica with a picture attached and a note that read, "Don't turn your back on this guy." The picture was old, and Norm assumed it had something to do with the evil clown Johnson. But as he looked closer, he could tell that it was in fact something very different.

Culled from the opposition research database of high school yearbook photos was an image of a pimply-faced teenager holding a tuba. It was not Johnson or Goldfarb, or anyone else Norm had expected, but rather, Greenbeaux's nemesis in the race, Lester Pulcinella. Norm ran over to get Virgil when he first received it.

"Oh my God!" Virgil exclaimed. "Lester Pulcinella is a self-loathing clown."

But the response from Greenbeaux was not at all what Norm had expected to hear when the two spoke by phone later that night.

Pulcinella had clawed his way up to second place among the Republican contenders in a newly released poll of South Carolina voters, largely on the strength of the case he was making that violent clowns had become a national embarrassment and a distraction from a proper conservative agenda for the country.

His argument didn't hold water with a majority of voters around the country, but he was getting through to a segment of the population that blamed the country's cultural shift to the left on the mainstream media. There would be time to move to the center later, but for now, Pulcinella was doing a masterful job of slicing a large piece from the right-hand side of the pie.

When Norm excitedly mentioned the tuba picture, Greenbeaux laughed it off.

"Oh yes, Les and I go way back. I used to see him at Clown Underground parties. But that was many years ago, before he ran for office."

Norm was dumbstruck. "You mean you knew this whole time and didn't say anything? That would have been useful information for us to have."

Greenbeaux could hear an edge to Norm's voice, but he brushed it off by explaining why he had not, and would never, reveal that Pulcinella was a clown.

"Look, there are a lot of hardworking clowns in Washington with good hearts. If we start going after the ones we don't like, then the floodgates will open and the decent ones will live in fear that they're next. Pulcinella has the seeds of his own destruction planted in his heart, just as all evil clowns do, and it's only a matter of time before his downfall comes. But the sunlight those seeds need to grow will not come from me, and it will not come from my campaign, directly or indirectly. Do you understand what I am saying?"

Norm did. Pulcinella was as hypocritical as they come in Congress, but Greenbeaux was not one to let political expedience stand in the way of principle, and that was the difference between the two presidential candidates. It made Norm's life as a strategist more difficult, but it was also refreshing for him to see integrity playing out in a game where the alternative offered far greater rewards.

Norm could hear Ruth's voice in the words of her son, and the echoes were starting to reverberate inside his own conscience.

*   *   *

Beneath Johnson's pristinely stylized surface was a kernel of concern. The listening devices that had been planted around the office before the campaign moved in were now yielding valuable clues into what the candidate and his advisors were thinking. He knew that his own past had been discovered and what Greenbeaux and his staff thought of him, but that was not why he was worried.

The investors had not expected the campaign to amount to much from the outset, but they were gamblers who liked to have a lot of bets on the table. As it was with members of Congress, so it would also be with presidential campaigns. Small favors granted once often yielded large dividends again and again, and they were happy to spread their money around in the expectation that a few flowers would bloom.

The editorial in the *Des Moines Register* had sparked their interest, but it was Greenbeaux's debate performance that had really captured their attention. Such a persuasive man arguing against their interest in the status quo could become a dangerous adversary if he ever attained power, and so they had increased their investment as a hedge against the risk.

Goldfarb was a good street lieutenant, but Johnson was their go-to man in situations like this, and they had planted him on the ground to wrangle the beast into the corral and forever brand him with their mark. The investors thought it a happy coincidence that they had two clowns working for them when Greenbeaux emerged on the scene. But it was not uncommon to find evil clowns on K Street, where certain jobs required naked sociopathy to be done correctly.

It had been a happy day when they found Johnson, and for him as well. His years as a pitchman had honed his skills as a master salesman, but the events of the Bear Aware campaign had damaged him in many ways that even he could not fathom.

That night in the tent had changed him forever. The bears had been tranquilized and there were sharpshooters stationed around the perimeter of the enclosure. But the foul-smelling product had made them angry, and Johnson knew that he would have been shredded if the sedatives wore off and the aim of the shooters was not true.

Whatever sense of empathy for others that might have been lurking in his limited conscience disappeared that night, and was replaced instead with a determination that he would look out for himself, and only himself.

When it became apparent that his career as a pitchman was over, he contacted an old acquaintance who connected him with someone else who, in turn, introduced him to Naomi Winston. She was working in the offices of a small political newsletter publisher at the time, but had aspirations to use her journalism training and beautiful face in a more visual medium.

Naomi recognized a kindred spirit in the deeply damaged pitchman, and she made it her mission to introduce him to the kind of K Street darksiders who could use his unique brand of manipulative persuasion. He asked what was expected in return for her help, and she replied: "Someday, I will ask you to do a favor for me. Deal?"

The two shook hands and agreed to the terms. Johnson soon had a high-paying job that suited his talents, and Naomi had the promise that a cunning ally would be in her corner should the need arise.

Now, that time had come.

When she learned that Johnson was pulling the strings behind the Greenbeaux campaign, her plan to dismantle Norm Brodie from within took form. And Johnson was all too happy to repay his old debt, in large part because he didn't like Norm and the ends suited his own needs.

It had seemed like a good idea at first for his people to vouch for the brilliant young strategist looking to get an introduction into the campaign. But Norm was proving to be difficult to manipulate. Not only had he discovered his pitchman's past and turned the others against him, he was now taking steps to block Greenbeaux's support for CAPA. That was more than just worrisome; it was unacceptable.

Johnson had personally assured some of the wealthiest men in the world that Greenbeaux would come around to endorsing their legislative agenda. He had wrapped it in a nice little package with a circus animal motif to secure the candidate's endorsement and the support of his followers.

Thanks to Norm Brodie, the campaign was not going to follow willingly. But Johnson would make sure that Team Greenbeaux would come along for the ride whether they liked it or not. He had gathered incriminating evidence to extort the candidate's sign-on, and as an added bonus, serve up the takedown of Norm Brodie that Naomi Winston so desperately craved. All the pieces were in place and the wheels were now in motion.

*   *   *

The small car weaved its way through the nearly deserted streets of a small Central Iowa city, the driver intent on his mission of death and destruction. It was to be murder, and not an accident, that would most please the devil on this night.

Three other passengers who were crammed into the two-seat car accompanied the driver. But nobody seemed to mind. They liked being in confined places, and found kinship and comfort in the close quarters. The passengers had been given half a bottle of rum to numb and prepare them for the heinous deed. There was not enough of the spirit to fully intoxicate them, but it was sufficient to loosen their inhibitions for what must be done.

A dog ran out in front of the car and three horns were instinctively honked, not including the driver's. The car swerved and then corrected itself. The animal was to be left off the night's body count, and he wandered toward a light in the distance while the clowns continued their drive toward a much darker place.

They could see what looked like a large red and gold circus tent looming in the distance as they neared their final destination. The scene seemed eerily still and quiet, and was not what the clowns had expected when they were told where they were going, but they had imbibed just enough to no longer care or raise questions about what was to be done.

When they pulled to a stop, the three were again briefed on what to expect, and the driver got out to accompany them on their careful walk up to the front door. He tugged on a seam in the tent that concealed the entrance, and guided the others to the door with the lock he had picked earlier. Then, he let one of the clowns turn the knob to avoid leaving his own fingerprints on the chrome surface. He stepped back slowly, and gave one final instruction as he watched the circus performers disappear into the tent with their backs turned to him.

"Keep walking into the darkness until you see a light, and then move toward it."

The driver moved delicately back toward the small car, being careful not to leave footprints that could later tie his large shoes to the scene. He waited for a few minutes to make sure the plan was working and drove off into the night.

CHAPTER 24

Carrie Rollins was sitting in the newsroom in the late morning when word spread that something unusual had happened in Bondurant, a small city 10 miles northeast of Des Moines. Workers from a pest-control company had found three bodies when the tent was removed from a house that was being treated for termites.

Details began to emerge that the victims had suffocated when they entered the house, which should have been sealed during the fumigation. A nearly empty bottle of liquor was found with them, and the early speculation was that the three had been intoxicated and broke into the tented house seeking shelter from the cold.

While Carrie was at lunch, she received a call asking her to get back to the newsroom quickly, and she hurried back to find colleagues looking for her. As she approached her desk, one friend ran up to her and exclaimed: "You are not going to believe this. They were clowns. The three guys found dead in the tent were clowns."

She quickly sat down to work, digging for clues on the Clown Underground message boards. Word had not leaked to the public about who was involved, and she didn't find any mention of clowns dying under these unusual circumstances. Instead, most of the recent posts on the boards were angry rants about the handshake between Greenbeaux and the mime.

She tried a news search to see if anyone had reported more details about the story, but saw only the summary briefs from local stations and the *Register* mentioning that the Polk County Sheriff's Department was investigating the death of three individuals in a Bondurant house.

Carrie got the address from a fellow reporter and drove to the scene in search of more details. Many of the same news trucks that had been at Cedar Point to capture the protest the day before were now here reporting on the grim scene inside the two-story house that was still partially shrouded in a red and gold tent.

She sidled up to a deputy sheriff she recognized, reintroduced herself, and started chatting him up in the hopes of getting some information. He was reluctant to share anything, but he did reveal a few details that helped her piece together what had happened.

The house was vacant and was being tented under orders from the owner, who was going to put it on the market after having just evicted a tenant. It appeared there had been some form of forced entry, and the investigators were analyzing the front door lock, which showed signs that it may have been picked.

Carrie asked if he could tell her whether the victims were clowns. The deputy had revealed a lot already, and he wasn't willing to confirm that level of detail for the reporter. Instead, he suggested that she talk with a public information officer who would be on the scene shortly. She thanked him, made her way to another deputy standing near a cluster of patrol cars and started the process all over again.

The public information officer arrived and spoke privately with investigators. Carrie could see deputies wearing latex gloves pointing to the curb, and then signaling a path with his arm from the street up to the front door. After 10 minutes, the information officer stepped to the other side of the crime scene tape and summoned the half-dozen reporters milling about.

The news cameras aimed toward her, but she waved them off. This was to be an informal briefing only to keep speculation in check. She couldn't answer many questions, but she indicated that the sheriff and other law enforcement officials would hold a press conference later in the afternoon.

"Here is what we know. Three individuals arrived at the house behind me at some point between 4:00 p.m. on Wednesday and 10:00 this morning. The subjects gained entry into the house, which was properly secured, through a locked door without using a key."

The officer checked her notes to make sure that she had the next part right. "Sulphuryl fluoride gas had been pumped into the house, and was at a sufficient level of concentration to cause asphyxiation. The subjects were found this morning when employees of the pest-control company arrived to remove the tent and ventilate the house. We have not ruled out the possibility that this was an accident. However, we are calling this a suspicious death investigation at this time."

The collected reporters were anxious for more information and started firing questions at the officer, who was reluctant to release too many details before her boss arrived to hold a press conference.

"Have you identified the victims yet?" asked one reporter.

"Yes. We have determined their identities, and law enforcement agencies in other states are attempting to notify their next of kin.

"Is it true that the three people found inside were clowns?"

"Yes."

"Do you know if they were associated with the Greenbeaux campaign?"

"We have not yet contacted the campaign. However, I can tell you that we have reason to believe that the subjects were briefly detained earlier this week in another state following an altercation that involved the band from Mr. Greenbeaux's campaign. Given the complex nature of the forensic investigation and the subjects' association with that incident, the FBI has offered to assist and will be joining the investigation."

Carrie was now certain these clowns were from the campaign, most likely as part of the band. After the information officer finished, Carrie returned to her office at the *Register*. Word would spread very shortly that clowns were involved, and she wanted to be on the message boards when news hit the wires.

*   *   *

Ruth was sitting at the control tower when Special Agent Michael Watanabe stepped off the elevator. His wife was expecting a baby in a few weeks, and he didn't like being too far from his base in Omaha. There were agents stationed closer, but he had met the leadership team at Cedar Point earlier, so the assignment fell to him.

He identified himself again, and asked Ruth if they could talk privately. They went to the conference room, and a few minutes later she emerged in tears looking for Virgil and Norm.   She rounded them up and they listened somberly as Watanabe explained the situation. The three circus clowns used pseudonyms, and so only one of the names the agent listed -- William Tuck -- rang a bell. But from the description the agent gave, with the signature bicycle horns strapped to their belts, Ruth, Virgil and Norm knew right away who had died in that house.

Watanabe revealed very few details of what was known at that point, given the possibility that someone inside the campaign had been involved.   The investigators were following multiple tracks, and the initial impression deputies had on the scene was that the inebriated men spotted the tent and had mistaken it for a circus. The pest-control workers were very insistent that they followed safety procedures to prevent people from getting in, and detectives were trying to determine if any of the men had experience picking locks.

There was also the question of how these men got from Des Moines to Bondurant, and a neighbor told investigators she had seen a suspicious car driving on the street with its lights off when she came home from work after 2:00 a.m. If the car was associated with the dead circus performers, then it meant that a fourth person had been at the scene, and it was not yet clear whether this was a suspect or a witness.

Watanabe expressed his condolences to the individuals involved in the campaign, but also indicated that they would like to talk with members of the campaign staff individually. And as a routine part of the investigation, he wanted to gather fingerprint samples from everyone working in the office.

He knew there was nothing routine about collecting fingerprints en masse at this stage of an investigation, and he suspected that they did too. But evidence had been left at the scene, and they would need to start excluding people who were close to the clowns.

On the other side of the wall behind the elevator, Johnson listened carefully to the conversation, which was being captured on a hidden microphone in the conference room. He was anxious, but this whole affair could not be dismissed as an accident if his plan was to proceed. There was certain evidence he could insinuate into the investigation later to ensure that the blame was properly affixed, but he thought it best to lay low in the meantime.

Ruth readily consented to allowing investigators into the offices, and within 20 minutes, two people from a Division of Criminal Investigation forensics unit descended to gather fingerprints from everyone they could find in the office. The backlash from the mime handshake was still reverberating, so most of the people hanging around were not clowns, or were too heavily invested to walk away.

Puck, Pluck and Tuck had not been popular figures around the office, but their sudden and mysterious deaths had jolted and saddened everyone there. Ruth called her son and told him about what had happened. Greenbeaux immediately canceled the rest of his planned activities in Florida and headed to the airport with his media interns to catch a plane back to Iowa. Rachel and Skip were soon recalled as well.

As news broke that three clowns associated with the campaign had died in Bondurant, camera crews began setting up camp in the parking lot at Cedar Point. Local reporters and national correspondents alike huddled in their vans and came out periodically to file live reports about the events.

The video of eight clowns emerging from a port-a-potty in Charleston graduated from social media to cable news, with red circles now added to highlight Puck and Tuck. Their families had been informed of the deaths, but the police would not release Pluck's name because they could not find any next-of-kin to notify. But everyone close to him knew that he had died in Bondurant as well, and it was not long before Pluck was identified in the video too.

With word spreading, the Clown Underground boards lit up with heartfelt messages of grief and conspiracy theories about the role that mimes had undoubtedly played in the tragedy.

Carrie watched the messages stream through with interest. She had a story to write about the political angle of this story, and there was little from the boards she could include except a brief mention about how the clown community was reacting. But she still found herself searching the threads long into the night after she had filed the story.

Memorial boards dedicated to each of the clowns were soon erected. Puck, whose birth name was Francis Mulvaney, was from Minnesota, and had earned his nickname after suffering head trauma during a hockey game.

His friends remembered him as the life of the party who loved cotton candy, funnel cakes with powdered sugar, and small animals. In his early years as a performer, his sidekick was a Chihuahua named Pickles who died tragically when he was accidentally shot out of a cannon and hit the broadside of an elephant at close range. It took Puck years to get over the grief, and he opted to join a performing team rather than replace his dear companion with another dog.

William Tuck came from a prominent New England family, and was one of several heirs to a small candy manufacturing empire based on Cape Ann, north of Boston.

One of his ancestors had been a philanthropist, and his family had tried to use that connection to get him into Dartmouth. But Tuck was not Ivy League material, and instead went off to clown college, where he flunked out after spending his time going from one tanker to the next in a high-pitched, helium-fueled haze.

Very little was known about Pluck, though authorities eventually let the press know that his name was Wayne Ruttinger. He was born in Texas and grew up in a hardscrabble family of carnival workers. There were no relatives left to notify or claim his body, and after a brief discussion with Norm's campaign finance consultant, Ruth authorized payment of his final expenses and personally took on the task of organizing his funeral.

While the posts gave Carrie a glimpse into the lost souls behind the greasepaint, they provided no insight into what might have gone wrong. She tried using the search term Bondurant, but it seemed like almost all of the posts to the board that day used the name of the town, and she was having trouble wading through all of the memorial comments to find any information of value. Then she tried sorting the list by date and found something interesting.

In more than a decade of existence before the murders, the Clown Underground site previously had only one message containing the word Bondurant. And that had been posted the night before the bodies were found.

"Big tent party in Bondurant tonight!!! Bring your horns!!!"

Carrie had a restless night and didn't sleep very well. She knew that this was important to the investigation, and she struggled with whether she should release it in a story the next day. When she awoke, she knew what she must do, and called a friend at the state Division of Criminal Investigation who met her at the *Register's* office.

None of the investigators had ever heard of the Clown Underground before, but this was indeed an important clue. A computer forensics expert with the FBI was given the task of examining the thread and could see that the message had been sent through a proxy with a masked IP address. But the cloaking had been done carelessly, and it didn't take long to figure out that the message had been posted from a wireless network residing inside the building at Cedar Point.

Perhaps one of the clowns had made the post, but it begged the question: Why would they go to the trouble of masking their identity when writing about a party? Even if one of the clowns had gone to that length for the sake of privacy, it now seemed quite likely the clowns went to Bondurant expecting that there would be a party involving a tent.

The press was now reporting that the whole tragic scene appeared to be an accident involving clowns who had picked the wrong tent to party in. But to investigators behind the scenes, it was beginning to look more like someone inside the headquarters of the Greenbeaux for President campaign had lured the men to their deaths.

* * *

Two men in dark-colored casual clothing moved quietly behind the building at Cedar Point, being careful not to disturb the news trucks that were staking out the front parking lot. It was three o'clock in the morning, and all the lights were off in the building, indicating that everyone had gone home for the night. They entered the back stairwell through a fire exit and retrieved a ladder and small bag that had been positioned there earlier. Then they went upstairs and unlocked a little-used back door to the office that led into the war room.

They made one quick pass through the offices to make sure that nobody was there, and then went to work. Moving from room to room, they methodically planted small wireless listening devices around the headquarters. Their warrant was very specific about the number of devices to be used and where they would be placed. The conference room got one, as did the war room, and most of the enclosed offices, including the one that Ruth had assigned to her son.

The men navigated their way around, aided by the signs with the names and titles of the senior staff on each door. When they reached the elevator, they noticed there was a newly finished office located on the floor that was not on their architectural schematics.

They had additional devices with them, but took the precaution of calling in to get the warrant revised, just in case anything was uncovered in this new office that the prosecutors would later want to bring into evidence. As they waited, they started testing the units already installed.

Pretty soon they realized there was something wrong. They were getting interference and could detect a slight electronic buzzing coming from a corner of the conference room. They pulled out a signal detector and homed in on the radio frequency, then raised an acoustical ceiling tile to find a device that was eavesdropping on the room.

The two agents were surprised. "Looks like this place has already been wired," said one. They called back to their supervisor and received clearance to sweep the entire office for additional bugs, take pictures, and disable whatever they found. They made quick work of it and were done before the word came back that they were good to go with the revised warrant.

They did a quick sweep of the Clowns United office, but didn't find any listening devices planted there. Whoever had wired Greenbeaux's headquarters was not interested in what happened on this side of the building.

Johnson's office was spartan, with only minimal finishing. There was a desk, a chair, a laptop computer, and a large locked cabinet. The agents placed a bug in close proximity to the desk, then exited.

CHAPTER 25

Monday morning was cold, a thick cloud cover creating a gloomy atmosphere matching the mood of the mourners at graveside in Des Moines. Ruth had spared no expense for Pluck's funeral, flying out Tevye, the most famous of the sad-clown virtuoso violinists, to perform at the service.

Word of the arrangements had been posted on the Greenbeaux for President website and the Clown Underground boards. When it became clear the crowd would be much larger than the small cemetery could accommodate, Ruth rented a hall that seated 350 people.

There was still some lingering anger over Greenbeaux's betrayal with the mime, but it was subsiding, and the mourning clowns flocked around the candidate at the public service. He was still the undisputed leader of their community, and the campaign's thoughtful handling of Pluck's memorial had helped with the healing.

Greenbeaux did not feel it would be right for him to eulogize Pluck. He had grown frustrated with the antics of the three circus clowns, and he thought it would be disingenuous to add his voice to the chorus of praise for a life he did not know or understand.

To be sure, he was mourning, and had been deeply shaken. He had not asked for the clowns to be imposed on the campaign, nor had he appreciated their antics. But nonetheless, three of his people had lost their lives, and he felt a duty to be there.

The incident had forced Greenbeaux to look deeply at himself. Puck, Pluck and Tuck represented everything he detested about the exaggerated clown stereotype he had dedicated his life to eradicating, and he was now trying to understand his negative reaction to them specifically, and to circus clowns in general. They were just being themselves, and had done nothing to intentionally harm him.

He was feeling far from presidential.

The whole campaign had been a publicity stunt to draw attention to clown rights, and he had never thought he would even want the job until people started jumping on the bandwagon. Now, he wondered whether he should -- or even could -- continue on in the race.

Ruth and Virgil had suspended all of Greenbeaux's appearances and other campaign activities until the services were behind them. Norm, all too familiar with the feel of campaigns on the edge of the abyss, had supported that decision. The little time he had spent in the office over the weekend was focused on relaying messages to reporters about the somber state of emotions inside the offices at Cedar Point.

He was positioning the campaign to return to full force after the funeral. But the deference was not just a show. Norm had felt the suddenness and depth of the loss as well, and he had spent a lot of time trying to process what had happened. Jessica called as soon as she heard that three people associated with the campaign had died under such strange circumstances, and she had served as a sounding board and shoulder to lean on through several conversations over the weekend.

Norm made discreet pleas to members of the press that they not show up in force at the funeral, and that request had been honored, for the most part. Two news vans arrived to report, but they kept their distance at the edge of the parking lot during the public service, and did not go to the cemetery for the burial.

Virgil volunteered to deliver the eulogy, both at the public service and the private graveside burial. As the campaign manager, he felt a duty to say words that gave meaning to the life of a volunteer. For all their faults and annoying pranks, the three were committed to the cause. They had come to Iowa excited about meeting Greenbeaux in person. They could have gone back to the circus afterward, but they stayed on in an effort to help the campaign by entertaining in the only way they knew how.

He had given a lot of thought to that conversation with Ruth in the conference room about treating others as one would like to be treated. It was a simple concept that transcended political ideology and religious boundaries, but one that many people never acted upon. He had seen too many Riley Booths in his day, people who were so oblivious to the needs of others that they made the world a darker place. He would deliver the type of eulogy that he would want said about himself if the only one left to mourn him knew little of his life.

The graveside service was to be a private affair for the campaign. The core leadership team invited the volunteers who showed up regularly to the office, as well as Johnson and Goldfarb. They found the lobbyists distasteful, but had no desire to make the ultimate showdown with them about who had the right to come to a funeral. The band was also invited, though few chose to attend. The tuba section and drummers had no use for the circus clowns, and most of the sad clowns were just too depressed.

The highlight of both services was the performance of the virtuoso, Tevye. His violin captured the sadness of the sudden loss that was weighing so heavily on everyone's heart. There had been no doubt about what Pluck's favorite music was, and Douglas recomposed the Linkin Park song *Skin to Bone* that had played endlessly outside Greenbeaux's office, this time as a solo for Tevye's violin. Stripped of its electronic elements and pounding bass, the new version of the song was melodic and mournful.

Greenbeaux had sat in Douglas's office to hear the composition that would serve as a tribute to the clown who had died without a family to claim his remains. He listened with fresh ears to the song that had so annoyed him just a few days earlier, and heard the lyrics take on a new and ominous meaning.

He had wanted the clowns gone, and now they were. As Tevye stood by the side of Pluck's grave playing the composition, the full force of the week's events engulfed Greenbeaux. He had failed to treat the circus clowns with compassion in his own heart, and had instead dismissed them for what they represented to his ego.

The graveside interlude proved too much for Greenbeaux as he finally surrendered to the emotion of the past few days. Each note in Tevye's haunting performance amplified the meaning of lyrics that had been stripped away in the new rendition of Pluck's favorite song.

* * *

Goldfarb walked uncomfortably into a dimly lit club and looked around. He had been in these types of places before, but the dancers had always been male, and he was not sure exactly how to act. As his eyes adjusted, he could see half-naked women milling about.

They were moving from table to table looking for men willing to pay for a few minutes of companionship. The men were moving around too, looking to get the attention of certain ladies they fancied. The sharks were circling the sharks, each predator on the hunt to get something out of the other.

He would have preferred not to be in this club, but there was a threat to the plan, and action was necessary. The stakes were high, and Johnson was very tense. His electronic eavesdropping equipment wasn't working properly, and he no longer had inside access to what Greenbeaux and his staff were saying. Goldfarb knew well the rage his boss kept hidden beneath the perfectly polished surface, and he thought it best to just follow orders without asking questions.

But most of the other aspects of the plan were working smoothly. One half of the operation would be as good as done within a couple of days, and the second part was about to commence. Someone close to the candidate had been careless, and they now had everything they needed to wrap him in a box and deliver the present to the clients with a little green bow on top.

Goldfarb walked up to a table and sat down. Two dancers in the corner saw him and jabbed at each other in a variation of the rock-paper-scissors game to decide who would get the first shot at extracting cash from the clown-shaped ATM.

A cocktail waitress in skimpy shorts and a skintight tank top came up to him and asked him what she could get him.

"Get me Debbie," he said.

"There is a two-drink minimum," said the waitress, slightly annoyed.

"Okay then, bring me water and Debbie," Goldfarb said, pulling a hundred-dollar bill out of his pocket.

The server's eyes lit up. "I'll get Debbie for you," she said, moving swiftly off to a dressing room door in the corner with the money in her hand.

The dancer's real name was Mercedes, but she used the stage name Debbie to maintain a measure of anonymity. Goldfarb's sources had told him that she was the one he needed to reach, and he had come prepared with a pocket full of the tools of his trade to aid in his persuasion.

A dancer with long flowing red hair approached from behind him and sat down in his lap. She reached out to shake his hand and asked, "What's your name?"

"Are you Debbie?" he asked.

"No, I'm..."

"Go away," he said, cutting her off.

It always amazed her how much the customers' tastes varied. Everyone always told her she was the prettiest girl in the place, but sometimes the men wanted something else. A little darker, a little shorter, a little rounder, a little different. And so she quickly got up and moved on to the next empty lap.

Less than a minute later, a woman with bobbed, sandy blonde hair and a button nose came to the table. She was not quite as pretty or tall as the first dancer, but she was certainly desirable to most of the men who came to the club looking for a fresh face.

"I'm Debbie," she said. "What's your name?"

"I'm… uh… Max," he said. Debbie wasn't the only one who preferred the veil of anonymity.

"What can I do for you?" she asked. Usually when men requested her by name, it meant someone else had found their encounter satisfying and told a friend.

"I need a favor," he said.

"Okay…" she said, slowly looking him up and down. "But judging by the size of those shoes, I'm going to have to charge you extra."

Goldfarb grew flush with anger at the thought of having to pay more for something because he was a clown, but then he quickly composed himself. "It's not that kind of a favor."

The server came back to the table carrying a small tray with a bottle of water and $95 in change, mostly one-dollar bills.

"Keep it," Goldfarb said as she approached.

"The water?" the waitress asked.

"Everything. Just go away," he said.

"You got it," she said, exiting quickly and doing a little happy dance as she made her way back to the bar with the cash.

Goldfarb turned his attention back to Debbie. "I was told that I should speak with you. I have a business proposition."

Debbie was intrigued, but cautious. "What type of business?"

"We can't talk here," he said.

"My shift doesn't end until 2:00 a.m.," Debbie said, "and I'm supposed to stick around.

He pulled a roll of $100 bills out of his pocket. "Does this change anything?"

"I'll get my coat," she said, and quickly disappeared in the back.

Goldfarb waved off another dancer who approached. When Debbie came back, he stood up and she tucked her hand gently under his arm to lead him out through a side door so the manager wouldn't see her leaving.

The cold air hit their faces when they left the steamy confines of the club and walked into the alley. As they made their way around the building to the parking lot she asked again: "What kind of business proposition is this?"

"It involves making some of the wealthiest men in the world happy," he said. "I will share more when we're in the car."

After a few more steps, Debbie saw something familiar. Goldfarb clicked a button to unlock the door to a small black Smart Car. It looked just like the one she told the police she had seen leaving the house where the clowns were found dead.

* * *

George Sommer was having another bad day, which was not unusual. The Republican National Committee and its staff had enjoyed only a few good days since 2004. Despite the party's success in the last midterm elections, he could see disturbing shifts in demographics and social attitudes coming to pass that were endangering the viability of the Republican Party. It was as if someone had switched on a mind-control machine that reinforced the Democratic Party platform in the belief system of younger voters.

Adding to that, the party that had once embodied the term family values was bracing for yet another scandal that raised questions about the character of one of its leaders.

The picture that was about to go public had already circulated around the office. It showed Lester Pulcinella unmasked as a member of the clown tribe he professed to loathe, and engaged in acts with his fellow clowns that offended some people in the office.

If somebody had gone to the trouble of looking, they might have noticed that there was a small green bow tie tattooed onto the left butt cheek of a very tall man among the mass of bodies in the background. But the image was fuzzy, and it would have required digital enhancement software and a magnifying glass to find it.

Pulcinella was about to make the short drive to the political graveyard, but Sommer still had to deal with the living. And so he tried to forget about the looming scandal and focus on his problem in Sacramento.

The police union had long since relented and allowed their officers to clear a path so that people could come and go from the Republican headquarters, but there were four men in the basement bunker who didn't want to leave. They had repeatedly worked their way through the checklist in the red packet and, upon each reading, they thought of more evidence to support their conclusion that the apocalypse was nigh.

It was clear in their minds that all seven signs were taking place at once, and they were expecting that at any moment they would be lifted toward the heavens and on to a better place, where there would be no sorrow or suffering or Democrats allowed.

A week earlier, there had been reports of a 5.0 magnitude earthquake farther south near Paso Robles. One of the men took it as a sign and stripped naked to await the momentary arrival of the rapture. He knew from the Good Book that all of his possessions and clothing would be left on earth, and it had just seemed like a good idea to save someone upstairs the trouble of disrobing him when it was his turn to be lifted to the sky.

That had been another bad day for George Sommer, and he had spent the better part of an hour on the ham radio trying to persuade the man to put his clothes back on before the mainstream media got wind of the story. But today was no better. Not only was Pulcinella about to go down in an inglorious blaze of hypocritical self-immolation, the fax machine was now broken, and they were having trouble receiving messages from their operatives in the field.

Fortunately, they had redundant methods of communication for just such an eventuality. Their spy inside the Greenbeaux operation didn't have a secure carrier pigeon with him, but the boy from Berkeley was resourceful. After nearly two weeks of silence, he had sent a message through a channel that worked.

The telegram read: "AND THUS I SAW HORSES IN THE VISION. STOP. HAVING SEVEN HEADS AND TEN HORNS. STOP. NOR OF THEIR SORCERY, NOR OF THEIR FORNICATION. STOP. SHALL HAVE THEIR PART IN THE LAKE WHICH BURNETH WITH FIRE AND BRIMSTONE. STOP. AND SHALL BE FOUND NO MORE. STOP.

Sommer had run the message through both the Republican Party's secret King James and New American Standard ciphers, but kept getting the same puzzling message from Skip Bancroft that he could not understand:

"I PUIT."

As it turned out, bad days were being had elsewhere outside the stuffy walls of the Republican National Committee headquarters in Washington.

Hill Heller had just been deposed as the head of his army. The coup had come from an aide who seized on the perception that the leader was weak, and rallied the followers around a new vision that didn't involve a man who sweated profusely on national television or have a name that could be easily confused with Hitler.

This was a ringing defeat for the man who had cobbled together a ragtag group of prison gangs and some of the more antisocial elements of certain militias. He had poured his heart into the movement, and despite his best efforts to rally the troops to make threatening phone calls to the Greenbeaux campaign, he was being summarily dismissed.

Heller had moved his family to the edge of a lake in Idaho to take the leadership reins of the movement, and now it had all crashed down. He wasn't sure what he was going to do to make a living, he just knew that he didn't want to go back to being a kindergarten teacher again. That would be a fate worse than death.

A similar story of fleeting power was playing out in Cleveland. At the IXM Systems headquarters building, Sharon from Human Resources was talking in a hallway with Noah, a lawyer who had the good fortune to be an expert on the subject of discrimination and to work in the home city of the company that employed Riley Booth. His billable hours runneth over.

Booth was not a happy man. He had been served with divorce papers and he had just received conclusive proof -- a confession, no less -- that his wife was having an affair. Sharon and Noah found him listening to a voicemail when they entered his office.

"Mr. Booth," Sharon started, "we are here to talk about the Pawlak case with you." This was just one of what was now becoming a torrent of suits being brought against the company as a result of the dense man's ignorance and incompetence.

But Riley Booth was in no mood, and instead wanted to play the voice message on his phone. "Here, listen to this," he said to the two.

Sharon and Noah gave each other a look, not quite sure what was coming next. The speakerphone button had been pushed and the two could now clearly hear Riley Booth's soon to be ex-wife rambling angrily.

"... So you caught me. Well, I'm glad you finally found out. Yes, he is a clown, and I just wanted you to know that what they say about clowns is true. He has an enormous..." Click.

Sharon did not want to hear what she suspected was coming next, and she had reached over and cut off the speakerphone, triggering a moment of awkward silence.

Noah reflected about what he had just heard -- not as a lawyer, but as a man -- and he couldn't imagine what curious logic had compelled Riley Booth to play that embarrassing message for others to hear. The tension was getting to him, and he said the first thing that came to his mind.

"Ouch."

Riley's eyes lit up and a smile emerged on his face.

"I know," he said. "That's exactly what I'm thinking too! If this guy is so big, sex with him must be really painful." Then, as an afterthought, added: "She's finally getting what she deserves."

Sharon had spent far too much money and too many hours on her therapist's couch asking unanswerable questions like, "Why me?" and, "What did I do to deserve this?" The time for questions had passed, and she was ready to take action.

With a certain member of the board of directors now past the tipping point of frustration with his soon to be ex-son-in-law, the protection from above had vanished. Sharon looked over at Noah, and he nodded back and tapped the desk with his index finger to signal that she had his blessing to do what was necessary.

She reached into her briefcase and pulled out a separation packet. Normally she liked to do this discreetly while others did the talking, but this was a cathartic moment of empowerment. She looked Riley Booth in the eye, slammed the packet on the table and said, "You are FIRED."

CHAPTER 26

Michael Watanabe was distracted as he sat in the Polk County Sheriff's Department headquarters listening to the briefing of the multi-agency task force, set up to solve the case of the clowns in the tent. His wife had experienced contractions earlier that day, and he really wanted to be back in Nebraska with her, but he had a big role to play in the meeting, so he tried to stay as focused as he could.

A homicide investigator with the Sheriff's Department started with a summary of key background details in the case:

> "We believe that the three victims were driven to the scene at approximately 2:00 a.m. A fourth individual arrived with them in the vehicle and accompanied them as they made their way up the front walkway.

> "That person opened a seam in the tent, leaving palm and finger prints that did not match any of the victims or workers employed by the fumigation company. The lock was picked, but the fingerprints found on the doorknob matched one of the victims.

"The victims entered the house and became incapacitated almost immediately. All three bodies were found within eight feet of the entrance point. A 750-milliliter bottle of rum was found with them. Toxicology reports indicated that the victims had blood-alcohol levels ranging from .05 to .07, suggesting moderate impairment but not legal intoxication."

"After the decedents had entered, the fourth subject returned to the car and left the scene. A witness returning home from work shortly after 2:00 a.m. saw a vehicle that she identified as a black, two-passenger Smart Car leaving the scene with its headlights turned off."

The detective then yielded the floor to his counterpart at the Des Moines Police Department:

"Last night at approximately 10:45 p.m., a subject dressed as a clown asked to speak with the witness at a gentleman's club where she works as a dancer. The witness engaged in a conversation with the subject, who enticed her to leave the business with him after he showed her a large number of $100 bills.

"When they reached the parking lot together, the subject unlocked a vehicle that she identified as being a black Smart Car, similar to the one that she had seen leaving the scene of the incident in Bondurant. She became alarmed, and made an excuse to return to the club, where she called 911. The subject departed the scene before our units arrived and could not be located in the area.

"A review of footage from the security cameras located at the front door and in the parking lot showed the subject arriving in the vehicle and entering the club, and then returning to the car with the witness next to him approximately 15 minutes later. We have an image of the individual's face, and we are working with the FBI to digitally enhance the security footage to get a readable view of the license plate.

The Des Moines police detective went on for another ten minutes, briefing the task force on other witness interviews and talking about additional evidence that he thought might be important.

When he finished, Special Agent Watanabe stood up and moved to the front of the room, turned to face nearly two dozen investigators, and began his presentation.

"We were invited to join the investigation shortly after the bodies were identified and it was learned that they had been detained by the police in Charleston, South Carolina. The three victims were involved in a highly publicized fight during a rally for Presidential Candidate Russell Greenbeaux. We had identified the threat to the campaign in advance of the event, and I went with Agent Baker of the Secret Service to brief members of the leadership team and inform them of the risk the day before the incident.

"I returned to the campaign headquarters following the identification of the clowns who were found deceased in the house, and initiated the collection of fingerprints from members of the Greenbeaux staff who were present at the time. These prints were subsequently compared with those collected at the scene, and all of those subjects were excluded from consideration.

"The following morning, we were contacted by members of this task force and asked to investigate a message that was posted on an electronic bulletin board frequented by clowns. The message indicated that there was to be a party involving a tent that evening in Bondurant. Our examiner quickly identified that the message had been posted from a device using the wireless network at the campaign's headquarters."

"At that point, we obtained a warrant to allow the placement of listening equipment inside the headquarters, and a team was brought in from our Chicago office to affix the devices. In the course of the operation, it was determined that an additional, previously unknown office was located on the floor behind a door marked Clowns United. There was reason to believe that office had access to the campaign's wireless Internet network, and so the warrant was revised to include the new office on that side of the second floor of the building."

"During testing of the wireless microphones that our agents had installed, it was discovered that listening devices had already been placed around the office, indicating that another party was illegally eavesdropping on conversations within the campaign headquarters.

"Monitoring of the communication in the office commenced the next morning when people returned to the headquarters for work. No statements of an illegal nature were overheard within the Greenbeaux campaign headquarters itself. However, we did intercept conversations originating within the offices of the Clowns United office which suggested that an individual there was engaged in conspiratorial activities with two other subjects, a male and a female, identified in their coded conversations as 'G' and 'N.'

"The sole occupant of the Clowns United office was identified as one Robert Johnson Shipley, who was referred to as 'J' by the other co-conspirators. There were discussions about the failure of electronic listening equipment, and that led us to conclude that Mr. Shipley was the one who was engaged in the illegal eavesdropping."

Most of what Watanabe had said to that point was known by the other agencies represented in the room, but the Special Agent had some new information to share that would explain the motive behind what had taken place.

"Prior to the death of the three victims in Bondurant, Mr. Shipley recorded the following conversation between Russell Greenbeaux and a political consultant affiliated with the campaign named Norman H. W. Brodie..."

Watanabe placed a small digital recorder on the table and turned up the volume before hitting play.

"Greenbeaux: I hate these circus clowns. I want to get them out of my campaign altogether.

"Norm: Don't worry. I'll take care of making them disappear. By the time you get back from Florida, they will be gone.

The Special Agent explained that voice analysis showed that the candidate had spoken first, and that it was the consultant who had been heard saying that he would take care of making the victims disappear. He played the recording one more time for effect, and then concluded his presentation.

CHAPTER 27

Ruth was already sitting at the control tower when Virgil stepped off the elevator at 7:30 in morning. He had gone to bed early the night before, and was feeling much better after a good night's sleep. Greenbeaux and Norm were to join them at eight for a meeting to discuss the campaign's future, and he was expecting that they would be renewing the battle soon.

Voting was under way in the South Carolina primary, and they would know by the end of the day how much the events of the past week had damaged or helped the campaign. They didn't have any organized volunteer effort at the voting precincts this time, and the polls coming out of the state only asked voters about candidates in the two major parties, so they had no way of knowing which direction Greenbeaux was trending.

It had been one full week since the marching band had squared off with mimes on a street in Charleston, but it seemed like an eternity to Virgil. He took one last moment of reflection, then gathered a notebook and headed over to the conference room.

Everyone was there shortly after eight, but the meeting hadn't really kicked into gear when Rachel ran into the office and summoned them all to the war room. CNN was trumpeting the return of Naomi Winston to the air in an hour, and hinted that she would have exclusive information about the clowns who had died. Most surprising of all, CNN now had a graphic that said, "Murder in the Tent," with ominous background music.

Johnson, who was lurking behind his door to the Clowns United office, could hear the commotion and he knew what it was all about. Very soon, Naomi would make her triumphant return with a special report pinning the murders squarely on the man nicknamed Dr. Death. She had the recording of Norm saying he would make the clowns disappear, and the whole world would soon believe that he was capable of killing far more than a political campaign.

The time had arrived for phase two of the plan. Johnson wanted to be the one to tell Greenbeaux that his lieutenant, Norm Brodie, was about to enter a very difficult period in his life. He felt that this would give him more power and control when he placed the sealed envelope with a photograph on the table. The weakened candidate would then crumble under the weight of the extortion, and would naturally see the virtue of endorsing the Circus Animals Protection Act.

Johnson grabbed the 9x12 envelope from his locked cabinet and strode calmly into the headquarters. Everyone was standing in the war room, waiting anxiously for any hint about what was coming. The media had been reporting under the assumption that the whole thing was a terrible accident, and that the clowns had simply wandered into what they thought was a circus tent. But now CNN was calling it murder. And certainly, the network wouldn't ask its overworked graphics department to put together a slide like that if they weren't pretty sure about it.

One by one, other news programs starting to pick up the scent of dead bodies again, and a local news station that had seldom left the parking lot was now telecasting live pictures of the Cedar Point front door in anticipation of some big news to come.

Johnson came up behind Greenbeaux and tapped him on a shoulder.

"We need to talk."

Greenbeaux turned around, visibly annoyed and said, "Not now, Johnson."

"This is important," the lobbyist said, moving closer and lowering his voice to just above a whisper. "It is about our friends who died in Bondurant. I know something that is about to be reported on the news."

Johnson now had the full attention of Greenbeaux, Virgil and Norm, and he signaled for the candidate to follow him. The campaign manager and the consultant also started to follow along, but Johnson waved them off. "Just Mr. Greenbeaux, please."

The two went to the conference room and Johnson shut the door.

"There is something you should know," he said. "Naomi Winston is about to report on national television that there has been a break in the case of the murder of our poor friends, misters Puck, Pluck and Tuck."

Greenbeaux could feel the hair on the back of his neck stand on end, anticipating that nothing good would come out of the mouth of that loathsome lobbyist.

"It appears that somebody in the office murdered them," Johnson said.

This just didn't sound right to Greenbeaux, and he arched his eyebrows, narrowing his focus on the other man.

"Somebody caught Norm Brodie on tape saying that he would get rid of them," Johnson said. "The recording found its way into the hands of the reporter your marching band ran over, and she seems very keen to put it on the air."

This all seemed surreal to the candidate, and he exhaled deeply as he slumped back in his chair before speaking.

"That is just not possible," he said. "Norm is a good guy. He wouldn't do something like that."

"I wouldn't have supposed it myself," said Johnson. "But then again, he's not a clown like you and me. He doesn't think like we do, and he doesn't value our lives as he does others of his kind."

Greenbeaux couldn't believe it. How could it be that Norm would kill Puck, Pluck and Tuck? They had all found the circus clowns annoying. But murder?

Johnson could see that the candidate was now under duress, which was exactly where he wanted him. He wanted to turn the screws just a tiny bit more and so he added: "Do you know what Norm's nickname is?"

The candidate fumbled, not recalling right away, so Johnson stepped in to help him.

"His nickname among politicos is 'Dr. Death.' Did you ever wonder how he earned that name?"

Greenbeaux couldn't stand it any more. He didn't know what to believe, and wanted to talk with others instead of the evil clown lobbyist. He got up and started to move to the door, but Johnson intercepted him.

"I wouldn't go out there if I were you," he said. "Any minute now, the police are going to come marching through that door to take Mr. Brodie away, and I think it would be better for your campaign if you're not in the way. You know, just in case there are news cameras with them. It might also hurt Mr. Brodie if the police are eavesdropping and you were to ask a question that incriminated him."

Greenbeaux froze, trying to think of what he should do.

"As the President and Chief Executive Officer of Clowns United, I cannot tell you how to run your campaign, Mr. Greenbeaux. But as a friend, I can tell you that I believe it would be a mistake for you to go out there."

The candidate seemed to shrink well below his great height. The lobbyist was most certainly not his friend, but Greenbeaux was wounded and he couldn't find the strength to run away. Johnson recognized that the trap had been perfectly set, and he gently put his arm on Greenbeaux's shoulder to lower him into a chair.

It was time to go for the kill.

"And Mr. Greenbeaux, I am afraid that there is some more very bad news."

What could be worse than hearing that the police might be ready to break down the door and arrest your trusted advisor? The now-sad clown raised his head, his eyes boring into the messenger next to him.

"I'm afraid that an unfortunate photograph of you has surfaced."

A fresh jolt went through Greenbeaux, and he could feel the air leave his body. "What kind of photograph?" he asked, knowing full well what the answer might be.

"Well," said Johnson, "let's just say, you are not wearing your clown suit. It is very unfortunate, and it could bring embarrassment to you and the campaign."

Greenbeaux was reeling. He looked down and saw that there was a manila envelope on the table that had been marked with a red rubber stamp saying, "Photos. Do Not Bend." He was hoping that Johnson was not planning to pull anything out for a show-and-tell session. That would be just too much to bear in his fragile state.

In the space of a few minutes he had fallen from a tall and mighty perch, and there was no sign yet of the bottom he was bracing to hit. He had started the day with a decision to make about whether to stay in the race. He was a popular national figure who spoke truth to the most powerful forces in Washington, and he had done a lot to bring respect to his fellow clowns.

But now he was staring down the very real possibility that his chief political strategist was about to be arrested for the murder of three clowns. And on top of that, there was a skeleton preparing to stand up on its own legs and walk straight out from the closet where he stored his deepest shame.

In the back of his mind, he had always known that this moment might come. It had weighed on him for many years, simmering on a subconscious level and threatening to boil over if the right heat and pressure were applied.

Greenbeaux told himself that he didn't want to be president because it was a thankless job, and to a large extent that was true. But in a moment of clarity he now realized that there was more to it. He could imagine nothing worse for himself -- or for the country he loved -- than to have a picture surface that would show the President in a compromising position.

His divorce had come at a time of both weakness and strength in his life. Greenbeaux had just built and sold his first software company for a lot more money than he ever imagined making, and his ex-wife's lawyer had picked up the aromatic scent of green in the air.

There were indiscretions that came with the kind of life that new money allowed, both in private and in public under the protective veil of the Clown Underground. Things sometimes happened at certain types of parties where privacy and confidentiality were normally valued above all else.

But others did not always follow the code, and some people had fallen victim to secret cameras stowed away by evil clowns. He had never actually seen a picture of himself as such, but his ex-wife's lawyer had been explicit enough in describing what had been found that Greenbeaux assumed it was true.

And now he was confronted by what had been placed on the table. Even if Johnson was bluffing and there was no picture in the manila envelope, he would go through life with a renewed fear that there was incriminating evidence out there to undermine the public perception of his moral character. He hadn't spoken to his ex-wife in years, but he suspected that she would be all too willing to share what she knew if anyone bothered to track her down and ask.

"You know," said Johnson, "problems like this can be fixed."

"What do you mean fixed?" Greenbeaux asked. He had never borne witness to extortion before and this was all new to him.

"There are people who can be paid to make this picture go away, for now and forever." Johnson said. "And seeing as how you are the victim in all of this, I don't think it would be right for you to be the one who has to pay out of your own pocket. But I do know some people, some very powerful people, mind you, who might just be able to help you make this disappear."

Johnson was ready to put the deal on the table: "As you know, my clients feel very strongly about the merits of the Circus Animal Protection Act, and if you were to say a few kind words in support of their position, they would consider you a dear friend. And friends help each other. That's the way Washington works."

Greenbeaux's eyes bored into his adversary. He knew that whatever was in the envelope had not just fallen out of the sky into Johnson's outstretched arms by accident. The snake had slithered his way down a dark path in the garden to find this shiny apple, but Greenbeaux wasn't going to bite.

"No," Greenbeaux said.

"Excuse me?" Johnson couldn't believe what he was hearing.

"I would rather drop out of this race than tell the people of this country that I endorse what is in that bill."

Johnson was taken aback, surprised that his perfectly laid trap wasn't working. "Mr. Greenbeaux, if this picture gets leaked out, there will be no graceful exit."

Special Agent Watanabe had heard enough. From his command post in a van parked on a side street, he gave the command over the radio: "Go."

Greenbeaux's staff was startled as the back door to the stairwell burst open and eight agents wearing jackets emblazoned with FBI in gold lettering rushed through the war room with their guns drawn. The strike team exited the room and took a quick left so it could approach at an angle where it couldn't be seen from the glass-walled conference room.

When Robert Johnson Shipley was at a crossroads in his life, he had made a deal with the devil for a job where he could have his talents realized. But now, the door behind him burst open and he was greeted by men who were coming to collect for his sins.

Watanabe hustled out of the van and ran to the building with his gun drawn. By the time he reached the back door, the code word "Ringmaster" was shouted over the radio, telling him that the arrest had been made without incident. He holstered his weapon and jogged up the stairs and into the war room.

Ruth saw Watanabe walk briskly through the open back door and tried to intercept him, asking, "What just happened?"

Watanabe was focused on getting to the conference room and he moved past her without saying anything. But when he reached the door, he turned and announced to Ruth and others in the frightened group: "Everyone just stay put. The candidate is safe now."

That was all she needed to know.

* * *

Naomi Winston was putting the finishing touches to her makeup. She applied another coat of red lipstick, double-checked the mirror, and picked up her purse, preparing to leave for the set. She was ready to present the most satisfying story of her career.

The anchor was to lead the hour with the news that there had been a big development in the investigation of the mysterious death of three clowns who worked on the Greenbeaux for President campaign. She would introduce Naomi with little fanfare, so as not to draw attention to the embarrassment earlier in the month, and then the special report would start.

The script was tight, and Naomi went over in her mind the words she longed to read on the air:

"We have received word that the three clowns who worked for Russell Greenbeaux were, in fact, murdered. A source close to the campaign has told me they believe that someone in the office lured the three men out of the headquarters with the promise of a circus party, and then let them into the tented house where they died. The source has told me that suspicion is falling squarely on a consultant to the campaign, Norm Brodie, who is known in Washington circles by the nickname Dr. Death."

She had the recording ready to be played, complete with graphics to show who was speaking, so that there wouldn't be any confusion about who had said that he would make the clowns disappear.

As she made her way down a corridor leading to the newsroom, she could hear a commotion ahead. An intern came running toward her. "Ms. Winston. A local station in Iowa broke the story ahead of us."

Naomi didn't completely trust Johnson, and it wouldn't have surprised her in the least if he had given the recording to someone else if it suited his own interests. Norm Brodie would still fall, and that would be good, but somebody else would get to break the news, and she would be denied the full measure of satisfaction.

She heard a distinctive ringtone and reached down to retrieve a second phone from a zippered pocket inside her purse. She answered it and started talking before she could let the other person get a word in edgewise. "What the hell Johnson, that story was supposed to be MINE!"

The call was dropped and she threw the phone back into her purse in frustration, picking up her gait to get into the newsroom and find out who had scooped her.

Ahead there was a monitor that had a live feed from an affiliate in Des Moines with its cameras fixed on the front door of the Cedar Point headquarters. She could see a large black SUV parked by the entrance. Some people were standing around, and then there was a flurry of activity as the front door to the building opened and FBI agents emerged to escort a man in handcuffs to the vehicle.

A wave of shock overcame Naomi as she realized that the face had makeup with an overdrawn smile. It was Johnson, not Norm Brodie.

Watanabe and his team had done their job well. They had determined that it was Goldfarb's palm print on the fumigation tent, and they had used cell tower data to track and identify the disposable phone Johnson called to talk with the mastermind of the operation.

Naomi was unaware that behind her was a woman in a navy blue pant suit who had visual confirmation when the phone was answered. Two men in dark suits emerged from another hallway and moved into place.

The realization that something had gone terribly wrong hit Naomi with full force when the three agents converged and she heard words that she could not have fathomed in her worst nightmare:

"Naomi Winston, you are under arrest."

*　　*　　*

Investigators remained at the Cedar Point headquarters for several hours, collecting evidence and interviewing members of the staff. Everyone was walking around in a daze, conscious of the news cameras still trained on the front door.

It was a big news event.

A well-known political reporter and a familiar infomercial pitchman had been arrested in connection with the headline-making death of the three clowns. Agents soon arrested Goldfarb at a motel in southeastern Des Moines, and the news vans arrived just in time to see a black, two-passenger Smart Car being hoisted onto the back of a flatbed truck that would tow it away to be searched for further evidence.

Ruth sent most of the volunteers in the office home for the day after the FBI agents conducting the interviews excused them. She preferred to keep the company of Virgil, Norm, and her son, and chose to ignore the phones that continued ringing nonstop. The media and curious onlookers would have to wait another day for the campaign to comment.

By midafternoon, the investigators were gone and it was just the four of them left in the headquarters. They moved over to the conference room from which Johnson had been permanently removed. They talked, trying to understand and process their feelings, and nobody made mention of what to do next with the campaign until Greenbeaux finally spoke up.

310

"I want out."

Everyone knew exactly why he felt that way. They didn't argue. The campaign's sudden rise had been exhilarating, but the deaths and funeral had taken every ounce of fun away from the ride. Norm asked a few probing questions to confirm that Greenbeaux did indeed want to withdraw from the race for the right reasons. When he was convinced of the inevitable, he smiled and said, "I can help with this. Graceful exits are my specialty."

Norm's phone had been ringing quite a bit lately, and he had been fielding inquiries from candidates who were in need of his services. He was no longer just Dr. Death, the man who knew how to kill campaigns before they suffocated under a pile of dirty laundry. He had proven that he could take an obscure third-party candidate and turn him into an Internet sensation and a viable presidential contender. Now everyone wanted a piece of that magic.

One call he chose to ignore was a desperate plea for help from the Pulcinella campaign. They needed Norm's services quickly to come in and save the candidate from the impending release of the embarrassing clown photo. But Norm wasn't interested in that particular job. Ruth's subtle way of conveying her lessons had gotten into his head, and he now felt he had a higher standard to maintain.

CHAPTER 28

The media were notified early in the morning that they should show up at Cedar Point for a press conference at 2:00 p.m. sharp. The back room -- where the marching band had first practiced and the FBI had come storming through -- had been cleared of everything except a podium that had been brought in, some chairs, and microphones that the news media had been allowed to set up an hour beforehand.

Virtually all the volunteers had been turned away that day. Only those closest to the campaign were allowed in. Douglas Goodwin was there, and so were Rachel and Skip. Ruth was serving as the concierge at the control tower to welcome the press, and Norm and Virgil were sitting quietly with Greenbeaux behind the closed door to the war room. Everyone had slept well the night before, and there were no changes of heart.

Virgil was feeling like a sad clown on this day, and he had drawn a very slight frown in place of what was ordinarily a happy face. There was no doubt in his mind that if Naomi had been successful in getting the recording of his friend Norm on the air, he would have come to work painted as a very angry clown.

He was preparing to check out of his hotel the next morning and drive back to Ohio. A reporter from the *Cleveland Plain Dealer* had been in touch, wanting to feature him in a story. The paper had sniffed out the local angle of the top national news, and they were eager to feature the Cleveland native who had been Greenbeaux's campaign manager.

Without tipping his hat at what Greenbeaux would say that afternoon, Virgil told the reporter that he would be free to speak later in the day. The reporter then commissioned a freelance photojournalist in Iowa to take pictures of Virgil at the press event for his story.

Norm, too, was feeling a little sad. He was used to being there when a campaign died -- usually by his own hand -- and so he understood more about this type of event than anyone else in the office. But this experience had been very different from the others. He had spent more time with this team of people and the experience had made him a wiser man.

Whenever he had helped to prepare an exit speech, he always encouraged the candidate to inject as much truth as possible into the message so there would be a ring of sincerity. In this case, there was no elaborate cover story to concoct.

At 1:59 p.m., Virgil stepped to the podium and announced to the wall of reporters and cameras that the candidate would be arriving shortly to make a brief announcement. Greenbeaux was still in the war room and heard that as his cue. He took a few deep breaths and steeled himself to make his final speech.

After a minute, he opened the door, walked out and turned left, starting on the same path that the FBI strike team had followed the day before. But instead of making a right turn to sneak along a wall to the conference room, he kept walking until he reached the podium.

He started by thanking the press for coming, then launched into his prepared remarks.

"Last fall, I started my campaign for President because I saw that too many of my people -- clowns -- were living in fear. People in this world with good hearts had no idea of their own prejudice against us. They assumed that what they saw at the circus or in movies was all there was to know.

"But there is more. There are far more of us than most people have ever imagined. We are their co-workers, their family members, their next-door neighbors, hiding in fear of what others would think if they knew our secret.

"As time went on, the campaign became about so much more. As I listened to voters, I heard a common theme emerge that rang true in my own heart. People are sick and tired of what is happening in Washington, and I found my own voice to call out for more civility, more bipartisanship, and more willingness to listen to each other's side of the story without judging or looking for the best opportunity to undercut our opponents.

"We are a nation built upon laws and rules, but sometimes we forget the most important one: the golden rule. There have been times when I was guilty of lumping all people in Washington -- politicians and lobbyists alike -- under one umbrella. I was wrong to do that; I am very sorry and I apologize. There are many good people who work on and around Capitol Hill. They come from all different political persuasions and they are committed to public service because they love our country and want to see it become a better place.

"But the game does not always reward those with the best intentions, and power and money often flows to those who are willing to do the bidding of the special interests who want to maintain the status quo or move us in the wrong direction for selfish reasons. This must change, but I will not be the one to lead that fight now.

"The events of the past week have taken a toll on me and the members of my staff, and we have all agreed that it will be in our best interest to disengage and allow ourselves time to heal. Therefore, I am suspending my campaign, effective immediately, and I will step away from the spotlight so that the country can go on with the very important business of selecting the next president of the United States."

With that, Greenbeaux stepped away from the podium, walked back to the war room, and shut the door. There would be no questions answered by the former candidate. Several reporters tried to get quotes from Virgil and Norm, but they had nothing new to add. Greenbeaux had said it all for them.

On her way out to the elevator, Carrie Rollins spotted Ruth and came over to talk. As a reporter, she had felt the need to keep a professional distance from a person she was covering. So many people in politics had tried to manipulate her over the years, to get her to write something that wasn't true for their own gain, and she had always thought it best not to get too close.

But Ruth no longer posed the same threat as others who were part of that cynical process. She was just a sad woman who was trying to put on a brave face, and when their brief conversation was over, it was Carrie who initiated the hug.

*　　*　　*

Early the next morning, Norm was on a plane to Washington and was met at the airport by Jessica. She wanted to be there for him, and she had decided to take a few days off so that they could spend some time alone.

He proved himself to be very different from the man she had suspected he was that night in Manchester. He was still as handsome and charming, but she had come to find more. He was thoughtful and humble, which was rare to see in the heat of political battles.

There was a question she had wanted to ask when she approached him that night in the bar. She wanted to know then if he was, as some suggested, a living breathing suicide machine who entered at the candidate's request to terminate the campaign, or if he was a saboteur -- a political assassin -- sent in by others to mortally wound an enemy.

Jessica had since figured out the answer on her own. Norm Brodie was the type of man who saved others, rather than destroying them. Despite what he had done to his brother long ago when he was a teenager, he had grown up to be a moral man who cared about people and was going about his job with integrity. This was not always the case with others in the business, and she had started to question whether she could rationalize what she did for a living for very much longer.

When the time came that night when they both wanted to pull back the covers, Norm did not care to have any ambient light glowing in the background from C-SPAN or any other channel. He still liked politics, but he no longer loved it. In that small way, Naomi Winston had accomplished what she set out to do. She had unwittingly caused Norm to see how his obsession for the game had blinded him to what really mattered. And what mattered most to him now was Jessica.

316

EPILOGUE

There was a lot of goodwill toward Greenbeaux after he withdrew from the race. People had been shocked by the crime, and felt sympathy for what the campaign team had endured. The dignified farewell speech had resonated with the American people, and there was a brief period of time when even the most jaded of partisan hacks spoke in more measured tones toward their rivals.

But that sense of congeniality didn't last long, and the bickering and gamesmanship returned in full force before the snow had melted in most parts of the country.

Greenbeaux soon found himself in demand as a public speaker and television pundit. He was seen as a nonpartisan presence, and was trusted as an objective voice with well-reasoned opinions. But the joy he felt at his new role was short-lived.

Soon after the election in November, his mother became sick, and Greenbeaux canceled all outside obligations to tend to her needs. Ruth had an aggressive form of lung cancer. She had been a heavy smoker for many years, and she recognized her inability to quit as one of her many imperfections. Her decline was rapid, but her son stayed at her side every step of the way, accompanying her on the endless treadmill of doctor's appointments, treatments, and two surgeries that, in the end, did not slow her decline.

Mother and son spent a lot of time talking, occasionally about politics, but more frequently about other things. Ruth would ask him to read her some of her favorite passages from the Bible, and she talked at length about what the words meant to her as she began to prepare herself for the inevitable.

Ruth knew her son well, and worried that after she died, he would idolize her without remembering the faults and frailties that made her human. Not a day went by that she didn't say to him: "Remember, Russell, nobody is perfect in the eyes of God."

Virgil had gone back to Cleveland, where he took a job as the chief operating officer at the Children's Hospital. The pay was far greater than what he had earned at IXM Systems, but more important to him, it was the type of place where he could work and people seemed to appreciate it if he was dressed as a clown. He visited Ruth, and they spent a full day laughing and remembering the good times they had together on the campaign, but not the bad.

Norm couldn't break away from the onslaught of work that came his way, but he always made time for Ruth whenever she called him. She was thrilled to learn that he and Jessica had become engaged, and vowed to be there when he got married.

But she didn't have that long left. She quickly reached a point where the doctors had to tell her there was nothing more they could do. Ruth and her son were both stoic about it, but she was stronger in such matters, and he had a hard time coming to grips with the fact that she would soon be gone. Her final weeks were spent under the loving care of a hospice team, who made sure that her pain was managed and that her son had respite to care for himself as well.

In the end, he was by her side, holding her hand as she started to let go. He listened intently as her breathing became shallower and her inhalations grew further between. Ten seconds apart. Twenty seconds. Thirty. Until, at last, he found himself waiting for one more breath that just never came.

Many old friends attended the funeral. Virgil. Norm. Douglas. Even Rachel and Skip, who were finding that their political differences were less important than the similarities that bonded them together. Norm took note, and told others that if those two could find love and common ground, then maybe there was hope for such a bitterly divided country.

The first few weeks after her death were difficult for Greenbeaux, but then he started to pull himself together, and began to think about what he would do next. He had enjoyed his role as a traveling spokesman for the cause of civility in the public discourse, and he started preparing to go back out on the lecture circuit.

After all the sensation and hoopla around the crime, the attention faded quickly when it became apparent that there would be no trial. Johnson, Goldfarb and Naomi Winston found the meticulously compiled evidence against them to be insurmountable, and they reached their own plea deals to preserve the small glimmer of hope that they might one day breathe fresh air beyond the barbed-wire fences that now encased them.

Greenbeaux thought he was putting that chapter of his life behind him, but then one day he received an unexpected package from the FBI. It contained a 9x12 manila envelope that was stamped "Photos. Do Not Bend." Special Agent Watanabe had included a handwritten cover note explaining that this evidence would no longer be needed, and that it was being returned to the candidate as the rightful owner.

Greenbeaux filed the envelope away for a few days, but then his curiosity began to get the better of him. He had enjoyed shaking hands and listening to people out on the campaign trail, and he started entertaining the idea that he might want to run for office again some day. But he had no intention of doing so if there was a photograph floating about that could easily be found.

One rainy afternoon, he sat down with the envelope in front of him and summoned his courage. Slowly, he broke the seal and reached inside. He had expected that if there really was a photograph in there, it would be an 8x10 inch glossy blow-up. But the picture he pulled out was much smaller.

It had all been a bluff. The picture was not the kind that could damage a political campaign, and Johnson would have had a hard time defending himself if Greenbeaux had opened the envelope and confronted him.

Greenbeaux stared at the picture, trying to understand what he saw. He recognized his own, much younger face. His mother was there too. He had heard about this picture, but he had never actually seen it before, and he knew what it had meant to his mother. It was her own private well that nourished her when she needed strength, and Johnson had stolen it away when her back was turned.

His mother was now in a better place, but seeing the image brought her back to life once more. She appeared far more beautiful and vibrant than Greenbeaux had remembered her from her final, difficult days. In her eyes he could see the compassion that had been her driving force, and he could almost hear her voice saying that it was okay to be a clown as she wiped the tears away from the little cowboy's cheeks.

Perhaps Ruth was right, and she wasn't perfect in the eyes of God. But she would always remain perfect in the eyes of her son, the clown who almost became President.

ABOUT THE AUTHOR

Greenbeaux author David Bergheim grew up inside the Beltway and he has never fully recovered from that trauma. He had the bad fortune of being born into a political family, and as a child, was put to work delivering campaign leaflets door-to-door for the candidates his parents fancied in his hometown of Alexandria, Virginia.

He moved to Tucson after high school, which was the farthest place outside the Beltway that he could think to go. Despite his best efforts to escape politics, he found himself being sucked back in during the initiative to recall a governor when he was a college student. After receiving his Bachelor of Arts degree in English Literature from the University of Arizona, he fled that state too (notice a pattern?) and moved to Connecticut where he earned an MBA at the Yale School of Management.

Flash forward to today… David successfully fled Connecticut and then Georgia, and now lives with his family in Southern California. After many productive years working in marketing and career services at prestigious universities, he is now quite happy to spend his time writing novels and strategic plans, rescuing kittens from trees, and occasionally coaching soccer. He is married, has two sons, one dog, and one cat that is not presently up a tree.

Contact:

author@greenbeauxforpresident.com
www.greenbeauxforpresident.com
www.facebook.com/greenbeauxforpresident

www.ingramcontent.com/pod-product-compliance
Lightning Source LLC
Chambersburg PA
CBHW071100250626
47159CB00002B/541